AS IF ON CUE

Also by Marisa Kanter

What I Like About You

MARISA KANTER

SIMON & SCHUSTER BFYR
New York London Toronto Sydney New Delhi

An imprint of Simon & Schuster Children's Publishing Division
1230 Avenue of the Americas, New York, New York 10020

This book is a work of fiction. Any references to historical events, real people, or real places are used fictitiously. Other names, characters, places, and events are products of the author's imagination, and any resemblance to actual events or places or persons, living or dead, is entirely coincidental.

Interior design by Hilary Zarycky
The text for this book was set in ITC New Baskerville.
Manufactured in the United States of America
First Edition
2 4 6 8 10 9 7 5 3 1
Library of Congress Cataloging-in-Publication Data
Names: Kanter, Marisa, author.
Title: As if on cue / Marisa Kanter. | Description: First edition. |
New York : Simon & Schuster Books for Young Readers, 2021. |
Audience: Ages 12 and Up. | Summary: It seems that aspiring playwright Natalie and musician Reid have been in competition all their young lives, but when they are forced to compete for scarce school budget dollars, they embark on an all-out prank war, which backfires; now they are forced to cooperate, pool their talents and ambitions to produce a school musical—and not only is cooperation an unfamiliar role, but they are suddenly starting to have feelings for each other.
Identifiers: LCCN 2021004822 |
ISBN 9781534445802 (hardcover) | ISBN 9781534445826 (ebook)
Subjects: LCSH: Musicals—Juvenile fiction. | Teenage dramatists—Juvenile fiction. |
Teenage musicians—Juvenile fiction. | Interpersonal relations—Juvenile fiction. |
Competition (Psychology)—Juvenile fiction. | High schools—Juvenile fiction. |
CYAC: Musicals—Fiction. | Theater—Fiction. | Dramatists—Fiction. |
Musicians—Fiction. | Love—Fiction. | Competition (Psychology)—Fiction. |
High schools—Fiction. | Schools—Fiction.
Classification: LCC PZ7.1.K285 As 2021 | DDC 813.6 [Fic]—dc23
LC record available at https://lccn.loc.gov/2021004822

For Sam—
it all started with a script

AS IF ON CUE

CHAPTER ONE

It is six a.m. and I am debating the opposite of frozen with Reid Callahan.

"It's 'melted,'" I mumble into my pillow, salty, because how dare he wake me up before the sun on a Monday? In my current state of bleary-eyed rage, I throw a pillow vaguely in the direction of my doorframe, where Reid is standing.

"No way. The opposite of frozen is definitely boiled. I'm serious. 'Boiled' is the only valid title if you're going for parody. 'Melted' is fundamentally flawed."

"*You're* fundamentally flawed."

He snorts, and I hear the clink of metal against ceramic. A spoon swirling in cereal. By now, I'm used to Reid in my house in the early hours of the morning, mastering complex arpeggios on the clarinet under the instruction of my father. Reid is pretty much the only person in the entire universe who matches Dad's intensity for a musical instrument. Which means he's *always* here.

It's kind of unbearable.

"Why are you here?" I ask.

"It's Monday," Reid says slowly, as if I don't know the days of the week. Monday morning lessons have been a thing since school started two weeks ago—and will continue to be a thing that makes Monday even *more* Monday for the duration of my junior year.

"I mean *here*, Reid. Why are you in my bedroom?"

"To pay up," he says.

He nods toward my desk, where a large iced chai from Kiskadee sits on top of an elephant coaster. Of course, he decides six a.m. is the perfect time to deliver my *Wow, you actually wrote a play* chai. Winning a bet against Reid Callahan is still always losing, in a way.

"Your timing is impeccable."

I fall back onto my mattress and roll over, facing the wall and closing my eyes in an attempt to return to my dreamscape. Before Reid woke me up with three staccato knocks, I was sitting at a table read for my big-budget Broadway play featuring the Chrises. We were staging a fight scene between Pine and Evans. Hemsworth leaned over to whisper in my ear, *You're bloody incredible, Jacobson.* And I didn't brush off his praise or downplay my talent—I owned it. Thor called *me*, Natalie Jacobson, incredible. I *felt* incredible. In my dream, playwriting is more than a high school hobby. It's possible.

Reid flips the switch next to my door and my eyelids twitch as synthetic light tries to push through them. "Don't want you to oversleep!"

"Thanks," I deadpan, sitting up because I am now officially awake and Reid has Won. I reach for my glasses while my eyes adjust, already plotting my revenge for his ruining of the epic Pine-Evans fight scene.

"You're welcome." Reid's hazel eyes meet mine. They seem to change color depending on what he's wearing. This morning, they pick up his green button-down. "The least you can do is be on time, considering you're wasting Mrs. Mulaney's."

It's so elementary, I almost laugh as I move from my bed to the adjacent desk and start weaving my disaster curls into two disaster braids. Any other day, I'd fire back a snarky retort. Not today. Because today is the culmination of an entire summer writing with my best friend, Henry Chao. Before homeroom, we'll enter scene and deliver a dialogue to Principal Mulaney about why *Melted* deserves to be our fall play—a performance that has the potential to shift the entire fate of Lincoln High School's drama department.

I can't afford to be distracted.

"Bye," I say.

I shut the door on Reid and reach for the chai on my desk. Straw between my lips, I take a long sip. It doesn't quite taste like victory, but it's still a Kiskadee chai. Therefore, delicious. I enjoy it, unfazed by Reid's basic insult because with *Melted* I have a chance—a *real* chance—at convincing Mrs. Mulaney that keeping LHS's drama department intact is just as valuable as new band uniforms.

Seriously, Reid's biggest problem is being an outfit repeater. When the school committee announced that "significant budget cuts" were coming for extracurricular activities at the end of sophomore year, the drama club had an emergency meeting. It was initiated by me and our former advisor, Miss Bryant, who quickly jumped our sinking ship of a drama program for a full-time faculty position teaching theater at Boston Arts Academy. But when Reid heard about the cuts, he didn't flinch. It's *that* obvious the band is relatively immune from total destruction, thanks to a passionate band director who, over the course of a decade, revitalized the music program from the ground up.

That teacher? It's none other than Aaron Jacobson. Reid's teacher. My dad.

It's complicated.

I pick up the pillow I launched at Reid and toss it on my bed on the way to my closet. Today's aesthetic is comfy and confident, like how Mom would style herself for meetings with her publisher. This is that important. I pull a new floral T-shirt dress off its velvet hanger, rip off the tag, and pair it with a denim jacket and white sneakers. To complete the look, I swipe a clear pink gloss over my lips.

Satisfied, I stuff my laptop into my backpack and I'm on the move. Downstairs, the kitchen smells like raspberry hazelnut coffee and burnt toast, the scent of creative anxiety.

I pause at the bottom of the stairs when I catch sight of the kitchen table scene.

Mom sits at the head of the espresso wood table, staring intently at her laptop screen. Reid's next to my mom, his button-down now unbuttoned to reveal a white graphic T-shirt that says MUSIC IS MY FORTE, with a spoon in one hand and *The Fundamentals of Musical Composition* in the other. Dad sits across from Reid, sipping on coffee and sorting through papers that spill out of his Band Bible—a three-inch blue binder with his certified nonsensical organization system. Last year, I created the most beautiful color-coded filing system for his monster binder. He was *not* pleased. How Dad transformed Lincoln High School's concert band and orchestra into a nationally recognized, award-winning program—yet cannot accept the convenience of alphanumeric order, page numbers, and *labels*—is beyond me. But no matter what, he's always in band mode, his back-to-school haircut still slightly too short, his salt-and-pepper beard slightly too long.

My stomach clenches, witnessing the comfortable quiet that is the three of them together.

"How's the solo coming?" Mom asks Reid.

Reid's eyes flicker up from his reading. "More work ahead. How's the book coming?"

Mom closes her laptop and smirks. "More work ahead."

He nods and raises his coffee mug. "Solidarity, Aunt Shell."

Reid is the only person who can get away with calling my mom any variation of "Shell." Aunt Michelle was one syllable too many for toddler Reid. I wish he dropped the "Aunt." It makes me feel like we're related—which, no, we absolutely are *not.*

Being the children of dads who were childhood best friends does not a family make.

"You're too hard on yourself," Dad says, looking up from his "organized" chaos. Is it the new music for the homecoming game? Is it a set for his jazz band, Lincoln Street Blues? Who knows! "Both of you."

Reid brushes off Dad's words with a shrug and looks up, his eyes meeting mine from across the kitchen. "Hey, Nat."

Enter me, the girl who always seems to arrive before her cue.

"Morning," I say, reaching for the box of blueberry Pop-Tarts above the stove. I take the entire box and slide into the chair across from my mom.

"You're up early," Mom says. Her hair is a messy bun of curls, now two shades darker than my own from the dye job masking her gray roots. Beside her laptop are a half-eaten apple and an elephant mug filled with what I'm sure is lukewarm coffee. Plastic purple reading glasses are perched on the tip of her nose as her eyes remain trained on her screen. "Nervous?"

My eyes focus on the apple, its exposed flesh already brown. Better than yesterday, when there was nothing left but seeds and core. On Mom's best writing days, the apple stays untouched, her fingers dancing on the keys, no chance of breaking their rhythm for a bite. On those days, Mom is Michelle Jacobson, *New York Times* bestselling author of *The Lola Diaries.*

I can't remember the last time Mom forgot to eat her apple.

"I'm ready."

"So, can I read it now?" Mom asks.

I perform the shrugging girl emoji.

If she reads it, she'll encourage me. She'll critique. She'll call me a playwright.

"You can read it when it's real," I say for the thousandth time. "That's what you'd say."

"I know, Lee."

Mom's voice begs me not to press further, so I don't. Before the pressure to follow up *Lola,* Mom was a force in publishing and proof that writing could be more than a hobby.

Now, I see my mom stare at a blank Word doc for hours. I hear the defeat in her voice when she says, *I know, Lee.*

And even though my stomach dips, everything inside of me is relieved to not love writing like that, to not be following in her footsteps. I love theater, but writing and directing are hobbies, and that's all they will ever be. I'm not sure what Adulting looks like for me—I don't even know what I want to go to college for—but I do know it won't be my parents' life. Dad's symphony orchestra dreams landed him as an overworked and underpaid high school band director. Mom's burnout is so intense there are days she doesn't get out of bed.

I've seen firsthand what art can do to a person who loves it too much.

The mental toll of tying your financial security and self-worth to a creative pursuit.

"Well I read it," Reid interjects. "The title needs work."

Mom's eyebrows shoot up. "*Reid* read it? Wow. That hurts."

I swallow a piece of my Pop-Tart. "It's not like I had a choice."

"You bet that I couldn't name every *Survivor* winner," he says, closing his book. "You basically handed it to me."

He even named them in order. It was bizarre.

I mean, who still even watches that show? It started before we were *born.*

I roll my eyes, but honestly? It wasn't the worst bet to lose. Last week, when he was reading my script at breakfast, he didn't even hear me come down the stairs, he was so absorbed in *Melted.* Before I made it across the kitchen, he laughed. Genuinely laughed. Like he got it.

It honestly did not compute. Because we do not get each other, Reid and me.

It's actually funny, Reid had said, his mouth full of Froot Loops. *You're funny.* Then he smiled at me and I almost forgot how much I hate him.

When I reached for the box of Froot Loops and it was empty, I remembered.

Mom stands. "I guess I'll have to take Reid's word for it."

"Off to do some productivity sprints?" Dad asks.

"More like prep," Mom says. "Now that my syllabus is approved, there is *so* much prep."

Dad waves at his chaos binder, like *exhibit A*. "Relatable."

It's going to be Mom's second year teaching creative writing at Emerson College, a side hustle that pays the bills while she impatiently waits for inspiration to strike. And bills we do have. Mom spent most of June in Ft. Lauderdale looking for a caregiver for my bubbe, after she fell down the stairs and broke her hip. In July, our air conditioner busted in the middle of the hottest Massachusetts summer in, like, two hundred years. And a few weeks ago my dad learned that his budget for new supplies got cut in half—forcing him to purchase new music for the fall Harvest Festival out of pocket. All summer, it has been one unexpected expense after another.

Mom always says bad things happen in threes.

I say don't pick a career that relies on creative whims to pay the bills in the first place.

"All romance writers this semester?" I ask.

Mom nods. Romance is her brand, the literary space where she has made her career. Readers have been waiting nearly four years to see how she follows up *The Lola Diaries.*

"Maybe it'll be inspiring," Reid says.

"That's the hope," Mom says.

"Nirvana always gets me through a long prep session," Dad suggests. "Just don't forget Delia has lessons with Rabbi Sarna at three." My twelve-year-old sister is in full bat mitzvah prep mode, eating, sleeping, and breathing Vayishlach 36:40.

Mom waves away his reminder. "We have a tasting with the caterer after."

Dad nods. "Four-thirty."

"Good luck today, Lee."

Mom squeezes my shoulder then tucks her laptop under her arm and retreats to her office in the name of class prep, leaving me alone with Reid and my dad. Pretty much the worst combination. Before I have a chance to form words, they're in their own musical world.

"Six weeks until the Harvest Festival," Dad says.

Every fall, the concert band performs at the Lincoln Harvest Festival in Pine Hill Park. The Harvest Festival is a community event filled with hayrides, farm stands with local produce, and so many cider donuts—pretty much peak fall in New England energy. A few years ago, Dad proposed that it also be a performance opportunity for the band, where the marquee event is a classic film score. Past performances have included *Casablanca*, *E.T.*, and *The Wizard of Oz*. It's an event that the town has come to anticipate and is excellent—both in terms of the local media attention it receives and the boost it gives to small businesses that participate.

Star Wars: Episode IV—A New Hope is this year's Harvest Festival score. The hype is already building, thanks to Aaron Jacobson's local on-screen news debut in a piece highlighting how the band's participation has increased Harvest Festival turnout.

The screen time has absolutely gone to his head.

It's a cool story, objectively.

But the school committee does *not* need another reason to obsess over the band.

Neither does the town, for that matter.

Because as a town, Lincoln is as average as it gets. Our sports teams are mediocre. We don't have a marching band. Our drama club is small. Our entertainment options are a movie theater, ice skating, a roller rink, and a mall with every store that's in every town.

But Lincoln's concert band and orchestra program?

They are exceptional.

Reid shifts the conversation to his current role: recruitment for the jazz ensemble.

"We need more percussion," Reid says.

"Makayla's—" I start.

"Rosalind Levy is sick on the snare," Reid says, cutting me off. "Which will make up for losing Tricia, I think."

Dad nods. "Cool. Good to know."

I wait for Dad to ask me about Makayla's sister, who is an incredible drummer. He doesn't. He continues talking to Reid like I didn't try to speak, like I couldn't possibly contribute something valuable to this conversation.

Like I wasn't once a musician myself.

"We won't know for sure until we hear how everyone meshes."

I am invisible.

Finally, after another Pop-Tart and what feels like endless band chat, Dad closes his binder and heads to his studio in the basement to set up for Reid's lesson. Reid stands and brings his cereal bowl to the sink, so I reach into my backpack for my laptop, ready for thirty sweet minutes of alone time, just *Melted* and me.

I open the file.

"It's not too late for *Boiled*."

I jump, my fingers jamming into my keyboard. "Why are you so fixated on this?"

"Imagine if Adina could instantly *boil* anything she touches. She'd be unstoppable!" Reid says. "Think about it. Artists need to be open to criticism, Natalie. Collaborative."

"Right. Except we're *not* collaborators."

Reid's jaw tenses. "I know."

"So why are you still standing here? Don't you have a clarinet to blow?"

Reid nods and takes a step backward. "As a matter of fact, I do."

He descends the stairs, not missing a beat. His cheeks don't flush, not even when I emphasize "blow." Reid woke me up before the sun and co-opted my parents . . . and I couldn't even make him blush? Everything makes Reid blush! I'm seriously off my game.

What a waste of a line, honestly.

CHAPTER TWO

An hour later I'm waiting in the wings, my cowriter cannot stop pacing, and our talent is late.

In this case, the wings are the bench across from Mrs. Mulaney's office, where I sit scrolling through my phone while Henry grows more annoyed with each step. Fitz is supposed to be here by now. As the de facto leaders of LHS's drama club, we're supposed to present *Melted* as a unit. Henry and I as the writing and directing duo behind the scenes, and Fitz representing on the onstage talent.

I stare at my phone, watching our Team Melted group chat light up.

Makayla Okoye
IT'S MELTED DAY AHHHH
7:29 AM

Arjun Patel
🔥🔥🔥
7:29 AM

Arjun Patel

Tell us everything ASAP. I know we subscribe to being a low stakes org but . . .

7:30 AM

Makayla Okoye

TODAY THERE ARE STAKES

7:30 AM

Arjun Patel

(no pressure!!!!)

7:31 AM

Makayla Okoye

(some pressure 🙃)

7:31 AM

I swallow the lump in my throat. Cool. Pressure. Cool cool cool.

I get it though. We've always branded ourselves as a low-commitment *come to have fun!* club. We're not serious thespians like the musical theater kids or intense musicians like the band. We're a mix of athletes and scientists, quiz bowl captains and future politicians, all bonded by our mutual appreciation for the *yes and* technique and putting together a solid production. For us, theater is in the B story in our life. But the best character moments are always in the subplots. So the thought of losing it?

It rattled us more than we expected it to.

So we came up with a plan. A low-budget proposal Mrs. Mulaney and the school committee cannot refuse.

I switch into my private group chat with Henry and Fitz as it buzzes with an update.

Fitz (Not Ava)
SORRY. OVERSLEPT. ON MY WAY!!
7:35 AM

"We should've told her to be here thirty minutes ago," Henry says.

"Fitz stopped falling for that years ago."

Henry exhales restless energy and pushes his clear plastic frames up the bridge of his nose before taking his own phone out of his pocket. He runs his fingers through black hair as he scrolls automatically through his phone. It sticks up in every direction, like he didn't bother to brush it. *Pillow Pet hair*, we call it, since his sleepover pillow of choice when we were kids was Ribbit the frog, which always left his longer-on-top style extra tall the next morning. That's how long Henry has been my best friend—since the era of Pillow Pets.

"She'll be here. Hey—" I pat the empty bench space beside me "—let's do a run-through?"

Henry takes a seat. "It's perfect, Nat. You nail it every time."

"I'm caught up in the fundraising logistics."

"You are absolutely full of shit."

But despite this, Henry presses his back against the wall, exhales, and begins.

"Thank you so much for meeting with us, Mrs. Mulaney. We know budget cuts are difficult to navigate. That being said, we—Natalie, Fitz, me, and every member of the drama club—have worked all summer to find a solution that cuts the budget without cutting the club entirely."

I jump in. "We made a checklist of all of the costs associated with producing a school play—and learned the biggest barrier isn't production costs. It's licensing fees. Over some emergency dumplings, the entire Lincoln High School drama program put their heads together and came up with something unique and original . . . but most importantly, something free. *Melted.*"

Henry stands. "And now we're at Fitz's part. We can't even rehearse without—"

I grab his wrist and pull him back down to the bench. "I was going to be Fitz."

"You should've said that before we started."

"Okay, well, I'm saying it now. Let's start over. Maybe this time, don't begin with the whole *we know budget cuts are hard* disclaimer?"

Henry frowns. "But they *are.*"

"Right. But I think stating it gives Mrs. Mulaney an auto-out."

"Okay. Fair." Henry nods and we rehearse the first part again. He takes my note and the introduction flows more naturally this time, leading me right into the Fitz portion of the presentation.

"*Melted* is the story of sisters Adina and Emma and a world where everything is on fire. It's part sister story, part an incisive commentary on the climate crisis, and loosely inspired by *Frozen*. Classic theater productions like we've performed in the past have their place, but didn't resonate with the student body and contributed to lower audience turnout. *Melted* solves the licensing problem *and* revitalizes audience engagement. I mean, who *wouldn't* want to see a *Frozen* opposite play? It's a show written by us, for us."

"We'll keep production costs low with homemade costumes and set design," Henry adds.

"And think of the publicity opportunities! Students proving that you don't need a big budget to make art that matters."

The closing argument.

"It's good," Henry says, the twitch in his fingers gone.

"*We're* good," I say.

Henry and I have been collaborators since middle school—but *Melted* marks a new era in our partnership as our first full-length script. The words poured out of us over one very long, caffeinated weekend in June. I write for character development and pacing. Henry is attuned to plot and overall hilarity.

We're a perfect team.

"It shouldn't even matter," Henry says. "*This.* The play. Yet the idea of *Melted* not being enough makes me feel like I'm going to vomit."

I snap the rubber band friendship bracelet Henry made me in sixth grade against my wrist. He is ten months older than me to the day, but it's never mattered until this year. Because now Henry is a senior, I am a junior, and we are in our final act together at LHS.

"We're supposed to have a final curtain call," I insist.

Our first was *A Christmas Carol.* The summer after third grade, Henry and I were thrown together at the elementary school's summer theater camp. I needed an outlet for my energy. Henry needed to break out of his shell. On the first day, he raised his hand and told Mrs. Tamorelli how weird it was to do *A Christmas Carol* in July. I agreed, it *was* weird, and raised my hand to say so, adding that it's also weird to assume everyone celebrates Christmas.

We've been best friends and collaborators ever since.

"Chao and Jacobson *does* have a nice ring to it," Henry declares.

"Not as nice as Jacobson and Chao."

"Wouldn't that be the biggest plot twist?"

Henry and I start laughing because he's right. It *would* be. But Henry is going full Business Bro at Babson next year. Sure, he'll write an entire one-act play just to make me laugh, perform Shakespeare monologues in the park for a passing audience, but it's all whatever he can fit in between track practice, debate team, and his shifts at his family-owned restaurant, Chao Down. Art makes him happy.

Henry taught me art doesn't have to be all-consuming, like my parents make it out to be.

It can be low stakes. It can just be *fun.*

"Shit." Henry glances at his phone. We are officially late. "Where is Fitzgerald? Homeroom starts in twenty."

Henry's white sneakers squeak against the floor when he stands. He pushes up the sleeves of his navy half-zip, readjusts his glasses for the second time, and holds his hand out for me to take.

"Natalie! Henry!"

I hear her voice first, followed by the clicks of block heels against vinyl.

Ava "Fitz" Fitzgerald, the person who completes our trio, appears before us, looking frazzled but fabulous in a white blouse with long flowing sleeves paired with a denim button-down skirt belted at the waist and black ankle booties. Her strawberry blonde hair is secured in a high ponytail with a scrunchie, rainbow drop earrings dangling from her ears. It's a total look she'd present on *If the Shoe Fitz,* her fashion-focused YouTube channel—sans the tiny drops of sweat that bead above her perfectly arched eyebrows.

"I'm here!"

"Finally," Henry says.

"I'm sorry! Luna's files corrupted in post and three hours of footage disappeared."

"Shit," I say. "Are they okay?"

Fitz shakes her head. "We were up until three a.m. trying to recover them."

Luna Blue is a teen BookTuber who lives in Anaheim. Fitz met them for the first time at a YouTube convention last year. Fitz called from that convention and came out to me as bi with the tipsy proclamation, *I'm kinda in love with Luna Blue!* They dated for half of sophomore year, until the long distance became Too Much and they decided that for now they're better as friends.

"Sorry. Anyways. Y'all ready?"

Her bubblegum pink lips break into a smile that's impossible to not reciprocate.

"So ready!" I knock on Mrs. Mulaney's door.

"Come in!"

I push the door open and we enter the office, seating ourselves in the wooden chairs in front of Mrs. Mulaney's desk. Her aesthetic—purple slacks and a floral print blouse—is *office chic,* according to Fitz. She tucks a rogue strand of her chin-length blonde bob behind her ear and plasters a welcoming smile on her cherry lips.

"What can I help you with this morning?"

Henry launches into our script. "Thank you so much for meeting with us—"

We deliver our proposal with the passion of a closing night performance. There is no way Mrs. Mulaney cannot be captivated by the possibility of the drama club putting together an epic, original, inclusive production that highlights issues that matter to us. When Fitz delivers the concluding line, my heart swells in my chest. We nailed it.

Except, there is no standing ovation. Mrs. Mulaney's expression morphs from intrigue to intense consideration to . . . I don't even know what. Her cherry lips turn upside down and my stomach drops because I have never seen an expression morph so quickly.

"I thought you knew." Her forehead creases. Not the reaction I anticipated. "I don't know how to say this, but we can't afford to replace Miss Bryant's position, not with the budget cuts. The turnout—between the number of participating students and the average audience sizes—just isn't enough to warrant the cost. I'm sorry, but there won't be a drama club. Not this year."

I blink, unable to process the declaration that has rendered an entire summer of work pointless.

"That's it?" Henry asks.

"Can't we recruit another teacher to take over?" Fitz asks.

Her words reverberate and I recalibrate. "Yeah, we'll find a new advisor!"

Mrs. Mulaney shakes her head. "I wish it were that simple, but there are other considerations. Beyond Miss Bryant's position being eliminated, the school board also cut down advisor stipends for after-school art programs. And *Barefoot* was not a helpful note to end on."

"Seriously?" I snap.

"I'm just stating an unfortunate reality, Natalie." Mrs. Mulaney shoots me eye daggers that rival my mother's every time someone questions the validity of romance novels. Which should be weird, but I'm used to it. Before she rose through the ranks and became the youngest principal in the district five years ago, Mrs. Mulaney was only Caroline, a history teacher on the LHS teacher bowling team with my dad. As a result, she's more quirky aunt than viable authority figure.

"But you took a meeting with us," Fitz says.

"I'm taking meetings for all extracurricular groups that have been cut," Mrs. Mulaney says. "Listening to how much these programs mean to students and building a case for the school committee to reconsider next year's budget is the least I can do. As for this year, I don't have anything left to work with."

"That can't be true. The band—"

Oh my God.

It hits me all at once. Even though his supply and music budget got cut, in the two weeks since school started, my dad has been able to secure buses for festival auditions, an honorarium to cover a visit from a member of the New York Philharmonic, and a new percussion set for his classroom.

An an arts budget *does* exist!

It just all belongs to the band.

I stand and toss my backpack over my shoulder. "This was such a waste of time."

"Can I be honest with you?" Mrs. Mulaney stands to

match my height, her palms pressed against her desk. "Lincoln High School has the top-ranked concert band in the MetroWest area. The festivals, the grant money they bring in, the positive press that comes with it—to the school committee, that matters. Also, band enrollment and retention has increased year over year, whereas participation in other extracurricular arts programs has declined across the board. I'm not happy about the cuts, I can promise you that, but I *am* happy that your dad and his students are surviving this mess. They've earned it."

I laugh. "And we didn't. Because all that matters is the bottom line."

My eyes sting with salt and I'm pissed, *so pissed.* Pissed at Mrs. Mulaney for admitting the one aspect of this school that brings me joy doesn't matter. Pissed at my dad, who sent me into a formality meeting with absolutely no warning. Pissed at the school committee for confirming what I've always known to be true.

Art is not a sustainable path.

Not even as a high school hobby.

CHAPTER THREE

Hosting a welcome back assembly two weeks into the school year feels like a delayed reaction.

Mrs. Mulaney destroyed our *Melted* hopes and dreams mere hours ago, and now I'm sitting in the gymnasium half listening to her school spirit bullshit. I'm stage left, sandwiched between Henry and Fitz and surrounded by the rest of the drama kids, all processing the death of our hobby.

"So, we're just supposed to sit back and be quiet through the desecration of the arts?" Makayla Okoye whispers behind me. Makayla, a junior like Fitz and me, is starting center on the varsity basketball team, has won a regional prize for her charcoal art, and can do a killer British accent. She's an athlete who arts, the embodiment of who my sister and I would be if we were smashed together into one person. If we were a five-eleven Nigerian-American girl from D.C. and not short Jewish girls who've never left Massachusetts.

"But first, a riveting lecture on the consequences of Juuling!" Arjun Patel says. He's sitting behind me, but I can *hear* his eye roll. Arjun is our senior stage manager whose main gigs are being student council vice president and captain of the tennis team.

My palms press against purple plastic bleachers as I lean forward to see over Ivan McGilvray, whose six-five frame is a serious problem at the moment. While Mrs. Mulaney moves on from Juuling to the budget cuts, I scan the bleachers—searching for my dad.

His eyes meet mine across the gymnasium.

Traitor, I mouth.

It doesn't matter that my dad is too far away to understand. It's cathartic, the word tumbling from my lips from a safe distance.

My phone buzzes in my hand.

Reid Callahan
how did boiled go?
8:45 AM

I make another face, this time at the back of Reid's head. He's sitting with a group of band kids a few rows in front of me. He bumps shoulders with Lacey Henderson, first flute, and laughs when she whispers something in his ear. His fingers tap against his thigh absentmindedly in five-four, to the beat of whatever song he and my dad jammed to this morning, most likely.

Fitz reads the text over my shoulder. "May I?"

I hand Fitz my phone.

8:46 AM

"Does anyone have any questions?" Mrs. Mulaney asks.

Her toothy grin screams *please don't!*

Henry chews on the inside of his cheek. Fitz raises her hand.

Mrs. Mulaney's lips press into a thin line, her expression neutral. "Yes, Fitz?"

"Can we talk about the 'across the board' arts budget cuts?" Fitz stands on the bleachers, her voice a decibel too high. "You didn't mention the music program."

Silence ricochets off gymnasium walls. That's a thing that happens when Fitz speaks. I mean, students never speak up at Mrs. Mulaney's assemblies. But Fitz, standing on the bleachers with her arms crossed and bubblegum lips pursed, demands attention.

Mrs. Mulaney's eyes meet Fitz's. "We're lucky to still have a core music curriculum and band program, but unfortunately there will be cuts there too."

Danica Martinez, a senior who is at the center of both the musical theater and a cappella clubs, raises her hand. Hell yes! *This* is Fitz's power.

"What does that mean for The Trebles?"

"It means . . ."

"No Trebles, Danica," Fitz chimes in.

Danica frowns. "Is that true?"

Mrs. Mulaney nods. "I'm sorry."

The choral students erupt into panicked whispers—and Fitz isn't even finished. "No Trebles. No theater or film classes, or advanced art classes, or lit mag, or broadcast journal—"

"*Enough*, Ava." Challenging Mrs. Mulaney behind closed doors is one thing. Calling her out in front of the entire student body? It's next level. "There is a newsletter in your student emails explaining the cuts and how to get involved in other LHS initiatives—"

"It doesn't explain why the band gets a pass," Fitz says.

Reid whips around to face us. "Because we're good?"

I blink. "Excuse me?"

Reid shrugs. "We put in hours every week. We deserve it."

I . . . cannot even right now.

Before I can overthink it, I stand beside Fitz. "No. Makayla's portraits win regional prizes. Over the summer, Danica spent a week in New York representing LHS in musical theater workshops. Fitz got second place at the state theater festival for her monologue from *Barefoot in the Park*. Don't tell me this is about quality performances."

My voice measured even though I feel hot, like a spotlight is beaming on me, center stage.

Reid raises one eyebrow. "We don't get second place, Natalie. We win."

"Art is *not* about winning!" I retort, my voice now an octave too high.

Mrs. Mulaney clears her throat. "Ava. Natalie. *Sit down.*"

Fitz sits. Smooths her skirt. "I'm good, *Caroline.*"

Silence transforms into collective *ooohs.* Now it's a scene.

"Okay. Everyone, please report to your first period class. Fitz . . ." Mrs. Mulaney's neck snaps to face us. "My office."

Henry's eyes narrow. "Good job, Fitzgerald."

Fitz stands, tossing her checkered JanSport over her shoulder, and shrugs. "What's she going to do? Suspend me from after-school activities?"

"You're my hero," I say.

Fitz blows me a kiss. "You were amazing too."

"Natalie!" Henry sighs, exasperated. "Don't validate this!"

I cup my hands around my lips and mouth *H-E-R-O* to Fitz as she saunters down the bleacher steps and follows Mulaney out the double doors, middle finger flipped behind her back.

"That went well," Henry mutters.

His voice drips with sarcasm, totally oblivious to the mini-movement happening before us. Because the non-band students straight up *applaud* Fitz as she exits the gym on Mulaney's heels. In my head, it's an aria, crescendoing from pianissimo to forte. In reality, it's a few dozen teenagers. But I *see* it. A clear division between band and the other arts clubs forming. Now that they know there's injustice in these budget cuts, they're not so willing to let them go.

It's an opportunity. I feel it in my bones.

This isn't over.

• • •

Independent Study now fills the empty block between AP Psychology and AP Chemistry.

It's not a plot twist, but even two weeks in it still hurts. Study period replaces Improv 101 in my otherwise aggressively AP junior year schedule. My low-stress palate cleanser between science classes has been rendered an empty space. A glorified comma, as Mom would say.

"Is this level?" Dad asks.

My study overlaps with Dad's prep period, so I'm spending it in the music room with him, seated first chair flute. Note, this is not a *choice*—Dad used his teacher power to have Ms. Rodkey, the school secretary, summon me to his classroom *via the loudspeaker*. Peak embarrassing. That's when I knew for sure he was not happy about the assembly.

I don't care. I'm pissed too.

I stuff my purple folder into my bag and look up. Dad's standing on a black metal band chair, arms outstretched to hang a poster above his desk. It features an animated treble clef—with *shoes*—that reads I KNEW YOU WERE TREBLE WHEN YOU WALKED IN.

I can't believe his students think he's cool.

"Tilt it a little to the left," I say.

Dad makes the adjustment and presses his palms against the poster, sticking it to the wall.

I press my lips in a firm line. I expected *traitor* to spill out the moment I walked into his classroom as easily as it did at the assembly. I'm not sure why. If the choice is stew in awkward silence or engage in an honest conversation, Dad and I will stew all day. So stew in the band room I do. With enough space for a full student orchestra, multilevel floor included—it's pretty much a dream classroom. Chairs are spaced evenly apart on the three tiers; music stands hang in racks on the back wall, which is decorated with a wide range of music theory posters.

Dad steps down, takes a seat in his rolling desk chair, and wiggles the mouse to wake up his desktop. The screen is angled toward me, opened to the roster for Composition, Beginner.

"So, that was quite a performance," he says, making the first move.

"I'd argue that the Tony goes to you this week, Dad."

His eyes meet mine, his expression softening. "Because I believed in *Melted*?"

I cross my arms, resisting the urge to ease up. "A reality check would've been helpful. At least a heads-up that they're not replacing Miss Bryant."

"I didn't want to burst your bubble on the basis of speculation. You and Henry were having so much fun this summer. I loved that you were writing together. I believed you had a real shot." Dad exhales a heavy breath and scratches his beard. "I'm sorry that you felt blindsided."

I pick at my chipped blue nail polish, frustrated. "Sorry enough to do something?"

Dad's silence in this moment is fortissimo.

"I thought so."

"Natalie, it is my job to make the band as valuable to this school as possible. To make *myself* as valuable as possible."

"Even if it's at the expense of every other arts student and their clubs?"

Dad frowns. "That's not my fault. I understand that you're upset. But you can't just go off the rails with an anti-band agenda. Do you understand how much trouble our family is in if the music program gets cut?"

Seriously? Dad speaks as if I don't know that this is his job and money has been tight. Like I haven't lived with the complicated tension of the band being a necessary evil in my life for years.

I'm aware of it. I deal with it. It doesn't mean I have to like it.

Besides, all I did at the assembly was state facts. That's hardly going *off the rails.*

"Reid started—"

Dad cuts me off. "Switzerland."

I exhale a frustrated sigh. All I want is for Dad to not be Mr. Jacobson for, I don't know, two seconds. Tell me that even though it's his department, Reid wasn't right at the assembly either. But Dad is *Switzerland.* "Neutral" on all things *Natalie vs. Reid.* What he doesn't understand is that his neutrality is, in fact, picking a side. I don't know why I even try.

I stand and swing my backpack over my shoulder, done with this familiar scene. "Whatever—"

The band room door swings open, cutting me off mid-exit.

"Sorry." Reid takes a step backward. "I'll come back later if I'm—"

"He's all yours," I say. "I'm out."

I push past Reid, crossing the tiered seating of the band room and swinging the door open before anyone can read my face. Except I'm not fast enough, because I hear Reid calling my name not once, not twice, but three times as he follows me through the hallway.

"Natalie," he repeats. "I'm so—"

I whip around to face him. "Don't. You're not. So don't."

Reid's fingers tap against his thigh in half notes, legato. The beat Reid taps in the minutes before a math midterm, or after the last lesson with my dad before a competition.

He exhales. "You got screwed. It sucks."

"He says before returning to the band room," I say.

Reid shrugs. "I'll just talk to your dad after Chemistry."

Before I respond, the bell rings and students flood the hallway. I make it a point to actively not engage with how much overlap there is in our schedules, but we have AP Chemistry together. I can't exactly storm off. So we walk together, our steps syncopated. Reid's mouth twitches, like the corners are trying to turn up. It's weird. Walking next to Reid Callahan is weird.

Of course the science wing is on the other side of the building, as far away from the band room as you can possibly get. We follow murals that depict the stages of mitosis toward the end of the narrow hall to Ms. Santiago's classroom. It's the last on the left, adjacent to an alarmed emergency exit. Reid's classes overlapping with mine is almost emergency enough to push through those double doors and bolt. Especially when he opens his mouth again.

"We could use another clarinet, you know."

His words stop me midstep. It's such a ridiculous statement, I wonder if I'm in a fever dream.

My laugh echoes down the hallway. "You're joking."

"It's too easy, simply being the best," Reid says. "Don't you miss the competition?"

I shake my head. "No. I really don't."

I just—this is why Reid and I will never have a normal conversation. His default setting is contriving a competition with me, even when there is nothing left to compete over.

"So you're just going to, what—?" He shakes his head. "Stats, chemistry, psychology, bio . . . your schedule is soul-sucking, Natalie."

"Why do you care?" I ask.

Reid stuffs his hands in his pockets. "I don't. But now that *Melted* is over—"

Nope. I cannot even. I lengthen my stride until I'm in front of Ms. Santiago's room and push the door open. I take the empty seat next to Fitz in the back-center table.

"Are you okay?" Fitz whispers, her eyes flickering in the direction of Reid's seat.

"I didn't get sent to the office. Are *you* okay?"

Fitz rolls her eyes. "Caroline puts on a tough show. But by the end of the lecture she was apologizing to *me* for not handling this morning better!"

I laugh, relieved that at least the consequences of our assembly performance were mild. As soon as the bell rings, Santiago rattles off her usual spiel about lab safety and handling chemicals. Our first lab of the semester is testing how aluminum and zinc react with hydrochloric acid. It's the only chemical the school allows the lab to stock that's actually dangerous, so Santiago reiterates every rule in the book. It's the same lecture we got in Honors Chemistry last year, but Reid is taking meticulous notes as if his life depends on it.

It's too easy, simply being the best.

Except Reid wasn't the best. Not when I played.

Now that Melted *is over . . .*

Reid's words echo in my head and I want nothing more than to wipe the confident smirk off his face. And it hits me—there *is* competition to start. It just isn't about the clarinet.

I spend the rest of class writing in my notebook, drafting and redrafting the perfect response to Reid's invitation to play the instrument that turned a childhood rivalry into a full-out war. My pen glides across the notebook paper, personal attacks composed in perfect script. Each version is a slightly different wording of the same simple truth.

I'd rather dump hydrochloric acid on myself than play the clarinet with Reid again.

And *Melted* is far from over.

Happy Birthday in Jazz Clarinet

In an alternate universe, I move through the world in quarter notes and four-four time signatures.

Dad and I spend hours in the studio together, just the two of us and our music. He corrects my breathing technique and coaches me through "Rhapsody in Blue" before abandoning the classics for improvisational jazz. Weekends are spent either preparing for auditions or attending festivals. Music is my blood, like Dad.

Sometimes I forget that before the clarinet was Reid's, it was mine.

The memory from third grade is a series of stills. Cake. Mom radiating excitement in a midlength purple dress, fresh off selling a new series. The final score after an intense game of Mario Kart with Reid, back when our relationship was a fun series of meaningless kid competitions. Dad holding his clarinet out to me with an encouraging smile. My back straightening like a marionette pulled by its strings, ready for the moment we'd been practicing for weeks.

Us playing "Happy Birthday," for Delia in jazz clarinet.

Dad blew through the mouthpiece while I sat on his lap. My fingers moved up and down the keys, barely big enough to cover the holes, but creating music. Dad's breath was staccato, giving me just enough time to switch between the notes.

In that moment, music felt like something that was Dad's and mine. Only ours.

Then the song ended. Reid tapped on Dad's knee, said, *You play a giant recorder!*, pulled out his green plastic tragedy of an instrument, and played the birthday song all by himself. Reid was *good*—as good as anyone playing a piece of plastic could be.

The clarinet was mine for one jazzy happy birthday before Reid made it ours.

Suddenly Reid was joining us in the studio every Saturday morning for lessons that were supposed to be private. He listened to jazz and practiced in my basement for hours. By the time we were twelvc, Reid had integrated himself into every minute of our intense schedule, accompanying us to recitals and asking my dad for intricate jazz pieces for extra practice.

I hated it.

Clarinet lessons had been the one space my dad and I shared, just us. My way into his studio and his musical world. He spent so much time in there—giving private lessons, prepping class materials, rehearsing with Lincoln Street Blues. If he was not playing music, he was *talking* about music, and I learned at a young age that if I wanted to spend time with my dad, the easiest way was to love the clarinet as much as he did. So I tried.

At least for the first year, Reid was catching up to me.

But then Reid crossed the break, hitting his high notes first, and everything got worse.

His presence became as grating as the high F he was now able to play.

And all of a sudden, I was the one trying to keep up with him. I'd play scales in my bedroom alone, in tears every time my high F fell flat. I worked so hard, spent so many hours on something that came so naturally to Reid.

I worked until I got that high F.

And in seventh grade, I beat Reid for first chair.

I didn't know at the time that it'd be my last year with our instrument—or that winning would mean so much more.

Today, my clarinet is in the back of my closet, in a case that is collecting dust.

CHAPTER FOUR

Chao Down is a landmark in Lincoln. Jenny and Michael Chao opened this location when Henry was an infant—and nearly eighteen years, twenty locations, and one guest appearance on *Top Chef* later, they are local celebrities. Perks of Henry being the future heir of Chao Down, I have a flexible part-time job that means getting paid to hang out with my best friends. Fitz and I hostess, while Henry works in the kitchen as a line cook.

Any minute, arts students will storm the restaurant, demanding justice with a side of dumplings. I think. I hope. We reached out to school friends from the other cut clubs in solidarity to build on the momentum from the assembly—proposing a meeting at Chao Down to start a conversation about our options re: fighting the budget cuts.

Come for the food, stay for the student activism! is Fitz's line of the week.

Will the message resonate? To be determined.

In the meantime, I'm ignoring my nerves by writing snapshots of dialogue from behind the hostess stand. Today's scene, scrawled on the back of a paper menu, is from *Lady*

M—a modernized black comedy starring sixteen-year-old Lady Macbeth, my favorite Shakespeare character. I love adapting my favorite works, taking something that exists and exploring it through a new medium or point of view. In *Lady M*, I've crafted an epic enemies-to-lovers arc between her and Macbeth, and it is so fun to get lost in their world and escape from the intensity of junior year. To lose myself in something I can actually control—something for only my eyes to see.

Because I love writing with Henry, but I also love having something that's just for me.

"Hey, Natalie."

Arjun's voice snaps me out of my creative zone and I flip my paper menu script over. Arjun is early, but he brought friends! Plural! Connor DiMarco, student council president and a baritone in The Trebles, and Kendra McKenna, a former journalist for the recently cancelled student news show, *Jag TV*.

I am cheesing *hard*, so relieved that people showed up.

"Hey! Henry's setting up some booths in the back."

"Awesome," Kendra says.

"Thanks for organizing this, Natalie," Connor says as they pass me, heading toward Henry.

My heart swells with validation as student after student enters Chao Down in the final minutes of my shift. Nearly every cut club is represented—drama club, visual arts, a cappella, journalism, lit mag, etc. We're up to nearly twenty attendees when the door swings open and Makayla and Fitz enter the restaurant with froyo.

"Natalie!" Makayla yells.

"You came!" I say, wrapping my arms around Makayla.

"Duh!" Makayla says. "But can we start ASAP? I have HIIT at four."

Of course. Makayla's aesthetic can be summed up as, *I can drop and give you twenty at any moment.* Today's look is compression leggings and her LHS varsity basketball track jacket.

"Your commitment to Saturday HIIT is aspirational. Truly," Fitz says, scooping a spoonful of M&M's.

Makayla shrugs. "It's easy when the instructor looks like Natalie Dormer."

Fitz swoons. "Wow. Okay. Saturdays at four, you say?"

"Do you even know what HIIT stands for?" I ask, folding my paper menu into quarters.

"I will learn in the name of Natalie Dormer," Fitz proclaims, and we burst out laughing as an elderly couple enters the restaurant, reminding me that I am still, in fact, on the clock.

"Kenny should be here any minute to take over, but everyone else is in the back. I promise we won't stand between you and a superior Natalie, Makayla."

Makayla laughs. "You're good people."

I seat two tables in the remaining minutes of my shift, giving the welcome spiel. In the lull between lunch and dinner, we seat patrons in the front room with the windows and maximum natural light. This time of day, midafternoon, the sun reflects on the gold foil artwork on the ivory brick walls. Chao

Down's aesthetic is elegant without being pretentious—even when the quality of the food is worthy of pretension.

"Hey, Natalie," Kenny Chao—Henry's cousin—says, approaching the hostess stand to relieve me. As always, I am grateful punctuality runs in the Chao family. Kenny is nineteen, has the most perfect smile, and always brings me a Thai bubble tea from the kitchen during our shift change. "Let the changing of the guard commence."

"Thanks! You're my favorite Chao," I say.

Normally, I'd stay for a few beats and flirt, because platonic flirting is kind of my thing with Kenny. But not today! I take the tea, tuck my phone into my pocket, and bolt toward the action at the back of the restaurant, untying my hostess apron. Everyone is crammed around six four-seaters pushed together to create one big table.

I take in the image, everyone eating and commiserating over their clubs.

Sipping my tea, I slide into the seat across from Henry, who is texting.

"Ready?" I ask.

Henry hits send and nods. "Let's do this."

Before we get everyone's attention, I'm interrupted by the one group not yet represented.

"Hey! I'm sorry we're late," Danica Martinez's melodic voice projects from behind me. It takes a moment to fully process that the most influential senior at LHS is *here.* In Chao Down. In shorts with fishnets under them, a ripped band T-shirt, her long brown hair in a mermaid braid down her back, as if her last performance was headlining a nineties grunge band.

"Hey!" Henry says. "We're just about to get started."

Danica's turquoise lips smile wide as Henry stands and goes in for a hug. Whoa. Fitz and I look at each other, her eyebrows shooting to the sky as we process the texting. The hugging. The stupid smile on Henry's face. It is all . . . a new development.

"Of course! My therapist says I need a healthy way to channel my negative emotions."

"Mood," Fitz says.

Not a new development? Fitz's crush on Danica. It dates back to post Luna Blue breakup, during the good old days of Performance Studies 101 with Miss Bryant. Danica, a junior at the time, convinced her scene partner, Jacob Linetti, to perform a gender-swapped rendition of the "Stella!" scene from *A Streetcar Named Desire.*

Fitz has been quietly pining ever since.

Danica pulls up a chair next to Henry. "Right? It's like, I can wallow over the fact that it is my senior year and there is no musical. But I'm tired of feeling *angry*. I want . . ." Danica's voice trails off, searching for words.

". . . to feel useful?" Fitz asks.

Danica smiles at her. "Exactly."

Fitz flushes. "I get it. It's how I feel thinking about *Melted.* Henry and Natalie's show. And not playing Not-Elsa in it."

"She's *not* Elsa," Henry says. "Her name is Adina."

Fitz winks. "Exactly."

"I have . . . so many questions," Connor says. His voice surprises me, as I was thinking he's mostly here for the dumplings. "Wait. *Melted.* As the in . . . the opposite of *Frozen*?"

Danica's eyes widen. "That's actually incredible."

"Right!" Fitz says. *"Genius."*

"How does it work?" Connor asks. "Is everything, like, *literally* the opposite?"

"It's about Not-Elsa, climate activist and Queen of Infernodelle," Fitz clarifies. "On the eve of her twenty-first birthday, a hot air balloon—"

I cut Fitz off. "This isn't just about *Melted.*"

"Can it be?" Connor asks. "Because I want to know everything."

"Fitz can DM you the synopsis," I concede, because honestly, I'm pumped that our basic-white-boy student council president is invested in *Melted* based on concept. "But we need to talk about the budget cuts. Has anyone tried proposing budget-friendly alternatives to their clubs?"

Everyone nods in unison.

"Mulaney turned down our art auction yesterday," says Cherish Montgomery, Makayla's friend and collaborator on all things set design for the drama club and musical theater.

"We can meet for lit mag, but it's now a lit *blogspot.* Can't even have a real domain!" Liliana Ortega, captain of the swim team and the head of the former literary magazine, adds.

Fitz winces. "I didn't know blogspot still existed."

Danica crosses her arms and rolls her eyes. "The Trebles can sing the national anthem at sports events. No concerts, no competitions."

Okay. Noted. I thought after the public callout at the assembly at least one club would get a sympathy win, but Mrs. Mulaney isn't even trying. That works for me. There is no better bond than that of a common enemy.

"Look around," I say. I'm typically a writer of impassioned speeches, not a deliverer of them, but I'm not about to waste a captive audience. "Look at who's here. More importantly, look at who *isn't*." I pause, letting the weight of the last word settle. "The band is sitting pretty. Why? Because they bring *prestige* and local media attention to our otherwise mediocre town. I'm not against the band. Or my dad. Just so that's on the record. But the band is—"

"—right behind us! Four o'clock." Fitz interrupts with an over-the-top nod in their direction. I follow her line of sight to a four-seater high top near the bar. It's The First Chairs. Lacey Henderson, first flute. Logan Price, first trumpet.

And of course, Reid. First clarinet.

I was one sentence away from blurting my entire plan in front of The First Chairs.

Fitz is a hero.

My eyes meet Reid's. Half of his face is hidden behind a menu, as if that's not conspicuous. Reid never comes to

Chao Down. It's my territory. If he's going to break the rules, it's disappointing that he's not even trying to be covert about it.

"Odds that this is a coincidence?" Arjun asks.

We disseminated the meeting details to a select group via a swift and effective word-of-mouth campaign, but people talk. If Reid and The First Chairs caught wind, they'd absolutely show up to see what we're up to. Definitely not a coincidence.

"It probably has nothing to do with us," Henry says. "Not worth a reaction from—"

I don't hear the last thing Henry says because I'm already gone, marching toward Reid and The First Chairs. Except as I approach the table, I overhear a genuinely animated conversation estimating the true value of a fire token and guessing the chances of an *advantageddon.* I . . . don't know what language they're speaking.

"Hey, Natalie," Lacey says casually, looking up from her computer.

"Hi," I answer, skeptical.

"It sucks. Your clubs getting cut," Logan says, brushing his too-long blonde hair out of his eyes. Logan Price is the first boy I loved in the most middle school way. I loved his chill confidence in his trumpet ability. I loved writing his name in my notebook—the swoop of the cursive L and looping the G. He held my hand during the hora at my bat mitzvah and I swear I didn't wash it for the rest of the night. "Trevor has been coping with excessive Mario Kart."

In eighth grade, Logan came out by re-creating the Ferris wheel scene in *Love, Simon* and has been in a relationship with Trevor Ryan, a junior on the swim team and in The Trebles, ever since.

"Yeah. It sucks," I repeat.

"Why are you here, Natalie?" Reid asks, placing his menu flat on the table. "I know it's not to talk about *Survivor* week one power rankings."

His tone is direct, with an edge. I can always rely on Reid to get to the point.

"Come on." I wave to the back of the room, to the movement that's underway. "You can't honestly expect me to believe that you're *here*. In Chao Down. To talk about *Survivor*."

Reid arches an eyebrow. "Yes."

"We do this every weekend," Lacey says. "I wanted to do lunch proper, but Reid insists it has to be after your shift because of some . . . rule book? I don't even want to know."

I blink. "You're here every Saturday?"

Logan touches his hair so much I'm not even sure he knows he's doing it. "Chao Down is our No Music zone, where we can focus on *Survivor* and not get sidetracked by band stuff."

I had no idea Reid managed to drag his friends into his *Survivor* fandom.

Or that he talks to them about anything besides, well, band stuff.

"I know what you're doing," Reid says, nodding toward our back booths, his raised eyebrows screaming *I know you're up to something!*

Lacey drums her pale pink manicure on the table. "Misery loves company. It makes sense."

I shake my head. "We're not—"

Reid cuts me off. "—against the band."

Of course, he has to let me know he heard every word.

Before I respond, he shoots me his most condescending smirk. "What a relief."

I press my lips together to silence my rage scream.

"What Reid *means* to say—" Logan says, brushing his hair out of his eyes for the umpteenth time "—is let us know if there is anything we can do to help."

That is *not* what Reid means and Logan is absolutely too nice to function.

"Noted."

I return to the booths before I can give any more away, with a mission to bring down the volume without snuffing out the passion or looking too sketchy. I slide into the opposite side of my booth so I can look over the restaurant and keep tabs on Reid and The First Chairs.

"It's *Survivor* Saturday. Allegedly," I say, my voice low.

Henry exhales a dramatic sigh. "See. Not everything Reid does has an ulterior motive."

Fitz shakes her head. "Really? Sounds fake."

Makayla raises her hand. "Not to be *that* person—"

"You are literally always *that* person," Arjun interjects.

"—but less than forty-five minutes until HIIT."

"Maybe we should reschedule," Fitz suggests.

I shake my head. "We'll never get this many of us in the same room again. They're far enough away that we just need to take it down. Do not project."

"Is that not a bit much?" Arjun asks.

"Reid and The First Chairs can't overhear this," I say, my voice just below normal dinner table volume. "I'll skip the exposition and get to the point. Would you be down to join forces with one proposal that we bring to Mrs. Mulaney and the school committee as a united front? A proposal for something that combines elements of all our interests and lets our clubs live on in some form? I think we can build a stronger case together. Make it impossible to say no."

I should be gauging my audience's reaction, but instead I'm indulging my paranoia—looking past Connor's head toward Reid. But he's just laughing at something Logan says and they don't seem to be paying attention at all.

"Is it worth it just for one night?" Makayla asks, snapping me back to the table. "We all have a lot on our plate."

Danica shrugs. "It does kind of seem like a lot of work and no guarantee."

"The annual budget is set. Why would anyone—Mrs.

Mulaney or the school committee—change their mind? The money would have to come from somewhere else," Connor says.

"It's easy to say no to a couple of students with a proposal." Henry's typical soft-spoken voice is so low that everyone has to lean toward him to hear. "But if we organize, keep the budget low, put our proposals together, and prove the community will invest in this event and climate change causes, like they do for band events, we can be great PR for the school too."

There is a beat of silence, everyone processing.

"So the money . . . would come out of the band's budget?" Makayla asks.

"Theoretically," I say.

Danica presses her lips together, her expression skeptical. "Are you really cutthroat enough to go up against the band? Against your dad?"

This is it. I can feel it. Whatever we say next will seal it or sink it.

"This isn't about the band. It's about Mrs. Mulaney and the school committee justifying what art should mean to us. As if the purpose of the programs they offer are to add to the school's image—like grant money, good PR, or fancy awards—not to give us a place to express ourselves or try new things. They could've budgeted a portion of the band's funds toward salvaging our clubs. The fact that no one even tried? It's messed up."

"We're not anti-band, we're anti-bureaucracy," Fitz emphasizes.

"Sorry, Connor," Arjun says.

Connor shakes his head. "I'm a glorified event planner with a smooth baritone, actually."

"If that isn't bureaucracy in a nutshell," Fitz says.

Henry coughs. "We're losing the plot. Are we following Natalie's lead?"

I look around the table, watch everyone's expressions as they silently work through this. I know we have to keep it quiet, but the silence is stressful. It becomes clear after a few minutes that everyone is waiting on one person's response.

Finally, she delivers.

"Okay, Jacobson. Let's join forces," Danica says.

Cherish nods in agreement. "What do we have to lose?"

Makayla smiles so hard her nose crinkles.

"Let's see what we can do," Arjun agrees, bumping fists with Connor and Liliana.

"The Trebles *have* to sing 'Let It Go' at intermission," Kendra says.

"Maybe we can do a short print run of the lit mag and sell it at the show?" Liliana suggests.

"Everyone wants to do *Melted*?" I ask, unable to hide the surprise in my voice. I had a pitch on deck, prepared for a hard sell.

"I mean. Yeah. Who wouldn't pay to see a *Frozen* opposite play?" Danica says.

Everyone else nods as the ideas of repressed arts students begin to pour out—and from there all eyes are on me as we exchange phone numbers and discuss next steps. I'm not used to this attention, to the spotlight being on me. Not that I hate it.

I actually *don't* hate it. Not at all.

CHAPTER FIVE

"Level four crisis."

My eyes shift from the biology flash cards I'm creating at the kitchen table to my sister as she drops her soccer bag on the floor and collapses into the empty chair next to me, her cheeks still flushed pink from hours of drills. Delia is the least dramatic person I know. Her crises are usually level two, at worst.

"What's up?" I ask.

"Hannah wants to go to the movies next weekend. Reid is driving us."

Relevant information: Hannah's last name is Callahan. Yup. As if Reid isn't on the periphery of my life enough *as is*, we both have twelve-year-old sisters who are pretty much inseparable. Worse, I know Delia thinks of Reid as a big brother. Worst, Reid *acts* like one.

But that's my crisis, not hers.

I scrunch my nose. "What aren't you saying, Dee?"

"Hannah invited The Monicas, too."

Of course this is about The Monicas. Hannah bonded with Monica Delgado and Monica Grisham over a mutual appreciation of grand jetés and the boys' basketball team this summer, while Delia was at Jock Camp. Delia returned from camp to a whole new Hannah, who has sleepovers nearly every weekend with her new dance team, cocaptained by The Monicas.

Delia is never invited to their sleepovers.

She undoes her French braids and ties her chestnut brown waves into a messy topknot before taking a seat at the table. "This is the first time I've been invited to hang out with her and The Monicas. I should be happy! Except today Monica D. asked me why a bat mitzvah couldn't just be in English. I'm used to people saying dumb stuff like that—I'm just not used to Hannah *laughing* at it."

My eyebrows shoot toward the sky. "Hannah did *what*?"

Delia looks like she's going to cry and I hate The Monicas. Antisemitism in Lincoln is disseminated through casual microaggressions. The Monicas, it's becoming clear, are two of the worst offenders.

"Hannah says she's joking and I'm too sensitive. Obviously, she's Jewish too, so it's like—am I?"

"*No.* Hannah is just . . ." I don't even know. Temporarily blinded by popularity? Internalizing biases? I don't know what Hannah Callahan is doing, but I need to protect her and snap her out of The Monicas phase ASAP.

"I thought we established this house is a Monica-free zone." Mom enters the kitchen, headphones around her neck, to check on the giant pot of matzo ball soup simmering on the stove. It's one of two meals that Michelle Jacobson is capable of pulling off, and she always makes it special for the first night of Rosh Hashanah.

Delia shrugs. "Hannah wants me to get to know them so I'll invite them to my bat mitzvah. Maybe if they get to know me, the microaggressions will stop. I don't know. I feel like I'm losing my best friend."

I shake my head. "You don't owe The Monicas anything."

"And you are *not* inviting them to your bat mitzvah. I am vetoing that now," Mom says.

Delia's shoulders relax. "Thanks. It's *so* confusing."

"What's confusing?" Dad asks.

He enters the scene just after his cue, emerging from a Lincoln Street Blues rehearsal in the basement.

"Hannah and The Monicas," Mom says.

Dad's expression is blank.

"Hannah's new best friends?" Delia pushes her chair back, scraping wood against wood. "The reason we saw the new Captain Marvel movie together last weekend instead of me going with her?"

"Right, of course!" Dad opens a cabinet and reaches for a glass. "And to think, I thought you wanted to go the movies with me."

I swear my dad lives in another universe that is composed of time signatures and treble clefs. Dad's recall is terrible unless it has anything to do with music or his band students.

I mean, who can forget The Monicas? There are two of them!

Delia rolls her eyes. "I'm *twelve.*"

Dad shrugs. "I'm an optimist."

More like oblivious, I think. There is a beat of silence, as if Delia is waiting for Dad to ask a follow-up question. It's the same beat I gave him in the days following *Melted*'s rejection, waiting for us to have a meaningful conversation about it.

It's been almost two weeks.

Delia shouldn't hold her breath.

"We're leaving for synagogue in an hour, Dee," Dad says.

Her shoulders sag. "The soccer uniform isn't quite temple couture, is it? I'll go get ready."

Tonight, Delia is participating in the service at Temple Beth Elohim, quietly chanting the chatzi kaddish on the bima with the other b'nai mitzvah students. She retreats to her room and Mom doesn't react until we hear the door close behind her.

"Really, Aaron," Mom says. "You could at least try to pay attention."

Dad removes his glasses and pinches the bridge of his nose. "I'm sorry that seventh grade drama isn't quite top of mind right now. There's so much going on. The Harvest Festival is right around the corner, I have to get our spring festival applications in, and Lincoln Street Blues needs to find a permanent sub on keys since Charlie tore his rotator cuff. Which is, you know, perfect timing while we're planning a bat mitzvah we can barely afford."

"*Aaron.*" Mom's voice is sharp. "I am finally working on a new book for Anna, one of my classes is filled with pretentious assholes, and I'm planning this *bat mitzvah we can barely afford* pretty much on my own. We all have a lot going on."

My parents are fighting. Mom is writing. This scene is impossible to process.

"You're writing?" Dad asks. "I had no idea. The extra pressure—"

"—is not an excuse to be so detached. Shana Tova." Mom plucks her oversized maple cardigan off the back of the kitchen chair and retreats to her office.

Leaving me alone with Dad.

I push my chair back and stand. "Every club *lost* their events . . . and you're complaining about how *busy* the band is."

Dad's expression instantly softens. "Natalie—"

"Shana Tova, Dad."

I exit scene in pursuit of Delia, before he has the chance to disappoint me. Again.

The first day of Rosh Hashanah falls on a Saturday, which is underwhelming for a variety of reasons.

1. I don't get to skip school in the name of religion.
2. It's Shabbat, so it's forbidden to blow the shofar on the first day of services. Seeing how long Eli Sarna, the rabbi's son, can hold the tekiah gedolah note is easily the best part of the service.

3. Though we are pretty much exclusively High Holidays Jews in this family, my parents enforce a strict no-tech rule on said holidays. As if that makes up for how relatively unobservant we are the rest of the year.

So not only am I spending my Saturday at Reid's house, I'm also cut off from any and all proposal progress this weekend. In the past week, my friends and fellow collaborators have created a massive group chat, drafted proposal objectives and a mission statement, and came up with the perfect group name:

HAVE A HE(ART): Save Our Art!

Fitz and Henry are ridiculously proud of it.

I am too. So not being up to date with proposal plans is slowly killing me.

The Callahans live twenty minutes across town, but their house feels like another planet with its high ceilings and a kitchen I'm convinced Bobby from *Queer Eye* designed. Its state-of-the-art appliances and clean white modern aesthetic are the total opposite of our dated wood cabinets, stove with a blown-out burner, and refrigerator with a jammed ice machine.

Currently, I am eating my feelings in apple wedges in said kitchen and lamenting about the lack of shofar in my life this holiday season with Delia and Hannah. Outside, Reid is officiating an intense game of cornhole: moms vs. dads.

"You're just upset you don't have an excuse to stare at Eli," Delia says.

"Hey!" I swat Delia's arm, but that's not *not* true. Eli has curly black hair that's a little too long and a one-dimpled smile that's insane. He's super involved with the Chabad at Boston University, where he's a freshman, so the opportunities for swooning are limited these days.

What can I say? Older, unattainable, unrequited crushes are absolutely my thing. It's not like there's anyone at my school to flirt with.

"Well, I for one *love* Saturday services," Delia says, dipping an apple wedge into the bowl of honey on the kitchen island we congregate around. "It's one less opportunity for the gentiles to mess up."

I snort. Delia's not wrong. In Lincoln, being Jewish means dealing with adults who are incapable of looking at a calendar. It's how Fitz and I became friends when she moved here from Dallas in eighth grade—we bonded over missing a field trip for Rosh Hashanah. Commiserating over Jewish feelings makes for an instant friendship.

"This is the first time we'll be in the class picture since *fourth grade*," Hannah says, pushing up the sleeves of her pink sweater and reaching for an apple wedge. Hannah is thankfully not acting like a third Monica at the moment. Delia begged me before we left to not make a big deal out of The Monicas situation and because I am an A+ sister, I oblige.

"And we only need to have the excused absence conversation

with the front office once this year. Sorry, Natalie, but I love Saturday holidays," Delia says.

"It's always *so* awkward," Hannah agrees. "Ms. Simpson acts like she's doing *us* a favor."

The oven timer beeps three times, staccato, and the moms rush into the kitchen through the sliding door that connects it to the back patio. It's coordinated almost as if they have a sixth sense, and not because Rebecca—Reid's mom—synced the kitchen timer with her phone.

"Girls, can you set the table?" Mom says to us, opening the long cutlery drawer.

"Best out of five?" Reid's dad, Leonard, shouts from outside. "Winner takes all after dinner?"

Rebecca smirks at Leonard and wow, it's *Reid's* smirk.

In case you're wondering where he gets his competitiveness from, look no further.

While Rebecca cuts the brisket and Mom attempts to assist, Reid enters the dining room to help finish setting the table, looking casual in a long-sleeve Celtics shirt and wearing his retro oval wired glasses. The shirt is jarring, like *Survivor* Saturday and pretty much any reminder that Reid has a personality outside of music.

"Shana Tova, Natalie," he says, taking a seat at the table next to me after we're done.

Bold move, speaking to me.

"Hi," I say, suspicious as I reach across the table for the challah basket.

"Thanks," Reid says, picking the *exact* slice of challah I was about to take. It was the ideal thickness and had the perfect crust-to-soft-insides ratio.

"No problem." I exhale, annoyed, and settle on a piece that's too thin.

"So—" Reid rips his piece of challah in half "—is it have a he*art*, like, emphasis on *art*?"

I choke on challah.

Like *I can't process what Reid jus said because I am in survival mode* choke.

I start coughing, but I swear my life flashes before my eyes! Delia hits my back repeatedly with gusto *after I'm already coughing*—inspiring little confidence in the effectiveness of her junior lifeguard training.

"How do you even—?" I try to ask but I am still coughing.

Reid refills my water. "Drink first. I will not be responsible for death by challah inhalation."

I need water more than I need to prove a point, so I listen and sip water until the coughing subsides. Shit. I should have been prepared for this. We attend a small school. People talk.

"I overheard Makayla and Arjun talking during gym," Reid says.

I frown. "Since when do you choose the real sport option?"

Reid makes a sarcastic *ha* face but otherwise ignores the comment. "I'd be organizing too, if the band was in jeopardy. I get it. And *Boiled*—"

"Reid."

I am not in the mood for *Melted* slander.

"I'm feeling festive! So I just want to say . . . it's really good. *Melted.* I hope you get to make it."

Reid's praise is so . . . earnest, I'm honestly taken aback. Suddenly it is too warm in here and I'm grateful that my hair is down, my curls masking the tips of my ears, which are surely pink. I don't flush, but my ears? They have a mind of their own.

"You don't mean that," I say.

Reid rakes his hand through his hair, frustrated. "I do."

I shrug, ripping my challah into smaller pieces. "So you'd support giving up some of the band's budget to fund *Melted*?"

Reid's jaw tenses and he looks at me like this is the first time this occurred to him.

It's easy to be all talk.

"The band—"

"Hey!" Dad proclaims as he enters the dining room with the salad. "It is Rosh Hashanah. We don't talk about work. We don't *think* about work. Tonight, there is no band!"

"Excuse me?" Mom enters the dining room with Rebecca and takes a seat next to Dad.

"It's called work-life balance, Michelle," Dad says.

Mom frowns. "Who are you and what did you do with my husband?"

Reid and I fixate on our own plates and actively ignore each other, now that dinner is served. It is a typical Jacobson-

Callahan affair—a cacophony of people talking over people.

"Natalie!" Rebecca says, calling my attention from the far end of the table. "How are classes going? Are you having trouble with Ms. Santiago?"

Out of the corner of my eye, I see Reid's eyebrows pinch together.

"She expects a lot, but as long as you follow instructions, you're good."

Rebecca smiles like I've impressed her and that always feels good. She's a child pediatrician doing research at Children's Hospital in Boston and who I wanted to be when I grew up . . . until I fell off a bike and learned the hard way that I get woozy at the sight of blood.

"Maybe you could teach Reid how to follow instructions," Leonard says. His tone is almost teasing, but not quite.

"I'm fine, thanks," Reid says, his ears burning.

"Don't take it personally, Natalie." Leonard leans back in his chair and scratches his beard. "Science is my specialty, but Reid won't accept my help either."

Leonard is an electrical engineer at an architectural firm and pretty much responsible for this dream kitchen. It's a kitchen that scientists get to have, a reward for their practical pursuits. Rebecca and Leonard are dominant in their fields—totally life goals *and* couple goals.

"Junior year can be an adjustment," Mom says.

Rebecca stabs her salad with her fork. "Oh, absolutely. SATs, college research, AP classes . . . I don't miss it."

Mom shakes her head. "Me either. I don't think I ever felt more lost."

"We had the luxury of figuring it out along the way," Leonard says, reaching for the breadbasket that has made its way down the table. "But in this economy? With tuition costs?"

And there it is, the feeling of existential dread that burrows deep in my bones whenever this subject comes up, which is more and more frequently. I like school. I like my classes. But when I close my eyes and picture the future . . . I have no idea what I see myself doing. Right now, the thought of listing a major on a college application is enough to make me break out in hives.

Undecided.

I hate that word.

If I'm going to college, if I'm taking on a lifetime of debt, I have to know what I want. Endless possibilities, *creative* possibilities, are not an option in that scenario. So I've been loading up on AP classes and peppering different electives into my schedule—Digital Marketing and Coding this semester, Economics and Anatomy next—hoping that something will stick.

"They still have time." Dad's voice is reassuring as he makes eye contact with me. In addition to our tendency to stew, we have the same *I'm spiraling* face—and mine is definitely on display.

"Exactly. Plenty of time to get that grade up, Reid," Leonard says.

Dad breaks eye contact to rush to Reid's defense.

"Reid is balancing a lot. For what it's worth, his grasp on the AP Music Theory material is as if he already took the class."

Leonard laughs. "You know that doesn't count on a transcript, Aaron."

Reid winces. Delia and Hannah's eyes widen. Rebecca looks at the floor.

I . . . even think that's harsh.

Dad frowns. "You've had too many beers, so I'm going to let that go."

"It's just good to have options, Reid," Rebecca says. "That's all we mean."

"Right," Reid says, but his voice is soft. "I know."

"Maybe the clarinet-school balance is what's off," Leonard says.

"Rule seven!" I exclaim.

It's supposed to be a joke, to lighten the mood. Everyone in our family knows the rule book. *Natalie vs. Reid.* Rule seven: Do not ruin family holidays. Art discourse will ruin Rosh Hashanah—especially when Leonard and Dad are not exactly sober and fall on opposite sides of the argument.

No one laughs.

Luckily, Delia shifts the conversation to bat mitzvah dress shopping—an important, all-consuming subject—and it works. My shoulders relax, grateful that the subject has moved away from Reid and me and the elusive Future.

Sometimes I wonder if Reid and I were born to the wrong parents. Mom and Dad would jump for joy if I wanted to pursue the whole playwright/director thing. My parents are the epitome of a *Dreams do come true!* Disney ad. They *actually* believe I could be a Broadway playwright and Delia can make it to the WNBA. I'm like, *Mom, you're five-four! Dad is five-ten! Delia is not going to be pro basketball tall.* I love that my parents aren't forcing us down a path. But sometimes I want them to be serious, like Reid's parents. To be honest about the reality of their creative dreams. Writer's block. Playing music to half-empty venues. Student loans.

But following Dad's path is what Reid wants. To go to conservatory and enroll in a composition program that will teach him how to score the next blockbuster film. The risks don't scare him. Sacrificing a chem grade is worth it, in the big picture.

"Santiago offers extra credit," I say under my breath. "If it's dire."

Reid shakes his head. "I got an eighty-one on the last quiz."

I frown. Ms. Santiago is tough. Most of the class is floating in the B range. I'm hanging onto my A- by a thread. Reid's parents embarrassed him . . . over an *eighty-one*?

"Oh," I say.

"Yeah. Hardly dire. *Melted,* on the other hand? Good luck."

Any sympathy evaporates. I don't give Reid the satisfaction

of a response. Because I don't know what my future looks like. But I do know HAVE A HE(ART)'s plan is probably the best shot we've got at getting some form of our clubs back.

We're not going to sit second chair to Reid and the band. Not anymore.

CHAPTER SIX

"Stars or pearls?"

I am balancing chemical equations at Fitz's desk when she approaches me with two chokers—one with delicate gold stars in her left hand and another with tiny pearls in her right.

"Definitely stars," I say.

Fitz nods, moving across her room to her standing full-length mirror, where she adjusts the choker's position until it's to her camera-ready standards. Dressed in high-rise ripped jeans with a white cotton T-shirt, tucked in, Fitz's look is almost plain until she adds the statement piece: a satin rose gold bomber jacket. It's an *If the Shoe Fitz* original, upcycled from a prom dress we found at Goodwill over the summer.

"Perfect," Fitz says, nodding in the mirror at her work.

As she scrunches out her curls and swipes rose gold gloss over her lips, I ask the portraits of Maya Rudolph, Timothée Chalamet, Stella McCartney, and Daveed Diggs that hang above Fitz's desk to send me the strength to finish my homework, even though I know it's already a lost cause. They make up her ever-growing collage of Low-Key Jewish Heroes.

A new celebrity is added every time someone says, *Oh, I didn't know you were Jewish.*

Because being Jewish isn't having a certain name or looking a certain way.

The Low-Key Jewish Heroes send positive vibes as I race to simply finish my homework before Henry, Makayla, Arjun, and Danica arrive in an hour to discuss all things HAVE A HE(ART)—our first meeting since the Rosh Hashanah hiatus. After Chao Down, we created a smaller executive board. Makayla represents the visual arts, Arjun represents the audio-visual and tech kids, and Danica represents the choir and musical theater students. Each of them are then coordinating and planning with their groups to ensure we're all on the same page.

"Natalie," Fitz says, her tone indicating that this is not the first time she's said my name. "Can you do the sound check?"

She turns on the mixer setup to my left. I close my textbook and accept that no homework will be completed. "What do you do without me?"

"Struggle," Fitz says, clipping the lavalier mic to her shirt. "I am a visual master, but sound is my nemesis! It is annoyingly easier to edit when you check the levels. Always."

There is no casual way to say this: Fitz is kind of internet famous.

I put on headphones as Fitz sets up the scene. Her bedroom is light woods and pops of pastel. She centers the shot on her bed, a white duvet with two blankets, lavender and mint, draped over the left corner. Two mannequins are in the background, one half-clothed in the bodice of a dress that Fitz is working on for her sister Tessa's twenty-first birthday. On the other side of the bed is a clothing rack filled with *If the Shoe Fitz* pieces.

I turn the volume down on the mixer. "Speak."

"What do you think is up with Henry and Danica?" Fitz asks, her voice still way too loud.

I wince, turning the volume down more. "I don't know. They have a lot of classes together."

"Okay. But Henry had literal heart emojis in his eyes when Danica showed up at Chao Down. I have never seen him like that before." Fitz moves into the frame of the video, sitting crisscross on the end of her bed. "Shouldn't we keep the dynamics between the HAVE A HE(ART) e-board members professional?"

"Sure. But what if Danica wanted to hug *you*?"

Fitz launches a pillow at my face. "I am a hypocrite."

"Henry would tell us if they were more than friends. You're overthinking this." I spin the desk chair to face the camera and fix the off-center shot. Through the camera, I notice her cheeks are a deeper shade of pink than the blush she's wearing. "Why are you overthinking this?"

Fitz runs her fingers through her hair and shrugs. "I don't know. Danica has always had big queer energy. But maybe I'm projecting. I'm *definitely* assuming, which is also not cool. Can I go back to pining from a distance? Ditch this alternate reality dream come true where my crush is *coming over to my house* in the name of *saving the arts.* Ugh."

"As she is coming over in—" I check the time on my phone "—forty-five minutes, it's a little late for that. If it helps, you look fabulous."

Fitz exhales her anxiety and fluffs her curls. "It does."

"Okay. Focus on your video. Pizza bagels will be waiting for you when you're done."

"Have I ever told you you're my hero?" Fitz asks.

"Not often enough," I say.

Fitz sticks her tongue out at me. Certain she has the frame and audio levels for a perfect video, I toss my backpack over my shoulder and exit Fitz's room, heading down the creaky wood steps that lead me to an empty kitchen.

I remove the baking sheets from the oven and preheat it before opening the fridge to compile everything I need to create the perfect pizza bagels. Dad always taught me the importance of mise en place, that the extra prep work is worth it.

Twenty minutes later, Henry enters scene with trays of bubble tea.

"I should have come sooner."

Henry takes in the scene that is now Fitz's kitchen: the empty jar of pizza sauce in the sink, the mozzarella cheese all over the counter, the vegetable scraps left on the cutting board, the three varieties of pizza bagels ready to go in the oven. His eyebrows pinch in an expression somewhere between amusement and concern.

"I'm currently at 'rewatch the "Flu Season" episode of *Parks and Rec.*' I didn't know you're at full Pizza Bagel Panic."

I shrug. "I kind of got into the zone."

"Fitzgerald's still recording?"

I open the oven and slide the first two sheets of pizza bagels inside. "Yeah."

Henry inhales. "Is that . . . *pesto*?"

I nod. "Chaotic, right?"

I wipe the rogue cheese into the sink with a paper towel, Henry scrapes the veggie scraps into the garbage disposal, and we settle into a steady rhythm. I'm a thousand percent more at ease with Henry by my side, and I'm pretty sure this is the definition of being a best friend—the willingness to clean up a mess you didn't make.

After we finish up, Fitz's kitchen populates. Arjun and Makayla arrive with cookies from Manuela's Bakery. Arjun's shoulder-length hair is post–cross country practice shower damp. Danica has church choir practice but arrives by our eight o'clock start time. We're discussing the general vibe among the clubs when Fitz joins us.

It's impressive how she even manages to be fashionably late *in her own house.*

"Cool jacket," Danica says.

She smiles, and I'm positive those two words just made her entire night.

"Thanks! And sorry! I kept tripping up saying 'rose gold goals' and . . ." Fitz pauses midstep and takes in the pizza bagels I am plating on a serving platter, her eyes widening. "Is that *pesto*?"

"Right?" Henry says. "It's worse than we thought."

"I mean—" Arjun starts slowly "—pizza bagels are delicious. Objectively."

"Not when they're a product of stress, Arjun!" Fitz says.

Arjun's eyes widen and his mouth snaps shut. Makayla and Danica look at each other and contemplate their life choices, presumably.

"Some people stress bake," Henry explains. "Natalie stress pizza bagels."

"Cupcakes are too sweet," I shrug, passing the platter around the table.

Danica raises one eyebrow at Henry. "Like how you made two pounds of guacamole last night?"

Fitz processes this new information without missing a beat, like the phenomenal actress she is. "Natalie and Henry are kindred spirits. It takes a stress chef to know one."

"I wasn't going to let five avocados go to waste," Henry says. "Five! Do you know how rare it is, to have five perfect avocados? I mean, it was more than a much-needed homework break. It was an *obligation*."

Danica laughs. "Maybe you're just bad at buying avocados."

I raise my eyebrows. Henry's passion for avocados is a . . . new development.

"Sounds like yesterday was productive," Fitz says, stuffing a pizza bagel in her mouth.

Yesterday, Henry and Danica couldn't work on HAVE A HE(ART) after school because of an AP Spanish project on *Cien Años de Soledad.*

"It was! After we finished, we also watched *Frozen,*" Danica says. "For inspiration."

Okay. Wow. Guacamole AND *Frozen*?

Maybe Fitz isn't so off base.

"Cool," Fitz says.

"Cool," I repeat, equally perplexed. When I asked Henry how yesterday went, his response was almost a nonresponse. "Danica is cool. It was chill."

I swallow my questions and open my laptop, ready to jump into HAVE A HE(ART).

Tonight there are three items on the agenda:

1. Outline the specific details of our HAVE A HE(ART) event
2. Write a petition to present to the school committee demanding that the budget be redistributed among the arts clubs
3. Strategize all things execution: how, when, and where to pitch this to the school committee

But when I log into Google Drive I'm . . . confused because the first item under recent files is the *Melted* proposal deck Henry and I created to prepare for our meeting with Mrs. Mulaney. I haven't opened that since . . . well, since the rejection.

I click into it.

The title slide reads: BOILED: AN ODE TO THE PLAY THAT COULD HAVE BEEN.

"Oh my God! I've been hacked. Reid!" I spin my computer screen around so it is visible to the entire table. I click through the presentation. It's gone. *Melted* is gone—replaced by a twenty-slide presentation listing every reason why there is no hope for *Melted* because, of course, it is not *Boiled*. Twenty! Slides!

"Callahan . . . hacked into your Google account?" Arjun asks.

"Why?" Danica asks.

"Reid and Natalie react to each other in pranks," Fitz explains. "It's been a while, but it's their thing."

"What did you do?" Henry asks.

"Nothing!" I protest. Henry and his victim-blaming are cancelled for the foreseeable future. I click on the presentation to edit and see if I can undo this travesty, but mine and Henry's admin access has been revoked and the presentation is marked "view only." I open a new tab and *shit*—the *Melted* script has also been freaking *Boiled*. I'm locked out of my own script!

"This is a message. He's worried about HAVE A HE(ART)."

"Wow," Makayla says, scrolling through the presentation as I gape at the screen. "'The ability to melt something is hardly unique. Boiling? It is a power less explored. Tons of potential.' I just—" Makayla's thoughts are interrupted by the collective laughter that overtakes the table.

"*Boiled* is an objectively terrible name," Danica chokes out, and I learn that she snorts when she laughs too loud, which makes her about ten percent less intimidating.

I close my laptop. "Reid is holding *Melted* hostage."

"I back up everything on my hard drive," Henry reminds me.

"*Hostage,*" I reiterate.

Obviously, I have to retaliate.

Henry shakes his head, as if he can read my mind. "Prank wars never end well."

He's technically not *wrong*, but my brain is already thinking ahead to the next move, how I can prank back in a similar—but unexpected—manner. Reid and I don't have a whole rule book established just for me to sit on my hands and *not prank back*.

"We're not twelve anymore, Hen," I say.

He raises his eyebrows. "Really?"

"I'm with Chao," Danica says. "There is a lot at stake. A final curtain call for the seniors. A chance for the juniors to prove that our clubs add just as much value to the school community as the band. If we want to be taken seriously, we have to take ourselves seriously."

Fitz nods. "Reid got us. It's annoying but . . . isn't the best retaliation . . . no retaliation?"

"Let's keep the focus on HAVE A HE(ART)," Henry pleads.

"Can we add an art showcase to the pitch? We can display art in the hallways, available for sale, like our auction proposal," Makayla says, attempting to get us back on track.

"Where would the money we raise go?" Arjun asks. "That will probably come up."

"We split it," I suggest, refocusing on HAVE A HE(ART). "Ticket sales, art sales, all of it. Between our programs and The Sunshine Project—an environmental charity created by our generation that is doing the work to fight climate change. We need the money, but I'm not about just performative activism."

"Me either," Henry agrees. "It's not like we can save all our clubs with one event anyways."

"I love that," Fitz says.

Everyone agrees.

"Perfect," I say, taking notes.

"And the pitch—" Arjun starts. "Do we really think going above Mrs. Mulaney is the best play? Shouldn't we try to appeal to her first?"

Fitz scoffs. "We did that already."

"My dad presents to the school committee all the time," I say. "Each meeting dedicates time to public comments. We just have to pick a meeting to attend and sign up."

Makayla raises her eyebrows. "It's . . . that easy?"

"To speak? Yes," I say. "Actually being *heard* is the challenging part."

"I'm in. I want to play Emma," Danica says.

"We'll have to do a chemistry read," Fitz says. "Since I'm Adina."

Henry swallows. "Can we cross that bridge when we get to it?"

Danica crosses her arms on the table, oblivious. "I showed it to Cassie and Toby and we're down to convince the musical theater troupe that *Melted* is worth auditioning for, even without music. Assuming this even works."

"It *will* work. HAVE A HE(ART) is a story. A message to the school committee that our clubs deserve funding too. That *all* art benefits the student body *and* the school's image," Fitz says.

I nod. "Drumming up good PR for the school is not just a band thing."

We spend the rest of the night unpacking our agenda items. I type meticulous notes while we brainstorm the event, and it's so exciting, feeling the proposal coming together and being able to *see it—Melted—*happening for real. A sold-out audience of students and parents and staff supporting the arts coming together. But as focused as I am on HAVE A HE(ART) and making *Melted* a reality . . . I still can't stop thinking about *Boiled.*

Mostly, how I can't *not* retaliate.

Prank wars with Reid are a recurring plot thread in our history. Okay, so the last one blew up in my face in a truly traumatic way, ending in a friendship breakup *and* a clarinet breakup. I can't deny it. But I have evolved. Reid's prank is so annoyingly good it is infuriating and has reawakened something in me.

Am I out of practice? Perhaps.

But not enough that I can't focus on HAVE A HE(ART) and distracting Reid from it.

I can't let him win by default.

Natalie vs. Reid

The summer before fourth grade, *Natalie vs. Reid* was signed into law.

I don't remember a universe in which competition did not define our relationship.

Who was better at Mario Kart. (Reid)

Who learned to read first. (Me)

Who could keep a fish alive longer. (Reid)

Who could solve a Rubik's Cube faster. (Me)

But the moment Reid picked up the clarinet and started joining my lessons with Dad? He shifted the entire nature of our rivalry. It didn't feel like a fun way to pass the time at family events anymore. Reid took the music I shared with my dad, the *time* I spent with him—and made it too intense, took it too far.

Childhood rivalries are cute until a doctor is setting your radius bone.

"This could've been serious," Dad lectured in the car, post-hospital.

"What were you thinking?" Leonard added.

I shrugged and cradled my broken arm. In retrospect, it was not the best idea to stage and race through a downhill obstacle course. But Reid's test run made it look *easy*. And he bet I wouldn't do it. I had no choice but to prove him wrong.

Also, I had just perfected the chromatic scale. Anything felt possible.

"Reid, when we get home I want your clarinet," Leonard said.

"What?" Reid cried.

The adrenaline from the crash was still wearing off and it occurred to me—my clarinet was being taken away too. I couldn't play with one hand! I'd be stuck in my purple cast for at least *six weeks*—and school started in four. I wouldn't recover in time to start my first year of band.

"For the rest of the summer," Leonard said. "It's only fair, since Natalie can't play."

"It's not my fault Natalie can't control her bike!"

Dad shook his head in the rearview mirror. "That's an interesting spin on it."

"Natalie." Reid looked at me, his eyes wide. "It was an accident, I swear."

"You didn't mention the *pothole*," I said through my tears.

The more I thought about the obstacle course, that kind of scary speed, how *hard* the crash was—the more it felt like Reid's fault. I couldn't shake the thought that he did this on purpose. Ever since he picked up the clarinet, he'd been obsessed with catching up to me. So he took me out to get ahead. Reid tried to have a whole summer of the clarinet to himself.

Reid and I cried the entire car ride home.

• • •

A week later, Reid came over with a first draft of *Natalie vs. Reid.*

"Six weeks without clarinet is torture. We need rules."

I'd been reading under the sycamore tree in my backyard, actually enjoying the break from clarinet lessons. At the sound of Reid's voice I looked up from my tattered copy of *The Lightning Thief.* Reid was miserable without the clarinet. It was the only explanation for the list he'd held out to me, written on wide-ruled notebook paper in red marker.

I dropped my book and took the list. "We can't tell our parents."

"Obviously," Reid responded. To say our parents didn't find our competitive streak endearing anymore was a massive understatement. "They'll take it away."

I read Reid's list and had some notes, of course. Reid rewrote the list as a book, each rule getting its own page of computer paper. He did the heavy lifting in terms of the creative, since I couldn't write with my cast, but I directed.

"Does it hurt?" Reid asked, nodding at my cast as he wrote "RULE 10" in his giant print.

I shrugged. "Not anymore. It's mostly just annoying now."

"That stinks. I'm sorry."

"Is that an apology for breaking my arm?"

Reid rolled his eyes. "*You* broke your arm."

I still wasn't convinced of that. But then Reid dropped my crayons and we admired his work of art, the result of every competition that had already passed and the code for all to follow.

Natalie vs. Reid: Pranks, Bets, and Everything Else

1. Never ever apologize.
2. They are between Natalie and Reid ONLY. Do not involve friends/parents!
3. They cannot end in a broken bone, even unintentionally.
4. Okay, sisters are the only exception to Rule #2. The best pranks will need some help.
5. School and clarinet lessons are safe zones.
6. The bus is fair game. Duh.
7. Do not ruin family holidays.
8. If you're going to yell at each other, do it in secret so the adults don't hear.
9. If you make the other person sad, you must make them an epic ice cream sundae.
10. Pranks are funny, not mean!

The Double Prank Clause: In an active prank war, the prankee has *three* (3) days to prank back. Once the three-day prank window expires, double pranks are fair game!

The Truce Clause: Truces are agreed on with a double pinky swear. No pranking can occur during the seven-day truce period.

Reid scribbled his name in pine green, his favorite crayon. Four letters. R-E-I-D. I signed mine next to his with vivid violet, an uncoordinated scribble thanks to my cast.

"Game on," Reid said.

"Game on," I repeated.

And it's been *Natalie vs. Reid* ever since.

CHAPTER SEVEN

Reid's forehead vein makes an appearance at breakfast. Between each bite of cinnamon toast, he searches his backpack. It's Wednesday—nearly a week since BOILED: AN ODE TO THE PLAY THAT COULD HAVE BEEN—and Reid has been on edge ever since. Monday night, his family came over to break the fast for Yom Kippur and I swear he kept tabs on my whereabouts *all* night. I mean, Reid. Chill. It was the Day of Atonement! I spent six hours in synagogue repenting every negative thought spiral and poor decision I have made over the past year—which includes but is not limited to forgetting to pick Delia up from her bat mitzvah lesson during *Barefoot in the Park*'s tech week, encouraging Fitz to cut her own bangs because of a TikTok challenge, and hoping Reid will bomb an audition . . . just one time!

I was never going to be diabolical on Yom Kippur.

Did I love seeing Reid think I would be, though? Absolutely.

"You good?" I swallow cold eggs and focus on reviewing the HAVE A HE(ART) petition Henry and I were up all night preparing. My eyes don't lift from the screen though, because Yom Kippur is over and a prank is now, in fact, mid-execution. Yesterday I swept all the extra reeds from my dad's classroom after school. This morning, while Reid was in the bathroom, I also took all the reeds out of his clarinet case.

Reid can't play the clarinet without a reed.

It's a stupid joke. Basic.

But if I make eye contact with him, I will laugh.

In my peripheral vision, I see Reid run his hand through his hair. "Did you—?"

"Morning!"

Mom's chipper voice cuts off Reid as she emerges from her office. She has spent more time there in the last two weeks than she has in *years* and it feels like writing might be happening. I hope. I'm too nervous to ask. Too nervous to ask about a brainstorming session, too nervous to knock on her door to vent about the band and tell her about HAVE A HE(ART). Growing up, a closed office door meant *do not disturb.* What if a simple knock bursts whatever creative bubble finally exists again?

"Is everything all right, Reid?" Mom asks, crossing the kitchen threshold for a coffee refill.

"Misplaced music." Reid's eyes meet mine, suspicious.

I keep my expression neutral, attempting to hide my surprise.

"Oh! I'm sure you already have it memorized," Mom says, her tone light.

"I don't," Reid says. "It's an audition piece for the pre-conservatory program at the Albany Institute for the Arts. I put it in my backpack last night and it's . . . not here."

"I didn't know you were auditioning for Albany, Reid. That's a really big deal," I say.

"I know," Reid snaps.

"I'm sure it'll turn up." Mom plucks a croissant from the bakery box on the counter and heads back to her writing cave before Reid can respond. She, too, can only take so much of Dad and Reid and Their Music.

Reid checks his bag for the millionth time. "Okay. Seriously. Truce?"

The desperation in his voice pulls me out of enjoying his anxiety. I mean, I'm a just prankster. Honestly. Summer Institute at the Albany Institute is intense. You have to *apply to apply.* It's, like, Julliard level, in terms of precollege programs.

"How could I have stolen your music if I didn't know you were applying?" I ask. "Not that it wouldn't have been deserved."

"I didn't think your password would actually be your birthday."

"So that makes it okay?"

"Identity theft is not a joke, Natalie. You need a more secure password. *Shit,*" Reid mutters under his breath. "I just received the packet last week. I've been so focused on preparing for district auditions and the Harvest Festival, I hadn't even looked over the pieces yet."

"Can't you request a replacement?" I ask. I stand and place my empty plate in the dishwasher before doubling back to pick up my textbook.

Reid shakes his head. "If I do that I might as well scream, *I'm not serious about this!*"

"No one is—"

Reid cuts me off. "You don't get it."

"What's that supposed to mean?"

"Come on, Natalie. Isn't that your whole thing? Not being serious?"

I step backward. "Not all of us have to make our one interest a personality."

Refusing to give my face a chance to emote, I exit the kitchen and take the stairs two at a time up to my bedroom. Reid has no clue what he's talking about and I can ride the early morning wave re: making it impossible for him to play the clarinet today.

Still, I can't stop thinking about the sentence he cut off.

No one is as serious as you, and that will be obvious when you play.

I almost complimented him. Me. Completely out of character.

I'm glad Reid interjected.

The rest of the week passes in almost equal parts HAVE A HE(ART) preparation and pranks.

Thursday I bask in the result of my reed prank, derailing an entire *Star Wars* rehearsal. At lunch, I ignore aggressive side-eye from Reid and the band as I'm approaching tables, asking for signatures for our HAVE A HE(ART) petition to prove there is solidarity and excitement for our proposal outside the arts clubs. Connor DiMarco's support is enough for the student council kids to sign; Cherish and Arjun emphasize *Melted*'s climate change themes to the environmental and STEM clubs and it is easy signatures from them. Makayla targets the jocks with surprising success.

"Mack filled us in on the situation," Ivan says, nodding at Makayla. "That shit is messed up. It's like if Mulaney cut basketball next week and said every athlete had to play baseball."

He encourages the entire varsity basketball team to sign, and it gets us to more than three hundred signatures! As Makayla and I return to our table, we're intercepted by Reid.

"What are you doing?"

My eyes snap up, meeting Reid's annoyed expression.

"Hey! Would you like to sign our petition?" I say in a clipped, professional voice. "We'd like the school committee to reconsider the one-sided allocation of the arts budget, as it is unfair to the equally enriching programming LHS is losing."

I hold the petition out to Reid, my smile sweet. He raises his eyebrows at the number of signatures. "Are you *trying* to get your dad fired?"

I refuse to give Reid the satisfaction of provoking me. "Nope."

"Whatever, Natalie. Do your petition. Hide reeds. Stage a whole protest if you want. It won't matter. The school committee has already chosen the band."

"So why not sign our petition? I mean, if it won't . . ."

Reid storms off before I even finish.

It's Friday when I receive my next prank—and Reid got the band to help with this one! More tech sabotage. Every time I open my web browser, the home page redirects to audio of the creepiest orchestral rendition of "Let It Go" that Reid could've possibly arranged. Did you know that all you need is an email address to set up parental controls on a computer? I do now! Reid parental controlled me and is torturing me with orchestral music, and I do not know how to make it stop!

It is diabolical.

I need to step up my game.

Fitz and Danica onstage together is going to be a revelation, whenever we have an actual stage.

"Damn," Makayla whispers in awe.

Henry groans. "How many times do we have to emphasize they're *sisters*?"

"It's pointless," I say.

Saturday is, for what feels like the first time since HAVE A HE(ART) started, all about *Melted.* While the band is having an extra *Star Wars* rehearsal in preparation for the Harvest

Festival next weekend, HAVE A HE(ART) takes the opportunity to have our own dress rehearsal.

The next school committee meeting is a week from Monday.

We'll be ready.

I will call out the school committee's messed-up valuation of arts programs.

Henry will share statistics on the correlation between robust arts programs and test scores.

Makayla and Arjun will highlight our ecoconscious message and fundraising plans.

And Danica and Fitz will deliver a riveting performance.

We even have a set concept! Since school committee meetings are open to the public, they take place in our auditorium. So Makayla and Cherish convinced Mrs. DiCarlo to let them take some giant wooden set panels for an *independent portfolio project* and they transformed it into a celestial canyon—all purple sky and a burnt orange scorched landscape.

I'd tattoo it on my face, I love it so much.

It's so massive, the art pieces live in the auditorium, onstage, drying behind curtains that have been closed since *Barefoot in the Park.* Imagine. An entire stage gone entirely to waste. At the end of the week we'll covertly put the pieces in place for our performance.

Since we don't have an auditorium for rehearsals and my parents are at Dad's gig, my basement is the next best thing. Our seats are the green microfiber couch that sags in the middle. The stage is a too-small area rug. It keeps the blocking close. Intimate. Two sisters, after a coronation that changed their lives. I'm sitting cross-legged on the edge of the chaise lounge, recording the rehearsal on Fitz's phone at her request, so she can analyze her own performance, and giving cues. It's effortless, my ability to slip back into being a codirector and block a scene with Henry by my side, and it feels *right*. It's exactly how this year was supposed to be.

And a reminder of what we'll lose if we fail.

"Then don't," Danica says, emotion thick in her voice as she storms off stage right.

Makayla and Arjun clap after every take.

"This is great," I say, flipping through my notes for eloquent critique. "You are great."

Fitz rolls her eyes, but a small smile tugs on the corner of her lips.

We're about to take it from the top when my phone buzzes in my lap.

"It's Delia," I say. "Take five?"

Danica swallows her sip of water. "But I am *in the zone*."

Fitz nods in agreement. "Fitzgerald who? I am Adina! Queen of Infernodelle!"

"We'll run it again," Henry says.

Okay. I can miss one run-through. It's no big deal. I hand Henry Fitz's phone and hop off the couch to take the call on the studio side of the basement. Pushing the door open to enter Dad's studio, I answer the FaceTime call and it's Delia and Hannah, together, at Reid's house.

"I switched out Reid's music," Hannah declares.

"You're my hero," I say.

It didn't occur to me until I saw Reid freaked over his Albany Institute music—which he found at home, on his desk, untouched by me, for the record—what an excellent and embarrassing way that is to mess with him. With Hannah's help, he'll have a selection of *Star Wars* songs transposed by yours truly into the entirely wrong key for his next rehearsal.

"Last week he asked me to mess with you, but I said, 'I'm not messing with Natalie. She lets me borrow her clothes and gives the best advice.' Ask Delia, she was there."

Delia nods. "It's true."

My eyebrows scrunch together. "You take my clothes?"

"The *point*—" Hannah pauses, now using the phone as a mirror to apply lip gloss "—is that he won't suspect a thing."

"Thanks for messing with him for me," I say.

Hannah shrugs. "This is an opportunity to smash the patriarchy. Plus, Sephora."

The sisters viewing Reid as a symbol for the patriarchy?

It's worth the obscene amount of money I will most likely spend on makeup for them.

"Natalie."

Henry's voice accompanies the knock on the door. I didn't realize I'd locked it. Subconscious. But I'm keeping my friends on the down low about the fact that Reid's pranks aren't entirely one-sided. So I say goodbye to Delia and Hannah and tuck my phone back into my pocket before I swing the door open.

"Sorry," I say, passing Henry and grabbing a pizza bagel on my way back to the couch. "Bat mitzvah Pinterest emergency."

"I don't even want to know what that means," Arjun says.

"You really don't," Fitz confirms.

"Should we refocus on *Melted*?" Henry asks. "I have some—"

"Yes! Actually . . ." I flip back two pages in my notes and find the point I want to emphasize. "Next time, Danica, don't start walking away until Adina says, 'It's enough pressure having a whole kingdom depend on me, without having to worry about you, too.' I don't want there to ever be too much physical space between you two. It's a big stage."

"But also, like, *some* physical space. You're *sisters*," Henry reiterates. "Cool it with the arm touching."

Danica and Fitz process the notes and ask a few questions, and we take it again from the top. This time, Danica keeps her feet firmly rooted in place, while Fitz is pure motion. The emotion in Fitz's performance is riveting—and when Danica as Emma, the younger sibling who tries *so hard*, has had enough, she pivots on her toes.

"Then *don't*," Danica says.

She holds the position for an extra beat and the energy in the room shifts. I swallow the lump in my throat and close my eyes to prevent any visible Emotions from happening. I'm not ready to let go of this feeling, of this show, of these people. *Melted* is small. HAVE A HE(ART) and the message we're sending to the school committee makes it bigger. Maybe we'll get a feature in the local paper—but it won't receive national accolades for the school the way that the band does.

So maybe I'm naive to believe in this.

But when Danica turns her back on Fitz and walks away, away, away—it is a performance that is worthy of a stage, of an audience to be single-tear-sliding-down-their-cheeks moved. It is devastating and perfect and something that we, students with our backs against a wall, created from nothing.

And that matters too.

End scene.

Hours after we perfect the coronation scene—and no, I am still not over it, not at all—I am working on a lab report for AP Bio because, unfortunately, homework is very much still a thing. Writing about plant pigments and photosynthesis is as inspiring as it sounds. It's difficult to shift my brain back to science after an afternoon in my happy place.

An unexpected knock on my doorframe makes me jump.

"You're up late."

I look up from homework, toward the threshold of my room and my father's voice.

"The AP grind never stops." I glance at the time and frown. It's not even ten o'clock. After dress rehearsal, Lincoln Street

Blues had a gig at Melville's. Dad is never home until at least midnight on gig nights. "You're home early."

"Shorter set." Dad's delivery is casual until he sees my eyebrows shoot to the sky in concern. "It's fine! It's only until we find a replacement for Charlie. Turns out that without a keyboard, our repertoire is limited."

"You can't just play the keys for now?" I ask.

Dad shakes his head. "I can teach piano, but I'm out of practice. You can always tell when a musician is playing an instrument that isn't their first love."

"Right." That's one of Dad's favorite lines, and I remember the first time he said that to me in his studio. In retrospect, I wonder how early he picked up on the truth of the clarinet not being my first love. That I wasn't there for the music—so much as for the conversations we got to have about music. Together.

"Anyway—" Dad crosses the threshold to my room and sits in my desk chair, spinning toward me "—we need to talk about the reed situation."

Damn. I thought I was off the hook.

"Which one?" I ask.

"Ha." Dad deadpans, his expression Not Amused. "I'm not sure what's going on between you two. Because Switzerland. But Natalie, what seems like a silly prank can derail an entire class period. You know how technically intricate the *Stars Wars* score is. The festival is next weekend. Every rehearsal matters. Next time, I'll have to write you up."

I make eye contact with my dad and call his bluff. "Okay."

"Is this about *Melted*? Every artist faces rejection. There are productive ways to—"

"Not an artist," I mutter under my breath.

"*Melted* can't be a school event. But what if you pivot? Film and post it . . . online?"

I shake my head, frustrated that once again I am living a scene that is Aaron Jacobson totally missing the point! "That won't work. Theater is meant to be experienced *live*."

"I'm just trying to help—"

I put in my earbuds and play my favorite theater production podcast to cut him off.

It does the trick.

Dad exhales and stands. "Goodnight, Natalie."

He backs off, whether he wants to or not. Either way, I'm glad he's gone. Dad loves to tell me how I'm supposed to feel, but never, not once, asks how I *actually* feel. Key distinction. It's why I haven't told him about HAVE A HE(ART) and our plans. He attends school committee meetings to advocate for the band. If he knew what we're planning, he'd shut it down so fast.

At first, I'm frustrated with my dad. Then I'm frustrated for being frustrated at all.

Whatever.

Next week, Dad will finally hear me.

CHAPTER EIGHT

One week later, I am sitting on a blanket in Pine Hill Park with Delia listening to the iconic score for *Episode IV—A New Hope*, eating cider donuts, sweating profusely, and hating the current reality that is eighty-two degrees in early October. In Massachusetts! So much for a Harvest Festival. I am born for sweater weather, but every year it feels like my favorite season gets shorter and shorter. Next week, the switch could flip and out will come the full parka.

Global warming. I wrote a whole play about it.

I wipe upper lip sweat with the back of my hand and check my phone for the time.

Two hours left of this family obligation. Then I am free. HAVE A HE(ART) is having a final dress rehearsal at Henry's house later tonight. The school committee meeting is two days away. We're ready. Our proposal is a low-budget compromise, our spin being HAVE A HE(ART) will give the illusion that the school committee cares about preserving the arts.

Have you considered the optics? The imminent backlash? Really, we're doing you a favor!

HAVE A HE(ART) will be taken seriously. It has to be.

Because every arts club in the school is taking a chance on HAVE A HE(ART).

On *me.*

"Where is Hannah?" I ask.

"Not coming," Delia says, plucking a cider donut from the paper bag between us. "It's Monica G.'s birthday. Her parents rented out the entire roller rink downtown."

Ah. "I'm sorry, Dee."

She shrugs. "I'm over it. At lunch yesterday, The Monicas called my Captain Marvel jacket 'basic'—and it hit me. On top of brushing off constant microaggressions . . . we have nothing in common, The Monicas and me. So it's, like, why do I even try?"

"Doesn't Hannah have the same jacket?"

Delia stands and crumples the empty paper bag. "It doesn't matter. Hannah becomes a different person around The Monicas. Like with me, her favorite movie is *Tangled.* But with The Monicas? It's *Hereditary.*"

"But Hannah hates scary movies."

Delia shoots her trash into the nearest recycling bin, basketball layup style. "Exactly."

Then Delia makes her way toward the main stage to join Mom, leaving me alone on my blanket. Anyone can come to the Harvest Festival to enjoy the music, but for a donation to the band program, folks can get a luxurious metal folding chair close to the stage. As always, Michelle Jacobson sits in the front row, her tripod set up in the aisle—which is cute and cringe and on brand. As tense as the energy can get between my parents in the lead-up to the Harvest Festival, at the end of the day Mom is always Dad's biggest fan.

Unable to focus on the music, I observe the audience—the sold-out seats by the stage, the groups of picnic blankets scattered on the lawn, the long lines at the food trucks. Plenty of townies who have no personal connection to LHS or the band are captivated by the magic that is *Star Wars* music live.

It's amazing.

It's also infuriating.

I mean, it is so bullshit, the school committee comparing any other arts club at LHS to the band. Of course the band is better! It has support, resources, opportunities. But seeing the way a community can come together and support a group of artists? It's motivating.

If anything is going to distract me from HAVE A HE(ART) and *Melted,* it is a well-executed prank. So I stand. Smooth down my floral print midi skirt. Start to walk in the direction of the sound tent. Consumed by tech week, Reid hasn't pranked back since my sheet music prank.

Giving me an opportunity to double down, per the double prank clause.

Honestly, the fact that creepy "Let It Go" is *still* torturing me deserves a double prank.

So I approach the sound tent with confidence. Cody and Jessica, Dad's Berklee friends who lead the technical sound crew, welcome me into the area FOR CREW MEMBERS ONLY.

"Natalie!" Jessica's tattooed arms wrap me in a hug.

"Aaron didn't tell us we had backup," Cody says, offering me a headset.

The sound tent is the motherboard of any outdoor event. Without its intricate setup and multiple tech checks, the band's music would not carry in an open space. I take in the main system and the dozen cables attached to it, powering the band and making sure the sound is crystal clear, as the performance is also being recorded for the public access channel for accessibility.

Memories of being backstage as a kid flood back and I am ready to make the most of this knowledge. Also, everything is labeled. While Cody and Jessica discuss volume levels, their backs to me, I unplug the mic line labeled CLARINET #1.

It's almost too easy.

I make small talk with Jessica and Cody about music (I haven't played in years!) and college (very much undecided!). Then I join my mom and Delia at the main stage, just in time for my favorite song, made even better by mild public embarrassment.

Dad raises his arms in the air to cue the music.

Reid brings his clarinet to his lips and straightens his posture.

A rogue curl falls into his eyes when he flips the page.

I exhale, attempt to keep it cool. It's a prank. It's a *prank.* It *is* a prank.

Cody or Jessica will hear the problem. It will be resolved in seconds. But five seconds is all it will take to rattle Reid, to make him wish he hadn't given me an opportunity to double prank.

"Look who decided to join us," Mom says.

"The sky is freaky," Delia whispers.

The sky, blue before I entered the sound tent, is now overcast. I hold my breath as the band shifts gears to the one song in *A New Hope* that is made for the clarinet: "Cantina Band." Dad's favorite arrangement has always been a clarinet quartet.

Today it features Reid as clarinet #1.

Except the signature melody is barely audible, apart from the steady beat of the drums. Because of *me.*

It sounds . . . worse than I imagined.

"Oh *no,*" Mom mutters under her breath.

Reid continues to play, either oblivious or assuming the glitch will be fixed.

Seconds later, the speakers blow.

Shit. My heart pounds in my chest. Did I—?

No. I unplugged *one* audio line.

Dad cues the band to stop and everyone lays their instruments in resting position, wide-eyed and confused.

"We'll take five to figure this out!" Dad yells, his hands cupped around his mouth because there is no microphone.

This can't be prank-related. One rogue XLR cable does *not* cause a speaker explosion.

Mom stands. "I'm going to see if I can help troubleshoot."

"This is high-key embarrassing," Delia says.

Five minutes become ten.

Ten become twenty.

Attention spans are short. The audience thins.

The sky darkens, ominous—as if given a directorial cue.

The timing of my prank is a coincidence.

"Natalie."

I look up to see Reid in his band tuxedo, rogue curl and all. Reid's voice is jarring, but when my eyes meet his, he looks . . . genuinely upset.

Not at all accusatory or suspicious.

"What's going on?" I ask.

"Technical difficulties."

"Obviously."

It comes out sharper than I intend it to.

"Obviously," Reid repeats, raking his hand through his hair, an edge in his voice. "Albany Institute faculty are in the audience, so the speakers blow. Obviously."

I didn't know that.

"That sucks."

"Extremely. Now it looks like it's going to—"

"Natalie—?" Dad's voice cuts Reid off. As my parents approach me, the sky gets darker with every step. It's only a moment before they are in front of us, arms crossed, Dad's right foot tapping in three-four. "The entire system is shot. They don't know what happened. Everything was set and tested, multiple times. It was ready to go. And they have been the only two people in the tent. Well, apart from you. Right?"

I swallow.

"Natalie." Mom's expression hardens.

Reid's eyes widen—and I *see* it, everything clicking into place.

The moment I open my mouth to respond, thunder cracks and the sky splits open.

The punishment violates the first rule in *Natalie vs. Reid.* Never apologize.

Therefore it cannot be done.

"No," I say. "Absolutely not."

It's later that night and Dad crosses his arms and leans against my door, my confiscated phone in his hand. Mom stands next to him, one hand on her hip. She is *quite frankly disappointed,* but I can see the gears turning in her brain. She is so desperate to get to her desk, to write this down, to keep it in her folder of miscellaneous scenes that could make it into a future manuscript.

"I'm not sure you're in a position to negotiate," Dad says. "Natalie, that wasn't some silly prank. You ruined a concert! The Harvest Festival's attendance *doubled* this year thanks to *Star Wars* excitement. You made us look amateur."

"Natalie didn't cause a flash thunderstorm, Aaron," Mom says, somewhat in my defense.

Dad shakes his head. "It's not about the *thunderstorm.* It's about the intent."

"It wasn't to ruin the concert," I say.

"Just Reid," Dad says. My non-answer is answer enough. He shakes his head and strokes his beard, the disappointment clear on his face. "Why? I know you didn't mean for the speakers to blow, but you still didn't even think *twice* about messing up a major event—"

Mom interjects. "Natalie messed up, but you're going to get a do-over—"

"—with even *more* pressure to deliver than before—"

"—and Natalie is still crushed over a play that should exist but doesn't because the school district cares more about a good publicity hit than what's best for their students. We're lucky they still value you, Aaron. We really are."

Mom doesn't even know about HAVE A HE(ART), but she summed it up in two seconds.

She is pretty much my hero.

"Natalie." Dad's tone softens. "If this is still about *Melted* . . . did it not occur to you that I could help?"

"Every artist faces rejection," I say, throwing his words back at him. "You wanted me to move on."

Dad shakes his head. "I wanted you to talk to me. Why don't you ever just *talk to me*?"

I shrug. Because we don't talk about real things anymore. Because it's pointless to talk to someone who will never listen.

"I'm keeping the phone."

"Aaron," Mom says, her voice sharp. They're supposed to reprimand as a team, but Mom is so not into this, so I know the sentence will be minimal at least.

"One week," Dad says. "I think that's pretty generous."

And suddenly, I am *furious.* Not at the phone loss, but because he's only ever my parent on his terms, and of course this—*Reid*—is the root of his anger. He puts so much time into Reid, molding him into the conservatory protégé of his dreams, and now he thinks he can just—what? Be my dad because I screwed up?

"I will never understand you, Natalie."

There it is. The truth of all truths.

Dad tucks my phone into his pocket and walks backward toward the door as tears stream down my face because he doesn't even try. Sometimes it feels like something is so broken between us, as if my clarinet past and its tumultuous conclusion snapped us in half.

I wipe my tearstained cheeks. "He doesn't get it."

"You blew out his concert, Natalie." Mom's expression softens as she sits next to me and rubs my back. "It's not an excuse, but he's in triage mode. It's not exactly getting . . . the sort of attention he's used to."

She shows me a video and . . . oh no. It is captioned "When the force says no!" It's only ten seconds, but it's brutal. Someone superimposed Angry Baby Yoda over the band! The clarinet quartet is barely audible! Then there is a *pop* . . . and the speakers blow.

Oof. TikTok is ruthless.

Mom locks her phone. "Never mind the previous forty-five minutes of excellence. These ten seconds are going to haunt your father for months."

"Me too," I say.

"Pranks are funny, not mean," Mom says, echoing the rule book. "I thought you two outgrew that and are strictly Awkward now. But maybe next time you're going to prank Reid . . . less public is the way to go?"

"That's fair."

Mom stands and sighs. "We'll talk in the morning."

Delia, who doesn't even pretend she wasn't eavesdropping, leans against the doorframe, her hair falling into her face as she scrolls through her phone, one earbud in.

"Henry thinks you're dead. I informed him that you're only technologically maimed."

Shit. Asking my parents to go to his house tonight is a nonstarter.

I'm missing the final HAVE A HE(ART) rehearsal.

"Tell him I'll relive it all in horrifying detail on Monday."

She hops into the empty spot in my double bed. "He expects nothing less. He also wants you to know that he's *got this*—whatever that means."

"Thanks, Dee," I say.

"You could text him yourself if you apologized," Delia says. "Reid has been extra stressed about his preconservatory audition thing—especially knowing that Albany people would be at the Harvest Festival. He didn't even quote all of Regina George's lines when we watched *Mean Girls* last weekend. It was weird."

"Weird," I repeat, the image of Reid watching *Mean Girls* with the sisters oddly endearing.

She places her phone down on my night table, yawns, and rolls over onto her side. "Are you nervous? About tomorrow?"

I shake my head even though Delia can't see it. "No. Yes. I don't know."

"I'm sorry about Dad," Delia says.

"I wish he were," I say.

Delia sighs. *"Men."*

"Men," I repeat.

Delia nods off and I stare at the ceiling, wishing I could stop thinking about Reid's face, his genuine confusion when he realized I had ruined his moment at the Harvest Festival.

The prank war was meant to distract Reid from HAVE A HE(ART).

But somewhere along the way, it became a distraction for *me.*

It is dramatic irony at its best. Because a petition all about how creating art doesn't need to be a tense and stressful thing . . . became a tense and stressful thing. I believe in HAVE A HE(ART) with my whole heart . . . but I'm also terrified of another rejection.

So I pranked.

And I went too far. I mean, it's supposed to be silly.

There aren't supposed to be actual consequences.

Henry was right. I am still twelve.

I reach for *Natalie vs. Reid* at the end of my bed. Flip through the pages until I'm at rule nine: "If you make the other person sad, you must make them an epic ice cream sundae." Followed by rule ten: "Pranks are funny, not mean!" For a millisecond, I wish we were still the kids in this book, writing down rules that would keep us safe.

Kids who pranked because maybe that was the only way they knew how to be friends.

The First Chair Wars

The First Chair Wars dominated the weeks before the start of seventh grade, triggered by an unfortunate rezoning initiative announced by our school district. If Reid hadn't infiltrated my life enough, between family dinners and weekly clarinet lessons, we now attended the same middle school and no longer would we be the first chairs, *plural.*

There was no way I could be second chair to Reid.

But by the end of the summer, it looked like that was a real possibility.

"Natalie, you're rushing," Dad corrected me.

I exhaled a frustrated breath. Dad could fixate on performance technique for *hours.* The lesson today focused on tempo and breath control—and the piece was Robert W. Smith's "The Tempest." AKA the worst song in the history of the clarinet. To me, at least. Because *eighteen measures* of the clarinet part is the same note! An A, in the same staccato rhythm. *One two and three four and one*—over and over. It is brutal.

"How are you *still* ahead of the tempo?" Reid asked, annoyed that we couldn't move on.

I shook my head. "I *wasn't.* Not at first."

Dad sighed. "Consistency is key, Natalie."

"Can we play it one more time?" Reid asked.

"Again? Seriously? We've been playing the same freaking note for an *hour*!" I snapped.

Winded from the repetition and the competition, I had to take a breath and a break. In preparation for the First Chair Wars, weekly lessons became daily and there was only so much I could take of Reid, in my basement, nonstop sucking up to my dad for extra lessons and tips. Most of my mid-lesson exits resulted in my dad coming upstairs to refill his water and nudging me, gently, back toward the music. But that afternoon?

I exited scene, and no one pursued.

So I didn't reenter. I avoided the studio any time Reid was in it. I avoided the studio any time Reid wasn't in it.

Practice time became me, in my bedroom, playing complex pieces I stole from my dad's high school lesson plans, with Madeline Park, my BBF (Best Band Friend). First chair, alto saxophone. We met at a summer woodwind intensive before fifth grade, when she introduced herself by asking if I had an extra reed and complimenting my Spider-Man T-shirt. Music came to her as easily as it came to Reid, but she was on my side.

"Can we call it?" Madeline asked three hours into our session. "My blisters have blisters."

I shook my head. "I'm *so close* to nailing the final movement, Madi. This is serious."

Madeline held out her hand. "So are my blisters!"

I winced. My hands weren't doing so great either, but I

wasn't going to stop. School started in two weeks. Time was running out. "You don't need to be practicing for me. I'm sorry."

"I *want* to," Madeline assured me, her deep brown eyes locking with mine. "You have to win. You're the best clarinetist in the whole school, Natalie."

"You haven't heard Reid play," I responded.

Madeline tied her shiny black hair back into a high ponytail. "I don't need to. You've got this. We'll practice every day until we fulfill our first chair destinies. Together."

So after a brief finger stretch, Madeline and I Mozart-ed for another hour. After she left, I played for two more, until *my* blisters had blisters and I cried frustrated tears because I hadn't nailed the movement yet. I loved Madeline and it meant the world that she would be so intense with me—but the person who could actually teach me was downstairs teaching the competition. After Reid left, Dad knocked on my door and entered in the middle of my weekly Clarinet Cry.

"It's not supposed to be like this, Nat," Dad said, wrapping his arms around me in what was supposed to be a comforting embrace while I cried into his Manchester United jersey. "It's supposed to be fun."

"This is the opposite of fun."

"Don't put so much pressure on a chair," Dad suggested.

"I have to. Reid is already better than me," I admitted into his shirt. "Why are you teaching *him*? He doesn't even need the extra lessons!"

Dad pulled away so I could see his face, pinched together in a frown. "Where is this coming from? You're the one who walked away from lessons."

"Practice with the competition?" I shake my head. "No way."

"Nat, it's just a chair. First? Second? It doesn't matter. I'm proud of you no matter what."

I cried myself to sleep that night because of all the things he'd said, I'd noticed what he hadn't.

He hadn't contradicted me when I said Reid was better. He hadn't said he'd make time for lessons just for me. He hadn't said he'd help me until *I'm* first chair.

He didn't *choose* Reid.

But he didn't choose me, either.

CHAPTER NINE

I take it back.

Every thought I dared to think the rest of my guilt-ridden weekend, every millisecond of a moment I spent driving to and from the only sweet shop that stocks Reid's favorite peanut butter hot fudge sauce, every second I lay awake last night plotting my totally sincere apology-adjacent thing instead of being consumed by the imminent school committee meeting and *Melted* feelings . . . I take it all back.

Because Monday morning, the auditorium is a crime scene.

Black paint is smeared all over our celestial canyon.

Paint cans are overturned on the stage.

We're supposed to be staging a scene for the school committee.

Putting the pieces into place for a coronation.

"How—?" Makayla's eyes widen. "My *set.*"

"What the hell?" Arjun says.

Henry's expression is withering. "You started a prank war."

"*Reid* started a prank war," I clarify.

"Reid finished it, too," Arjun says.

Shit. I am so pissed at the peanut butter fudge sauce in my backpack. I thought we were being careful. Covert. I thought even if the prank war blew up the Harvest Festival—it had *worked,* keeping Reid distracted. Clearly, it did not. And, okay. I know I ruined the band's concert. But it was an accident! A prank gone wrong.

There is no point to this destruction except cruelty.

Behind us, the auditorium doors swoosh open and Danica and Fitz emerge into this disaster with both Mrs. Mulaney and my dad. Mrs. Mulaney takes in the scene, her expression hardening when we make eye contact. Dad's eyes pop open at the sight of our ruined stage.

"Nat-a-lie," Dad says slowly, enunciating every syllable. "What did you do?"

"There isn't a drama club," Mrs. Mulaney says, pushing her glasses up the bridge of her nose. "Yet there is a set. Interesting."

My jaw drops.

The stage has been vandalized! What did *I* do?

"*Was* a set," Fitz corrects, her turquoise nails digging into her palms. "Past tense."

"Natalie," Dad repeats. "Explain. Please."

"We're presenting *Melted* to the school committee tonight," Henry confesses.

I sigh. Henry is always the first to crack.

Mrs. Mulaney frowns. "Have you been conducting unauthorized drama club rehearsals?"

"Not at school," Henry says.

"But there is a set," Mrs. Mulaney says.

"Was," Fitz repeats.

"It was a project for Mrs. DiCarlo's class," Makayla explains.

"That Reid totally ruined!" I blurt out.

"Natalie," Dad warns.

I shrug. "What? Reid knew about HAVE A HE(ART). He has motive."

"No thanks to you," Danica mutters under her breath.

Mrs. Mulaney crosses her arms. "Can someone please enlighten me?"

I pull the completed proposal out of my backpack and hand it to Mrs. Mulaney. "Look. We're using the limited resources we have to show the school committee that we don't need a budget to create art. Inside this packet is a play, a petition, and a vision that brings all the cut arts clubs together for a charity event."

Dad's expression softens. "You've all been working together on this?"

We nod in unison.

"It's not only us. We've just been leading the quiet revolution," Danica says.

"But we're not anti-band!" Makayla says.

"Just anti-bureaucracy," Arjun adds.

I continue, feeling empowered by my dad's full attention. "If HAVE A HE(ART) is approved, the school committee gets good PR and will seem invested in finding creative solutions to retain arts programs. We'll create something fun and meaningful. It's a win-win."

"No." Mrs. Mulaney pinches the bridge of her nose and takes in the set, the stage, the *mess.* "You never should've been in the auditorium without an advisor. That cannot happen again."

"We were just trying to—" Henry starts.

Mrs. Mulaney cuts Henry off. "You were just being defiant."

I swear Henry's teacher-pleaser heart stops.

"First period. Now."

We march up the aisles of the auditorium and I just cannot even. I swallow my snark. Mrs. Mulaney is more focused on our so-called defiance than *literal vandalism.* I mean, seriously! Paint on waxed wood should be a felony. HAVE A HE(ART) is taking a stand. It's creating something from the ashes of our programs. Not *destroying—*

"Natalie," Dad says, standing by the door and stopping me in my tracks.

We make eye contact, my dad and me. He reaches into his back pocket and pulls out a phone, *my* phone. It's a small victory, the weight of my phone in my hand, plucked from my dad's palm. Maybe for the first time ever, Dad's recognizing his perfect protégé isn't so *perfect* after all.

"Good luck tonight," Dad says.

He has the audacity to sound *hurt.*

"Thanks," I whisper.

"I hope, moving forward, you and Reid can set aside whatever—"

I don't hear the end of Dad's sentence. I'm already gone because once again it's got to be both sides. It's too much to hope an anti-Reid switch will flip in Dad's brain.

Outside the auditorium doors, I pause.

Exhale a shaky breath and press the heels of my palms against my eyes.

"Natalie?"

My eyes pop open. Of course, *of course*, Reid is here to witness the aftermath of his scheme.

"Are you okay?" he asks.

I don't even dignify that with a response, opting instead to unzip my backpack and take out the jar of peanut butter fudge sauce and two plastic spoons. I sit on the floor, my back against the pillar, and open the jar. Put a spoonful in my mouth and it's good, *so good*. Reid is missing out. I'm definitely not sharing.

"This is supposed to be apology fudge. For the Harvest Festival. It's no longer apology fudge."

Reid's expression softens. "Natalie—"

"The way we are—it's not supposed to be like this. We have *rules*."

Reid's nose scrunches and he has the audacity to sit next to me. His eyes are wide, his neck flushed pink. As if he is *concerned*. "Nat, I sincerely do not know what you are talking about."

"You can drop the act. You win, okay? You. Win."

I swallow my second spoonful and wrinkle my nose because it's not nearly as good as the first. Too sweet. Besides, it's for Reid. It's *Reid's* favorite ice cream topping. And that's what it's supposed to be—a topping.

Before I can think twice I flip the open jar and . . . *oops,* there goes his stupid perfect hair. Reid jumps back but it's too late—the sauce is everywhere, flattening his curls, dripping down his ears, landing on the shoulder seams of his crisp blue shirt.

"Shit! *Natalie!* What is *wrong* with you?"

Reid keeps trying to run a hand through his hair. He *can't.* Every time his hand touches his scalp he is reintroduced to the relentless sauce. Without a response, I exit the scene, tossing the empty jar in the nearest recycling bin on my way to first period.

Reid got his peanut butter fudge sauce after all.

During last period, Ms. Rodkey summons the core members of HAVE A HE(ART), plus Reid, to the office via loudspeaker. We're sat around a conference room table with Mrs. Mulaney and my dad seated at the head, deflated and waiting on consequences. Henry rakes his hand through his hair. Fitz fixes a chipped nail. Danica scrolls through her phone. Arjun fidgets with a pencil. Makayla reapplies peppermint ChapStick.

Reid enters the office last, in his LHS band T-shirt he changed into post-fudging.

He still has remnants of sauce in his hair. Good.

Mrs. Mulaney begins with a lecture about the mess and liability, but I care more about the vandalism investigation.

"We retrieved security footage of the incident," Mrs. Mulaney says. "The stage was vandalized by a group of underclassmen band members."

That makes no sense.

"How would they even know about HAVE A HE(ART)?" I ask, my eyes meeting Reid's.

"Natalie, it was the least subtle anti-band smear campaign on the planet. I mean, Ivan and his jock bros signed your petition!" Reid says.

"Everyone knew?" Dad frowns and strokes his beard. "And . . . no one thought to tell me?"

Reid shrugs. "We weren't worried about it. Not until Natalie blew out our concert, anyway. Also, if my innocence has been proven . . . why am I here?"

"You're all here because clearly the budget cuts have created more tension among the student body than we anticipated. So we have a solution," Mrs. Mulaney says.

"We read HAVE A HE(ART)," Dad continues. "The district needs another buzzworthy marquee event to make up for the Harvest Festival flop. Mrs. Mulaney and I believe that with some tweaks . . . *Melted* could be that event."

Holy shit.

Validation courses through my veins as I take in the tableau of reactions, everyone barely able to comprehend the words. Makayla and Arjun's eyes widen. Henry's eyebrows scrunch together. Danica and Fitz victory-pump their fists. Reid's forehead vein protrudes and I can almost hear the stress loop that is his brain.

Oh my God.

HAVE A HE(ART) . . . just got approved!

Mrs. Mulaney laughs. "They're speechless."

"*Melted* can absolutely be that event!" I confirm.

"Tweaks to the script?" Henry asks.

"Yes!" Mrs. Mulaney claps her hands together. "We love the premise. A student-written production is a compelling hook and the climate crisis cause will resonate with the community. We just have one small, tiny, reasonable note: to incorporate the band and present an event that is truly interdisciplinary. So instead of a play—you will develop and execute an original musical."

I . . . don't see this coming.

"A musical," I echo.

Mrs. Mulaney nods. "*Melted: The Musical.*"

I don't musical. I never have. Besides the fact that Reid is super into them and that they are very much his thing—the whole breaking-into-song-midsentence structure always takes me out of the story. I would be pulled into a monologue, invested, and then . . . cue music, reminding me that nothing is real.

"I can't write music," Henry says, so softly I barely hear him.

"This is where some collaboration comes in," Dad says.

"I can help," Danica says, and she has the audacity to look excited.

Henry's expression softens when Danica speaks, like the idea of collaborating with her fixes everything, and my heart flops into my stomach because *I am losing him, damn it.* I try to connect with Fitz, who cannot sing, to make sure we're on the same page, but she's focusing on the way Henry is looking at Danica and she's a lost cause too.

"Natalie and Henry, you are a fantastic directors and writers," Mrs. Mulaney says. I am instantly suspicious. "Reid, your musical skills are unparalleled. Your strengths are complementary. So, Reid will come on as a third director."

"What?"

No. No way. This is worse than apologizing!

"Mrs. Mulaney—" Reid starts.

I cut him off. "I'm sorry, Mrs. Mulaney. That will never work."

"This is nonnegotiable," Mrs. Mulaney says.

I lock eyes with Henry, my eyes screaming *save me!*

"It'll be fine, Nat," Henry assures me, and I want to scream. It will absolutely not be fine. The whole point of this was to do one last show, to direct something we wrote together.

Reid looks at my dad, his expression incredulous. "You're seriously okay with this?"

Dad nods. "Since it's a band event, I'm stepping in as

advisor. We'll use my classroom to rehearse every Monday and Wednesday. I'll conduct too, and tie it into the band curriculum."

"What?" I repeat.

Since it's a band event. Wow. Codirecting with Reid is enough of a plot twist. But Mr. Jacobson—my *dad*—calling our proposal, *my* show, a *band event.* It's too much.

"It's a perfect compromise," Mrs. Mulaney says. "Everyone can work toward the common goal of putting together *Melted: The Musical.* I am already imagining some of these scenes as musical numbers."

"I mean, it's based on *Frozen,*" Fitz says.

"Exactly!" Mrs. Mulaney latches onto the agreement, not willing to let in any more drama today. "Also, the school committee will be in the audience, assessing the execution. Next year's budget could very much depend on the success of this event."

I swallow. "Define 'success.'"

"A sold-out audience. Local media attention wouldn't hurt either. Think of this as an opportunity to prove how your art adds value to this community."

Mrs. Mulaney's delivery is so casual, I have to laugh. Adds value? We're *students.*

I see so many pizza bagels in my future.

We're dismissed and Henry bolts from the room first, unwilling to miss too much of AP Lit even in the middle of total drama catastrophe. Everyone else exits the office, dazed, while Dad, Reid, and I stare at one another for a four-bar rest.

Dad smiles at me. "Well, congratulations, Natalie. *Melted* is happening."

"I played a few harmless pranks. *You* ruined an entire concert! How did this even become my problem?" Reid asks.

"You'll want it on your resume, Reid. We're not going to D.C. this year."

Reid and I react in unison. *"What?"*

Every year, the band ranks high enough to perform at Nationals in Washington D.C.

"*Melted* is coming out of the band's budget and there is no way we can afford both. We crunched some numbers—and ultimately, *Melted*'s costs are low and revenue potential is high. Funding an out-of-state trip in a way that makes out-of-pocket costs affordable is pretty much the opposite. So this semester we focus on *Melted* and on delivering a great show . . . and then recalibrate for the local festival circuit in the spring."

"Wow. Okay. You really do win after all, Natalie," Reid says.

"This isn't winning," I insist.

Dad scratches his beard. "Can't you try to be open-minded?"

"About you turning *Melted* into *a band thing*?"

"Actually, I saw potential, stuck my neck out for you, and now have to tell my students that our biggest trip of the year is cancelled—and *still* it's not enough for you."

Dad's words feel like cold water dumped over my head.

I haven't felt this way since the last time I picked up my clarinet.

I open my mouth to retort, then close it because I do not have a comeback.

I *do* have a production. A chance to direct and change the fate of the drama club. I can't screw up again. I owe it to my friends and every HAVE A HE(ART) signature to see this through. Even if it means living my nightmare.

"So. *Codirector,*" Reid says, sarcasm heavy in his voice. "When should we meet to discuss the rewrite? I have notes. Specifically, curious about act two, when—"

I turn on my heels and book it down the hallway toward the final few minutes of pre-calculus. Theater has always been my one reprieve from the artistic intensity that radiates from Reid and my dad. Now, not even the thing that has always been *my* thing is safe. It's been infiltrated by Reid, by my dad, by *music.* But no way will I let Reid sweep in and make it his. He has already done that to me once.

I will not let it happen again.

CHAPTER TEN

Mrs. Mulaney does know we have to . . . write this musical, right?"

Reid is the first voice to speak up once Dad tells us the production schedule. It is Wednesday afternoon and we are in a circle of six chairs downstage center in the music room. Dad's classroom becoming the official meeting spot for *Melted: The Musical* is the worst. The creative team consists of myself, Henry, Fitz, Danica . . . and Reid. Makayla has preseason conditioning after school but promises to deliver an incredible set with the rest of the art team. Arjun is, quote, *down to stage manage when there's something to manage.*

Danica frowns at the schedule. "Five weeks to adapt a play into a musical? It's almost like she wants us to fail."

"I mean, we have a script," Fitz says, peeling the left thumb of her blue manicure. Her tone is bored and she doesn't look up from her nails, a stress defense mechanism because in musicals, the leads generally sing.

Reid's knee bounces in even eighth notes. "But it's more than a script now. We need lyrics. Music. I started writing . . . but I've never composed for a full orchestra before."

I frown. "You started writing?"

He nods. "It's only three songs so far but Logan and Lacey think—"

I cut Reid off. "*Only* three?"

Reid is supposed to be as annoyed as I am that this is even happening! Wallowing with his fellow woodwinds and whatnot! Not writing three full songs!

Reid shrugs. "It's not like we have time to waste. I reread the script and I felt inspired, I guess. I don't know. Do you want to hear them or not?"

No. Yes. I don't know.

"Yes," Dad answers on my behalf, reminding me that Reid writing songs isn't the worst part of this whole *Melted: The Musical* situation—that award goes to my dad, who is sitting directly across from me in total Mr. Jacobson mode. "I think that's a great place to start."

"Me too," Danica says. She reaches into her backpack and pulls out an Elsa notebook that says MELTED MUSIC in perfect block bubble letters. Her lavender lips break into a smile. "I don't write music, but as the resident musical expert, I have so many ideas. Luckily, we aren't working from scratch. We have *Melted,* the play. But we also have *Frozen* to vibe from."

Henry shakes his head. "It's not *Frozen.*"

"But I think we can lean into the *Frozen* opposite theme," Reid says, rummaging through his backpack and pulling out his composition notebook. "Add some familiarity for our audience."

"Yes!" Danica agrees, and wow I hate Danica and Reid being on the same page. "Exactly."

Reid nods and takes a seat at the piano. He opens his composition book and begins to play a medley of songs he's composed for our show. *Henry's and my* show. The songs have titles like, "Keep It In," "Do You Wanna Build a Fire?," and "Hate Is a Closed Window"—and while the names of the songs are inspired by the *Frozen* opposite concept, almost like it's a *joke* . . . the music Reid has composed is wholly original. Reid bops along to his own melodies and describes how each piece could fit into the show, since lyrics are still a work in progress.

I stand. "This isn't going to work."

"Nat, I was skeptical too, but these aren't bad," Henry says.

I swear, Henry sounds *impressed.*

Danica blinks at me. "I mean, this is obviously a rough draft. But it has potential."

Even Fitz shrugs. At this point, she's made significant progress with her left hand and has a pile of dried blue nail polish on her lap.

Henry nods. "Natalie, as a fellow codirector, I know this isn't what we planned, but it has—"

"Henry!"

"Can you maybe let me finish my sentence? Just, like, for *once*!" Henry snaps.

Wow.

What does *that* mean?

Silence.

"—it has the potential to still be great. That's all," Henry finishes.

"But it's already *so* wrong," I insist. "You cannot just start writing songs, Reid. That's not how a collaboration works."

Reid's fingers smash against the keyboard in C minor. "I'm sorry you inspired me!" The note fades to silence and I know the tips of my ears are pink. Reid swallows. "I always liked *Melted*. That was never a prank. Okay?"

I am suddenly aware that my friends—and my *dad*—are witnessing what very much feels like a private *Natalie vs. Reid* conversation. I pivot back.

"Henry and I should still have been involved before any writing happened. In fact, I want to be involved in the composition process too."

"Nat-a-lie," Reid says slowly, enunciating each syllable as his fingers start to move back up and down the piano. "I called you, like, twelve times last night. How can we collaborate if you don't answer your phone?"

I pull out my phone and click to see missed calls and . . . I have Reid in *do not disturb* mode.

Dad clears his throat, bringing the drama to a halt. "Okay. I'm calling it. Everyone can go home. Codirectors, pull it together. Mrs. Mulaney wants script approval by mid-November and a cast list before Thanksgiving. *Melted: The Musical*'s one-night-only performance will be February sixth. Is this tight? Yes. But it's doable, assuming we get our act together and start acting like professionals."

Except, we're not professionals. We're high school students.

That's kind of the whole point.

"Can I be honest, Mr. J?" Danica asks.

Dad nods. "Please."

"I think Henry and I should codirect," Danica says, and five sets of eyes snap to meet hers. "Look, I should've been president of the musical theater club. Henry would be drama club president too. As seniors, it is our last chance to be in a leadership role. For Natalie and Reid this is a punishment. I think we should consider that for some of us . . . putting on a show this year actually means something."

My eyes turn to Henry in disbelief but I can't read his expression. Is this serious?

"That's not fair," Reid says. "Yeah, Natalie and I were thrown together as codirectors. But we're the ones who are still going to be here next year. We have something to fight for."

Do I . . . agree with Reid?

Does Henry . . . want to abandon me for Danica?

Impossible. All of it.

I look back at my dad, who looks at me like he is so far out of his depth.

So our first rehearsal ends on an awkward and confusing note. I watch Danica and Henry packing up to leave. Danica tells Henry she'll see him at study group. Henry smiles and nods, zipping up his backpack and tossing it over his shoulder, exiting scene without even saying goodbye, and I'm really over the passive-aggressive attitude.

I follow him out of the band room and down the hallway.

"What was *that*?" I ask.

Henry pivots to face me. "I have to get to work, Natalie."

"You're pissed about the prank war," I say.

"Our play became a punishment and an exercise in team-building for you and Callahan."

"I'm sorry! But snapping at me in front of the group? Codirecting with Danica? I know you're friends . . . or maybe more? I don't even know! What's going on?"

"I wish I knew!" Henry admits. "I know we have fun together. Dani is going through the senior stress too. It's nice talking to someone who gets it."

Henry's delivery is so casual it *hurts*. We have been best friends for almost a decade . . . but now Danica *gets it*? I know I'm not applying for college yet, but Henry knows that I understand the stress of it—the monetary stress, the making-a-momentous-decision stress. I can be there for him if he *talks* to me. But I guess he has Danica now.

I can't figure out how to say any of that though—so I pivot back to *Melted*.

"We're supposed to be codirectors," I say.

"Honestly, I'm not sure I want to be a codirector at all," Henry admits. He exhales, as if saying these words out loud are a relief. "I'll still come to meetings, but I need to take a step back. I'm not qualified to direct a musical. I don't *want* to direct a musical. Or to be in the middle of you and Reid."

Henry doesn't want to codirect with Danica.

But he doesn't want to codirect *at all.*

"Are you . . . breaking up with me? Directorially speaking?"

"Three's a crowd," Henry says. "And I need to focus on college applications and taking on more at the restaurant."

"What changed?"

Henry shrugs. "Nothing. Everything. I don't know. I love writing and I loved our low-stakes drama club. It was always supposed to be chill. Just for us. Fun. But it can't be that now. Not with an entire budget on the line."

I shake my head. "We're supposed to be Jacobson and Chao."

"We still are," Henry insists. "Just meant to be a writing duo, I guess."

Henry walks away . . . and I'm so confused. We put in so much work. And I know we have to put in *more* work to adapt *Melted* into a musical. But still. Now that *our* show is happening, for real, Henry wants to . . . step back? Because *Melted* is no longer . . . chill? Is it not chill to want to put on a decent show? To protect what we created? Henry and I have always been on the same page about everything, especially theater, and for the first time . . . we're not.

But the whole point of writing and pushing so hard for *Melted*—outside of saving a flailing drama club—is so we can do this together, before Henry graduates and everything changes.

Maybe it already has.

CHAPTER ELEVEN

I am outlining *Melted: The Musical* at my kitchen table, attempting to envision a musical version. At its heart, *Melted* is about Adina and Emma trying to save a world on fire, about learning to lean on each other and reversing a climate crisis. *Melted* was inspired by the very real, constant anxiety my friends and I feel over the future of our planet. How does one . . . *musical* that? I don't have a vision yet. But I need one, ASAP. Because Henry, Reid, and I have our first attempt at *collaboration* this afternoon. I have zero expectations as to how this will go.

"Hey, Lee."

I minimize my screen at the sound of my mother's voice. "Hi."

Mom enters the kitchen, setting down her laptop on the table. "How's *Melted* going?"

"Okay," I lie. "How's writing going?"

She opens the fridge and pours cold brew from a pitcher over ice before taking the seat next to me. "I am . . . cautiously optimistic. My students are actually providing some inspiration."

"How so?" I ask.

"Well, one of my students, Travis, is in the wrong class. But he didn't drop it, and I think it's because he's into debating the validity of romance novels with Elisa. She absolutely eviscerated his first workshop entry."

"Literary douchebro in a romance class is a premise I need."

"I needed it too." Mom smiles at me and her energy is contagious—almost reminiscent of Before the Block. "I'm twenty thousand words into it . . . far enough that I need to outline before it all falls apart. Maybe we can have a brainstorm session soon?"

"Definitely," I say. Brainstorm sessions are a throwback to the time my love for playwriting emerged. We'd spend hours in a back-and-forth flow, pinpointing motivation, heightening stakes, finishing each other's sentences, and asking leading questions to inspire the next scene. Then we wrote. While Mom worked on her book, I adapted ideas we'd just brainstormed into short scenes, only caring about the dialogue and emotion conveyed in those moments.

Then came the writer's block. I thought brainstorm sessions would fix it but . . . they didn't.

I can't remember the last time we had one.

"I honestly need it for *Melted,* now that it's a musical."

"Does this mean I can read it?" Mom asks.

"Maybe." I relent. "If I can read your pages."

"Deal," Mom says with a smile. "Maybe. Sometimes I think you're the only person in the world who still believes in me, Lee."

Mom covers her ears with her headphones to get some work done as I swallow the lump in my throat. It's complicated. I believe in my mom, in her talent. I know how it feels when the words flow onto the page and writing feels so completely *right.* It's how I feel every time I write a perfect line of dialogue, how I felt all summer working on *Melted.* But Mom is an example of just how wrong it can go. It's everything I'm afraid of and dangerously close to how I feel now—stuck and stressed because the words are becoming work.

Maybe Henry is right. Maybe this is all just too much now.

But seeing Mom's fingers fly across the keyboard, her words returning like they never left, remembering how writing feels when it *works,* is the motivation I need to push through.

I have to at least try.

Hours later, music envelops the kitchen the moment I swing the basement door open. Reid is down there playing Mozart's Clarinet Concerto in B-flat. Somewhere in the second movement, I think. I used to know without thinking, in another life when instinct was reaching for the clarinet the moment I got home from school. I close my eyes and access the music part of my brain, trying to remember. Dad says it's all muscle memory. If I stack my hands left over right, like I'm holding my clarinet, will my fingers play along on imaginary keys? It makes me pause.

This is why I hate listening to Reid play. It always, *always* makes me pause.

I ignore the scratchiness in the back of my throat as I walk down the stairs.

When I push the studio door open, Mozart goes sharp.

"Already?" Reid asks, placing his clarinet on its stand, then moving to the electric piano in the corner. The clarinet is Reid's band instrument and his musical soul mate, but the piano came first, in the form of weekly lessons in elementary school. He only picked it back up in a meaningful way in high school, with his growing interest in music theory and composition.

"Unfortunately," I respond.

Reid begins to play scales as I take a seat at the desk on the adjacent wall. It's impossible to separate my clarinet feelings from this space, and memories resurface. Installing wood-paneled walls, just the two of us, the Chanukah I was in sixth grade. Watching hours of YouTube together at the computer—everything from music theory videos to animated shorts that made me laugh so hard tears streamed down my cheeks.

The clarinet was an entry point into my dad's world, but the memories aren't all music.

"Codirector! You could at least *pretend* to be listening."

Reid's snark brings me back to reality.

"I *am*," I insist.

He flips a page in his composition book and an out-of-place curl falls into his eyes. "Sure. Now this next one—"

"We should wait for Henry," I say.

I check my phone for the millionth time and I have an update at last.

Henry Chao
DONE WITH THE SATS FOREVER
12:10 PM

ALSO Dani was talking about wanting to see the new Mindy Kaling romcom and I said we should go see it and she's down!!
12:11 PM

. . . except she thought I meant we should see it NOW
12:12 PM

I'M SORRY. Stay strong! You've got this! It's not like I'd be much help on the musical front anyways . . .
12:13 PM

I blink at my phone. Henry is ditching me and *Melted* for a movie date with Danica?

I mean, this tracks. I should not be surprised. Still. Henry promised he'd be here. To support. Consult. Those were *his* words. For the first time, I thought I'd be battling Reid from a majority alliance with Henry by my side. Instead, he chooses a *movie* with his new . . . best friend Danica? Girlfriend Danica? Senior solidarity Danica?

Does the label even matter?

Now I have to deal with the situation on my own. I stand and roll my chair across the room to the piano, in a better position to collaborate or whatever, and sit cross-legged.

"Can you play 'Do You Wanna Build a Fire?' from the top?" I ask.

Reid's eyes met mine. They're more brown than green today. "Sure."

I place my phone facedown on the piano and wrap my arms around my knees.

Reid begins to play.

I stop him four measures in. "It's too whimsical."

Reid sighs. "I promise it's not."

"This doesn't sound like *grief*," I retort. "Maybe slow it down. Or—"

"Natalie, I will take any and all criticism after I play it through. Okay?"

"Fine," I concede.

As soon as I focus on Reid, I remember why I avoid the studio. Why I don't go to band concerts. Watching him play music makes me feel things in this disgusting way that is not compatible with the rest of my essence. His fingers move up and down the keys with ease, shoulders rising and falling with the melody. Curls keep falling into his eyes and it is so distracting.

So I close my eyes and force myself to separate the music from the musician.

I allow myself to hear the potential—from the warmth

conveyed in "Do You Wanna Build a Fire?" to the emotional slow burn in "Hate Is a Closed Window" that crescendos into Adina accidentally burning down the only home she has ever known. I feel the intention in every chord progression, down to the quiet intensity of the motif that ties the song together.

I'm not sure I understood what *Melted* could sound like until now. But I do.

It's the worst.

Then the key changes and he moves into the potential showstopper, "Keep It In." Adina's solo. Reid wrote the lyrics for this one and they're not quite right—the tone is a bit too insecure. Adina doesn't leave Infernodelle because she lacks confidence. She's *afraid.*

But with the right lyrics, the music could work.

Wait. No. There's one small issue—

"Adina can't have any songs," I say.

Reid stops singing, but he doesn't stop playing. "Adina is the lead."

"Fitz can't sing."

I whisper this as though Fitz is going to pop out from behind the piano to claim offense.

Reid's eyebrows scrunch, confused. "Everyone has to audition, right?"

I mean, yes. But not Fitz.

"Fitz is attached to play Adina," I say, firm.

Reid finally stops playing and runs a hand through his hair, frustrated. "Okay. I know she's your friend, but she was supposed to be Adina in the *play*. This is a musical now and I'm sorry, but we can't cast a lead who can't sing."

"Henry and I wrote Adina for *Fitz*. We're not recasting."

"Where is Chao, anyways?" Reid asks. "Didn't you say he should be here?"

I chew the inside of my cheek. "I know. But he'd agree."

"Agree on making something already hard impossible? This shouldn't even be my problem!" Reid says. "I should be spending my Saturday focused on my Albany audition. The chances I get in are low already, but with *Melted* on my plate? I'm totally screwed."

I roll my eyes in response.

What?" Reid asks.

I shrug. "I don't think that's a real problem. You'll get in."

"Oh. Thanks," Reid says, his voice piano.

Silence settles between us, one measure too long. I don't know what is wrong with me because complimenting Reid is the last thing I do.

So I pivot. "Can I hear another song?"

Reid begins playing chord progressions. "Yeah, sure. I'll play the start of 'In Winter.' It's not finished, but when you're listening to it, imagine it as your standard big Broadway tap number, okay?"

I raise my eyebrows. "*Melted* does not need a standard Broadway tap number."

He stops playing. "I didn't think so either, but after talking with Danica, I got sucked into some research last night—"

I frown. *Danica? Research?*

Reid reaches for his backpack leaning against the wall and pulls out his laptop. "Danica sent me some tap numbers and it feels necessary to include one now. I'll show you—"

"You can't just play me the song? We're nowhere near choreography."

"I mean, I can. But you need to believe in the tap. Otherwise you won't *get it.*"

Reid opens YouTube and scoots over on the bench, enough so there's plenty of space for me to sit next to him, as if we do this all the time. It's weird, seeing this totally different version of him. A Reid who writes original show tunes in front of me and sort of glows at the prospect of *tap* instead of smirking over Mozart.

"I wish I had the skill to do this," Reid says, gesturing to the screen.

It reminds me that musicals are Reid's domain. Music always came first, but a lot of the band kids also did the musical, back when the titles of those productions had *Jr.* at the end and they were less of a time commitment. Reid's half-hearted audition led to him starring in *The Music Man Jr.* in eighth grade—a role that was both his debut and final act.

He pulls up a sequence of videos so fast and we spend the next twenty minutes watching a mix of the classic numbers from *Anything Goes* and *42nd Street*, then move to Reid's more recent favorites—*Newsies*, *Aladdin*, and *The Book of Mormon*.

"See? It's music too," Reid says.

I shrug, but I get why Reid is into writing a tap number. Watching the dancers create music with their bodies is like seeing the words in a script executed flawlessly onstage.

Reid closes his laptop. "The dancers and the music are inextricably linked, right? So when I play . . . you have to imagine *that* adding to it."

I nod because despite myself, I am intrigued.

Reid launches into the song—a high-energy, whimsical ensemble number that has the cast daydreaming about experiencing a true winter, something Infernodelle has, of course, never seen before. I tap my toes to the music subconsciously, adding in where the taps would fit into the melody. Reid is as lost in the music as I am. His knee bumps mine when he presses the foot pedal and I stand, moving back to my rolling chair, suddenly very aware of how close we are, how intimate this feels, sitting on a piano bench with Reid.

He stops playing and looks at me expectantly. Like what I have to say matters to him.

"I like it," I say, and before I've even given it permission to, my mind is racing with notes, ideas. "What if the last bridge changed keys?"

I expect him to scoff and explain the virtues of keeping the song in F major, but instead Reid takes my note and tries it out, live, before my eyes. He tinkers with the chord progressions before shifting the bridge up a step.

"How's this?" he asks, and it sounds exactly like I imagined it would.

“That’s it,” I say. It surprises me how much I mean it.

Footsteps tap their way down the basement steps and Dad enters the studio, a scene transition I’m not ready for.

“Natalie! Reid! Are you *collaborating*? Be still my beating heart!”

I roll my eyes. “Barely.”

“I was just explaining the merits of a Broadway tap number,” Reid says.

Dad nods. “I have ten minutes before bat mitzvah errands. Hit me.”

Reid plays the new version of “In Winter”—*my* version. Dad stands over Reid and considers every chord. Reid straightens his back, a subtle subconscious adjustment because he is always my dad’s student, even on a Saturday afternoon. I swear, Reid is sustained by the words *well played* delivered by my dad.

“Smart key change,” Dad notes with an appreciative nod.

“Thanks,” Reid and I say at the same time.

Excuse me? “I thought—”

“Can you take it from the top of the second chorus?” Dad asks Reid.

He cuts me off. Like I’m not even here. I give Reid a note, I *try* to collaborate—and he takes the credit five seconds later. I reach for my phone on top of the piano and pull my oversized gray sweater closer to me, scrolling through Instagram and counting the measures until yet another collaboration between Reid and my dad is over.

"Good luck finding a dozen tap dancers," I mutter as my dad exits the studio.

Reid stops playing and gives me a withering stare. "You mean Danica and all of her musical theater friends?"

I clench my jaw but I won't concede. "Right. But we're not going to ice the actors who can't sing or dance."

Reid's shoulders tense. "It's a *musical*."

"The whole point is to represent all the departments that got cut. Not just the music ones. This whole thing is a compromise, so you and your 'vision' need to bend too. Speaking of which, this is an okay start, but we can't approve anything without Henry."

Reid frowns. "Okay. But where is he?"

"Caught up at the restaurant," I lie. Even if I'm annoyed, I'm not about to expose that Henry is caught up with the actress, not the show. Chao Down, at least, is a valid excuse.

Reid closes his notebook, his expression shifting. "I'm still wallowing a little on the inside. Clearly. But I promise that I'm serious about this. I'm going to show up."

"Okay."

"Natalie, I'm—"

"*Serious*. I know. You always are."

Reid frowns as he loosens the ligature on his clarinet to change the reed, already ready to get back to audition practice. "Is that a problem? Is everything I say going to be a problem? We are *codirectors*. We have to at least *try* to collaborate."

The laugh that escapes my lips is sharp. "So you can take all the credit? No way."

"So how is this going to work?"

"You write the music. I'll write the lyrics. Alone."

Reid frowns. "Natalie, that's not—"

I pull the studio door open and exit before Reid finishes his sentence, unable to stop my brain from looping back to my dad praising Reid. Especially after how I reacted to the songs. It makes me regret letting my guard down, even for a moment. I'm not going to let his musical talent overrule my vision. It's a necessary reality check, a reminder that codirecting with Reid is absolutely a problem with no real solution.

Because when it comes to Reid and music, it will always be a competition.

Even when we're supposed to be on the same team.

Outplayed

At the start of seventh grade, I, Natalie Jacobson, was the best clarinetist at Lincoln Middle School.

First chair was validation. The hours I spent practicing every day, the battle blisters I'd overcome—it was all worth it. According to Mrs. Sullivan, I was the best. *Me.* First chair proved that I was a talented musician, proved that my dad was investing his energy into the wrong student.

"Congratulations!" Madeline's arms wrapped around me in a surprise hug from behind, since alto saxophones sat in the second row.

"Good job," Reid said, disassembling his clarinet with a shrug. "You outplayed me."

I raised my eyebrows, suspicious, but decided to play nice. I mean, we'd have to sit next to each other all year, so might as well *try* to be civil. Plus, I won.

There was no point in being a jerk.

Except that ended up not being the case. Because of course, his sportsmanship was temporary. Within a week, it became clear that Reid was on a mission to make my band life as miserable as possible.

After class ended, Reid walked right up to Madeline as she was breaking down her saxophone. "Hey, Madeline—" Reid swallowed, nervous "—I was wondering if, um, maybe you . . . wanted to see the new Captain America movie this weekend?"

I hid my smirk as I was unscrewing the ligature on my clarinet to remove my reed, anticipating the look on Reid's face when he got turned down for the second time in two weeks.

"Sure. Okay," Madeline answered simply.

My reed snapped in half.

I turned around in my chair, *first* chair, so fast to see Madeline was grinning nervously at Reid and he was smiling back—not smirking, *smiling*.

Nothing made sense.

Madeline's eyes met mine after Reid walked away, wide with a hint of guilt.

"Are you mad?"

"I'm confused. We hate Reid. But you're going on a movie date with him?"

Madeline closed her saxophone case. "I know you have history. But I think Reid is cool. I . . . don't think I want to be a part of that."

In that moment, one of my deepest fears came true. Madeline didn't just tolerate Reid or laugh at his stupid woodwind puns. She *liked* Reid. Over the summer, Madeline was one hundred percent Team Reid Is the Worst. But since he went to another school, she only knew him through stories of our rivalry. Now Reid's mutant eyes and extra-floppy hair had morphed her into a total stranger.

Caught so off-guard, all I could do was stammer, "O-Okay."

I FaceTimed Henry after school.

"I don't understand. Reid is the *worst.* Madi knows this!"

Henry shrugged, his bangs (yes, bangs) falling into his eyes. "I think you need to let Madeline find out about Reid herself."

"So let her go on a *date*? Henry! What if Reid is using Madi to get back at me? For first chair? This could all be a *prank.*"

"That would be messed up, even for Reid."

I heard Henry's words, but still I clung to this theory. Reid messing with me? I was used to it. But messing with Madeline? Nope. Not okay.

Date night came that weekend, and I spent the entire evening hoping it was a disaster. But when Madeline Face-Timed me the next morning, she gushed about how sweet Reid is. *Gushed.* About *Reid.*

And then, just like that, he was her boyfriend.

We were literally twelve, so the "relationship" consisted of handholding and eating lunch together, mostly. But it was still complete torture. I ate lunch at the same table as Reid for an entire week! I kept waiting for Reid to mess up, to show his true colors, that this was all a revenge scheme.

But I couldn't wait forever. I had to double down.

Henry was right. I needed to let Madeline form her own opinions about Reid.

Telling her Reid was the worst clearly did not work.

But what if I showed her?

CHAPTER TWELVE

Assembling the invitations for Delia's bat mitzvah is a family affair.

Planning a bat mitzvah is like directing a play—the months spent organizing logistics, the slow burn of rehearsing the script . . . and then tech week, where everything needs to happen all at once. Except, it's tech *weeks.* Six weeks, to be precise. Crunch time. Invitations need to go out, centerpieces need to be designed, an over-the-top slideshow of Delia's life needs to be created (my job), speeches need to be written. The next month and a half pretty much consist of a never-ending list of bat mitzvah to-dos, which would be a lot without the never-ending list of *Melted* to-dos on top of it, now that I have to transform the script into songs.

It's a *lot.*

But the countdown to Delia's day—December fifth—is on. Delia stuffs her invitations, styled to look like season passes, into envelopes, Dad seals with a basketball sticker, Mom addresses with her perfect calligraphy, and I stamp. Episodes of *Gilmore Girls* that we know by heart run in the background. I will never not die when Luke pushes Jess into the lake, which happens just as Mom looks up from the guest list.

"Monica D.?" Mom frowns, pen poised above Delia's final list.

"I thought anyone named Monica is not invited?" Dad asks.

Delia swallows. "They're okay. We're . . . friends now."

I flash Delia an intense *since when?* look. "Dee."

"What?" Delia says. "They're invited. Can we drop it?"

"Sure," Mom says in her light *this is a test* voice, starting to write her name on the envelope.

"Wait—" Delia says before Mom has even dotted the I. "Can we skip them for now?"

Mom drops her pen. "Okay, Dee Marie. What is going on?"

Delia sighs. "Hannah says I'm not making an effort with The Monicas. So I want to try. Because otherwise I'm going to *lose* Hannah to The Monicas—and that would be a *million* times worse than dealing with them at my bat mitzvah."

Delia exits the kitchen, tears brimming under her lids. Mom drops her pen and stands, but I shake my head and tell her I've got this. I follow Delia up the stairs and through her bedroom door, where she sits on the edge of her bed and scrolls through her phone so fast she can't actually be looking at anything.

I sit beside my sister and wrap my arms around her until she drops her phone.

"Everything is trash." Delia wipes her eyes. "I don't know what's happening to us."

"Middle school," I say.

I remember it too well.

"But it's like I don't even know her anymore. Or like she doesn't know me the way I thought she did. She thinks I'm not inviting The Monicas because I'm jealous. Me! *Jealous.* I'm, like, no. I'm not inviting them to an event they're just going to mock."

"Hannah needs a reality check. Have you talked to her?"

Delia shakes her head. "It's hopeless."

"Hannah is your Henry, Dee. And we haven't been in the best spot either, so I get how you feel. I know confrontation is the worst. Trust me. But Hannah needs to know how much these microaggressions bother you, even if they don't seem like a big deal to her."

"We were supposed to go shopping today," Delia says, sidestepping my question. "Hannah cancelled at the last minute. She said she had too much homework. But she'll probably be in the background of Monica G.'s Snapchats later."

"Or she really has too much homework," I say. "I know I'm not Hannah, but I'm free this afternoon." Today is supposed to be a catch up on homework day. But homework can wait in the name of a sister crisis. "I can text Fitz, too."

"Really?" The mention of Fitz turns Delia's entire mood around. Truly, there is no bigger fan of *If the Shoe Fitz* than Delia Jacobson. "I still need a dress for my Friday service."

I send Fitz a message.

delia is having a friendship AND fashion emergency
11:10 AM

is your afternoon open for some shopping??
11:10 AM

Her response time to my text is the instant validation I crave.

MAJOR SAME
11:11 AM

(11:11 make a wisssssssh)
11:11 AM

this is a henry-free zone correct? we need to talk about that movie date???
11:11 AM

yes! ugh i know.
11:12 AM

i'm filming (stop distracting me) but i'll pick you up at . . . does 2 work?
11:13 AM

you distract yourself fitzgerald
11:14 AM

perfect!
11:14 AM

"Fitz will pick us up at two," I say.

Delia nods. "Thanks, Natalie."

"Shopping sprees don't heal all wounds, but they always help. I'm sorry Hannah is being such a butt. A third Monica. It will—"

A knock on the door interrupts my sister advice. Mom and Dad poke their heads in.

"You know, I remember vetoing an invitation to anyone named Monica," Mom says innocently. "Blame us."

We follow them back downstairs, and my sister takes a black Sharpie and crosses The Monicas off the guest list.

Shopping with Delia? It's *exhausting*.

"This is my *pro-cess*, Natalie," Delia says, drawing out each individual syllable as we enter the fitting room at Nordstrom Rack, the fourth store we've browsed in *four hours*.

"Respect the process, Natalie," Fitz says, her arms overflowing with dress options. She supports Delia's process with a handpicked selection of dresses, all sustainably sourced brands and from the sale rack. "You only get one bat mitzvah, you know?"

"What was yours like?" Delia asks.

"My theme was A Night in Paris," Fitz says, passing Delia a lavender chiffon dress over the door. "We had a local patisserie supply the cake and deserts. The color palette was pink and black. Tiny Eiffel Towers were the centerpieces. This is my truth: I am a cliché."

"It sounds perfect," Delia says, unlocking the dressing room door and swinging it open to reveal the lavender dress that swallows her in too much material. "Unlike this dress."

Fitz wrinkles her nose. "It didn't look so . . . ruffly on the rack."

"Not at all," I agree.

"Purple is my Saturday color scheme, anyway. I already have those dresses," Delia says.

Fitz nods. "Right! We should branch out."

She offers three more options to Delia—a gold striped maxi dress, a navy jumpsuit, and a teal dress with a lace bodice and tulle skirt. I attempt to offer sisterly thoughts and feedback on the fashion show, but Fitz's words are the only ones that matter.

"So, have you talked to Henry?" Fitz asks, her deep red lips blowing a raspberry as she sits next to me on the bench in the open fitting room stall across from Delia. "I feel like he's kind of ghosted us since the musical. Became all about Danica. I fully convinced myself I was imagining things during HAVE A HE(ART) . . . but a romcom? Starring my lord and savior, Mindy Kaling? Way to rub salt in the wound!"

I shake my head. "He left me *alone* with Reid yesterday—

after promising he'd show up! I tried to text him, like, twelve times last night, but I don't even know what to say to him. I don't think we've had a real conversation since *Melted* became a musical. He said *Melted* was supposed to be chill. Now it's not. Whatever that means."

"In all fairness, you are a stress monster," Fitz says. "So much Reid Rage."

I whack her with my purse. "I hate you."

Delia laughs. "Reid Rage. I love that."

"You're both cancelled," I declare.

Fitz rolls her eyes and turns to inspect herself in the fitting room mirror. "It's not even that I'm not happy for Henry. Dani and I were without question vibing during *Melted* rehearsals, but if she's into Henry I can live with that. He's just being *so* sketchy about it. I know he's your best friend—" Fitz reaches into her purse for a tube of mascara and twists off the wand "—but I guess I thought our friendship mattered too."

"*Of course* it does, Fitzgerald," I say. I don't know what it says about me, that even when I'm annoyed with Henry . . . I still defend him. "That's why he's being so weird."

"He needs to get it together."

"We all do," I admit.

"I think I'm in love," Delia says, opening the door to show off the navy jumpsuit, a smile spread wide across her face. It has a lace neckline with flutter sleeves and ties at the waist. "I never would've considered a jumpsuit, but now I'm obsessed. It's cute! It's comfortable! It doesn't need to be hemmed!"

"Spin!" Fitz says, and Delia obliges. "Wow. We love an accurate petite sizing! I have a whole vision that includes hair and makeup."

"Oh my *God.* Hannah will . . ." Delia stops whatever she's about to say next. Swallows. "You're the best, Fitz. I mean, this is it, right?"

"It's clearly speaking to you," Fitz says with a nod.

"One more spin," I say. The sight of Delia in her perfect outfit nearly brings me to tears—whether it's because she looks so grown-up or because this means shopping is *finally* almost over is anybody's guess.

Delia and Fitz high-five each other and Delia forces me to pose for her Snapchat story before she changes back into her clothes. They chat about all things *If the Shoe Fitz* as we make our way to the register, Fitz giving Delia a behind-the-scenes look at the lineup of curated posts for the next two weeks. I pay for the jumpsuit, and even at the sale price I'll still need to pick up extra shifts at Chao Down next week. But Delia is actually smiling so it's worth it.

We conclude the afternoon at the food court. As much as I complain about shopping, it's the most fun I've had in weeks and a break from *Melted* I didn't even know I needed. We order chocolate milkshakes and fries from McDonald's and make our way toward the seating area in search of an empty—and clean—table.

We're about to sit down when Delia stops and turns her head. "Is that Reid?"

Sure enough, Reid is sitting at a food court table with his own chocolate milkshake, reading *Read Between the Lies,* a popular YA novel, completely absorbed.

Why is Reid hanging out, alone, at the mall?

We follow Delia, who is walking over to Reid to say hi.

"Hey!" Delia says.

Reid looks up from his book. "Delia? Hey! Quick recovery."

Delia frowns. "What?"

"They're either at Francesca's or Forever 21," Reid says, oblivious to Delia's confusion. It isn't until she scrunches her nose, her *I'm trying not to cry* move, that it clicks with Reid what is happening. His eyes widen. "Oh. You were never sick?"

"I guess Hannah doesn't have *so much homework,*" I say, my hand on my hip.

Delia saw this coming. I hate that she was right.

"It's Hannah's loss, Dee," Fitz says, squeezing her shoulder.

"Can we just go home? I . . . can't run into them," Delia says, wiping a tear before beelining for the parking lot. Fitz follows behind Delia and I should too. Leave Reid with his book without another word.

But something keeps my feet in their place.

"I hate The Monicas," Reid says.

Of all the things Reid could say, I'm relieved it's this. "Right!"

"In the car, Monica D. kept asking me how much money I got for my bar mitzvah."

"Oh my God."

"I mean, I guess I hate their parents. They're *kids.* This shit comes from somewhere."

"Yeah." I take a sip of my milkshake. "So what are we going to do?"

The question slips out, unintentional.

Reid taps his fingers on the table in two counts, staccato. "We?"

"I mean—" I start, searching for a way to backpedal. If people face-palmed in real life, that would be me right now. "It's our sisters! The Monicas have been getting between them since Delia got back from Jock Camp."

"Really?" Reid's eyes widen with concern. "Am I that oblivious?"

"Yes." Reid is like my dad in that way. Everything else in the world—people, priorities, problems—fade into the background when they are absorbed in their music. "I need Hannah to snap out of this middle school spiral ASAP. Delia almost invited The Monicas to her bat mitzvah!"

"Seventh grade is the worst."

Reid's eyes meet mine and take me back to seventh grade. I squash down all the feelings that come with it. This is about Delia, not me.

"Swap?" Reid asks. "I'll talk to Delia. You take Hannah."

We nod in sync and I take a step back, retreating from

this conversation. As I'm crossing the parking lot, it occurs to me that I can't remember the last time Reid and I had a conversation that wasn't about *Melted.* Like, did I just make a plan with Reid? Not *against* him? I guess The Monicas are a common enemy. And Reid is somewhat tolerable when he's worried about our sisters. Still. *We?* The words spilled from my lips as if I can't handle this myself. As if I need him. There's got to be something wrong with me.

But then I see Delia's tearstained cheeks in the rearview mirror when I slide into Fitz's passenger seat—and some things are bigger than *Natalie vs. Reid.*

CHAPTER THIRTEEN

Mere weeks before a script is due to Mrs. Mulaney, Reid suggests a developmental edit. We're in a circle in Dad's classroom after school, meant to present a first look at the songs and structure of *Melted: The Musical*, when Reid goes rogue and launches into an idea that I, his codirector, in no way approved.

"I'm having trouble writing a Moritz song," Reid says. "What if we cut him?"

I frown. Cut an entire character arc—the *villain's* character arc—because Reid is blocked?

"What?"

"Hear me out," Reid starts, tucking his pencil behind his ear. "Moritz is supposed to be the *villain* . . . but isn't the point that the villain isn't any one character? That it's the *planet* and this external force that no one—not even Adina—can control? The *setting* is the villain."

I cannot even at Reid attempting to mansplain my script to me and getting it wrong.

So wrong.

Everyone is more or less unfazed by Reid's suggestion.

Fitz continues sketching costumes in her notebook, her eyebrows pinched together, focused. Henry scrolls through his phone and Danica punches numbers into her graphing calculator. Even Dad is in his own zone, grading quizzes on the chromatic scale at his desk. I know Reid and I have a reputation of our meetings devolving into unproductive bickering—but this is serious! This is beyond a key signature, a botched lyric, or shooting down the notion of Reid turning *Melted: The Musical* into a full ninety-minute opera.

"Infernodelle didn't randomly start over-burning," I say. "Your suggestion . . . implies that climate change is inevitable. It's *not.*"

"Obviously that's true," Reid says. "But we can take creative liberties with Infernodelle."

In my peripheral vision, Dad raises his eyebrows, an indication that more unsolicited feedback is incoming.

"You can't take creative liberties that impact the message," I insist.

"Natalie has a point," Henry says, looking up from his phone.

"Thank you!"

It's the most *Melted* interaction Henry and I have had in weeks. He shows up to every after-school meeting, but he tends to multitask with homework, never all that present. Until now.

Danica's eyes widen and she raises her perfectly shaped eyebrows, like she had a light bulb moment. "What if instead of one lead character who represents humanity . . . we use the ensemble instead?"

"I love that." Reid removes the pencil behind his ear. "We can convey how multiple small actions crescendo over time into irreversible damage. That's it. We make 'In Winter' darker."

Fitz stops sketching. Danica lights up at Reid's enthusiasm.

Henry shakes his head. "Can't we enhance the ensemble without losing Moritz?"

"Then the symbolism of the ensemble is less obvious," Danica says.

No.

The plan has always been to *adapt* the script that Henry and I wrote.

Not delete characters or change plot points.

Henry swallows, his Adam's apple bobbing. "I don't know. I'm with Natalie. I can't support the musical direction if it's going to change the heart of our show. Is there a way we can meet—"

"*Melted* doesn't work without Moritz," I reiterate.

"—in the middle?" Henry finishes.

I blink, processing the concept of *meeting in the middle* with Reid. I don't know why I'm surprised. While *maybe* Henry would outright object to a Reid idea, there's no way he's going to object to a Danica one.

Danica shrugs. "It works. It'd also give Emma's relationship with Kris more time to breathe in the second act."

"We're adapting. Not rewriting," I declare.

Reid runs his hand through his hair. "You're too invested in the play."

"I think so too," Danica agrees. "It's a musical now."

Dad stands and walks up to his whiteboard and reaches for a green dry erase marker.

"I love the passion everyone is bringing here," Dad says. He draws a line down the center of the board and writes "MORITZ" on one side and "~~MORITZ~~" on the other. "So let's work through this. Why keep Moritz?"

Dad holds out the marker and we all take turns listing our reasons to keep or cut Moritz.

MORITZ	~~MORITZ~~
He's the VILLAIN	Replace his role with an ensemble = a bigger cast = a larger audience = A BETTER CHANCE AT SELLING OUT
"Hate is a closed window" is a bop	
Removes a source of conflict between Adina and Emma	More time for Emma/Kris banter
He's! the! VILLAIN!	The symbolism is too on the nose
	Also the plot makes no sense, like WHY would Emma trust a dude she just met to protect her kingdom?

I become more protective with each new point added to the ~~MORITZ~~ column.

"You can't cut Moritz on the basis of wanting more banter!"

Danica's turquoise fingers drum against her arms. "Excuse me for knowing my strengths."

"The evil trash people ensemble makes sense," Fitz relents.

"What if we killed Moritz at the end of act one?" Henry suggests. "We're destroying ourselves. It's symbolic. It's a comp—"

"No!" I exclaim. Evil trash people make sense? Kill off our villain? *Nothing* makes sense. "We are so far past the point of character development. So can we *please* just . . . unveil the songs like planned and stay in our lanes?"

Dad clears his throat. "*Natalie.* Cool it with the dramatics."

His tone is *harsh.*

It pulls me out of my panic-induced spiral.

At school, Dad's cool teacher demeanor is strong. But the way he says my name? It's parental. It indicates another conversation to come. It's further proof that no matter how many times Aaron Jacobson feigns neutrality with his *Switzerland* and pro/con lists, that is never the reality. It doesn't matter the subject.

Also? I'm not *dramatic.* I'm protective.

Fitz's blue mascaraed eyes connect with mine. "Natalie, I love your script, but this change feels *right.* For a musical. You know?"

"We always struggled with Moritz," Henry admits.

"I felt that," Reid says. "On the page. His voice fell flat compared to the rest of the cast."

"Since when are you an expert on voice?" I ask.

"I know good writing when I read it," Reid retorts.

"Well, I know a bad *Melted* decision when I hear it."

Danica's eye roll is scathing. "Really? Because it's four against one. And what we need are directors who don't argue over *every* creative decision. Also, this isn't even about *Melted.* I can't tell if you legitimately hate each other or secretly want to kiss each other's faces but whatever this—" Danica waves at Reid and me "—is? It is embarrassing. I am embarrassed for you. Stop. In case you forgot, there are actual stakes."

Reid is silent.

Henry is silent.

Dad is silent.

I am silent.

"It *is* legitimate hatred," Fitz stresses, unable to handle silence longer than five beats. I appreciate the backup, because the second option makes my brain short-circuit.

Henry pinches the bridge of his nose. "That is all so beyond the point. Nat, I know ninety percent of the time Reid's editorial suggestions equate to *Boiled.* But there's merit to this one."

I don't even know what to say.

I expected Reid to swoop in, to attempt to put his stamp

on *Melted* in this unfamiliar format. But I believed when that moment came, I'd have backup. Reid would be outnumbered.

Instead . . . I am the outnumbered one.

Everyone agrees.

It's over.

"We . . . can work out a compromise."

It is *painful* to relent out loud. It feels like handing Reid a win in front of everyone. But Danica is right. There *are* stakes. I have to swallow my pride so we can move forward and ensure that *Melted* is a success so that maybe everything can go back to normal next year. Reid starts fleshing out the details of the ensemble plan while I sit in silence and process the reality that this is pretty much my worst nightmare. I know I'm not being objective. I know that if this suggestion came from *literally* anyone else, I'd be open to it. But I can't be. Seeing how receptive my friends are to Reid's suggestions is like watching him ask Madeline out all over again.

And to say that didn't end well is a massive understatement.

Cool it with the dramatics.

The weight of my father's words don't hit me until I'm in my bedroom, alone, attempting to decompress after a stressful rehearsal. But decompress, I cannot. Not when these words become a loop in my brain. It is so hypocritical. If Reid or my dad are stressed about anything music related it's because they are *passionate*. When I am stressed about a musician who has a history of co-opting everything that is mine, I am *dramatic.* Is my passion, my vision, less valid because it's not artistically in pursuit of anything greater than a high school drama club?

Because that is bullshit.

Cool it with the dramatics.

I can't let it go. I *shouldn't.*

But I will. I always do. If I open up about my *Melted* feelings, how difficult co-*anything* with Reid is, how deeply I'm afraid that this *partnership* and my dad's involvement is going to end the same way the clarinet did, he'll cry *Switzerland.*

So it's, like, what is even the point?

I don't know. But Mom will say the right thing. She always does when it comes to Reid, my dad, and their music. I exit my bedroom and make my way downstairs toward her office in the hopes that her door is open. It's a gig night for my dad, where he puts on his fedora and goes to town on the clarinet for a sixty-minute set with Lincoln Street Blues at Melville's. The perfect opportunity to unload my complicated feelings.

So I am not expecting the sound of my father's voice at the end of the hallway.

I inch toward the office, each step careful not to cause a sound.

"I just . . . don't know what we're going to do, Michelle," Dad says.

"This pressure? It's extremely helpful," Mom says, sarcasm dripping from her voice.

"It's not pressure! It's just . . . shit . . ." Dad's voice trails off. My heart starts beating double time in my chest. I am accustomed to Aaron Jacobson's stress voice, but his panic voice is less familiar. "If Tara is right, if the rumors are true, I don't even know what we'll do."

Tara . . . Mrs. Westfield? My English teacher?

"I'll start freelancing again. Or teach extra classes."

"But you're writing!"

"Well how else am I supposed to respond to this hypothetical situation?"

"The layoffs are hypothetical, but our Melville's gig getting cut is now very real."

Layoffs? Lost gigs?

"We'll figure it out if and when it's all real, Aaron. We always do."

"I feel like an easy target," Dad says, and my stomach drops to the floor with this admission. As many complicated feelings as I have about the band, having these feelings is a million times better than the alternative! "The Harvest Festival was a disaster. How do I make up for that?"

"I mean, *Melted.* Right?"

"At this rate I'm not sure there will even *be* a *Melted.*"

"Maybe if you talked to them. If they understood—"

Dad cuts Mom off. "No. They're *kids.* I don't want to worry them over a rumor."

"Then *you* should stop worrying over a rumor," Mom stresses.

"It just feels so out of my control. I stuck my neck out for *Melted,* but now—"

I back up from the door, from the conversation.

It's too much to process. I don't understand. I didn't think of the repercussions of my Harvest Festival prank gone wrong beyond a botched concert. Dad has always seemed so untouchable. I guess that's not true.

It reinforces what I have always known. No art is safe.

Dad has never projected anything other than confidence and security, so hearing the vulnerability in his voice *rattles* me. It must feel dramatic to listen to kids bicker over the legitimacy of a fictional character when your career is at stake.

Melted hasn't been low stakes for a while—but this revelation reshapes the importance of its success. I have to figure out a way to work with Reid. Our inability to collaborate can lead to a problem so much bigger than a stolen song key or a cut character.

I close my bedroom door behind me, vowing to *cool it with the dramatics.*

CHAPTER FOURTEEN

The night before my seventeenth birthday, I throw myself a party.

For the record, I've never been much of a birthday person. I am a Scorpio, after all. Really, I enjoy the simple birthday pleasures—homemade cards, eating takeout Thai food straight from the carton, and Mom's famous devil's food cake. An early November birthday means it's usually cold enough to deter any outdoor activities, so my tradition is just a movie night in with Henry, Fitz, and Delia, laughing and watching romcoms and being us.

But tonight my basement is full of people I semi-know.

Delia is sleeping over at Hannah's tonight and Lincoln Street Blues has a much-needed overnight gig at a wedding on Cape Cod, playing both at the rehearsal dinner and during the ceremony. Mom goes with them, promising on her way out the door to be back in plenty of time to have proper birthday festivities tomorrow night. I can't remember the last time my parents took a trip together, just the two of them, and it's kind of a birthday present itself.

Instead of hosting the chill birthday of my dreams

though, Henry asked if he could invite Danica and I said *of course!* because it is currently easier to swallow my *Henry abandoned me for Danica* issues than to deal with them.

As a result, the entirety of Lincoln's musical theater department has now ended up in my basement. At least they came bearing the gift of cheap vodka.

"Happy birthday, Natalie!" Makayla and Arjun—who I did invite—sing, competing with an unfamiliar show tune blasting in the background as they present a plate of pizza bagels.

"Pesto with spinach and tomatoes," Arjun says. "*Someone* almost made basic cheese."

Makayla rolls her eyes. "It's a safe choice!"

"Pesto. Always pesto," I confirm, taking the plate of bagels. "Thanks, Arjun. Makayla, your choices are forgiven because you look amazing!" I exclaim with a one-armed hug. It is an occasion when Makayla is not in athletic wear and she looks so chic in patterned flowy pants and a black cropped tank top.

"Thanks!" Makayla laughs over the music. "I guess I missed you. Even though we have classes together every day. Weird!"

"I missed you too!"

Over the past few weeks, Reid and I have resumed working together in a dysfunctional writing cave while Makayla has been preparing for basketball tryouts and Arjun has been planning the upcoming pep rally. I'm so glad they're here. I'm glad that in this sea of semi-familiar faces, HAVE A HE(ART) is reunited.

Makayla and Arjun head toward the folding table set up against the back wall to grab a drink and I, pizza bagels still in hand, push through a group of quasi-drunk thespians dancing to "Aquarius" and place them on the coffee table next to bowls of popcorn and Doritos. I assume that's the name of the song. I'm not sure what musical it is from or how they're performing an *actual choreographed dance* to it. So I just sip on a vodka cranberry, the white girl of mixed drinks, and accept whatever is happening.

I don't hate it, but I don't *love* feeling left out of the loop at my own birthday party either.

So I pivot and head upstairs to check on Fitz and the chocolate chip cookies she's baking—a birthday party tradition. When I approach the stairs, I have to blink once, twice, because *Henry and Danica are making out.* On the stairs. *My* stairs. I duck right and swing the studio door open, quickly tucking myself inside. I shut and lock it behind me, then press my back against the door, eyes squeezed shut as if it will erase what I just witnessed.

I've never been more grateful for soundproof technology.

Do I intervene? I mean, as someone who witnessed Henry take three tequila shots in a row I can guarantee he is definitely not sober. He also really likes Danica—and I'm going to be the one who deals with the blowback of Henry's Emotions tomorrow when—

"Hey."

The shock of the sound makes me scream and jump backward, whacking my head against the door, *shit.* My eyes pop open and adjust to the fluorescent lights. Reid is sitting at the piano, his back to me. Reid is *here,* working on songs for the musical, while our prospective cast is getting trashed in the next room.

Reid is sort of at a party I did not invite him to. A party he could totally expose.

He turns to face me, almost guilty, as his fingers move up down the keys. "I used my studio key." When my parents designed the studio, they chose the side of the basement that has a sliding door out to the backyard, so Dad's students can enter and exit the space without walking through the house. "I didn't know you were having people over."

I sit on the floor, back still pressed against the door. "Please, at least give me a heads-up."

Reid raises his eyebrows. "What?"

"You know. Before you tell my dad."

Reid stops playing. "It's your *birthday,* Natalie."

I nod and sip my vodka cran. "I'm aware."

"So it's a truce day." Reid starts playing a variation of the opening chords of "Hate Is a Closed Window," my favorite song because it is the most ridiculous. It is sharp and dark, and the song that allowed us to keep Moritz. Last weekend marked the first collaboration session where Reid and I—armored with the reality that is *Melted*'s stakes—were able to compromise. I convinced Reid that *this* is the true villain song and in turn we agreed to kill Moritz off at the end of act one, per Henry's suggestion. Progress. "Even if it wasn't, I'm not a total asshole."

"Just a little asshole."

"Are you drunk?" Reid asks, a smirk tugging the corner of his mouth.

"I wish."

I'm more buzzed than I think though, because a few seconds later I stand up and cross the studio, minimizing the distance between us, and ask Reid to *scoot.*

Like, I tap his shoulder and say, "Scoot."

He does.

"What're you working on?" I ask.

"Messing around with 'In Winter' some more. It's my favorite composition, but it's lyrically weaker than the rest of the score. I work best in the studio, so here I am." Reid flips the page of his composition book with one hand, to a page that is a mess of crossed-out lyrics. "Help?"

I shake my head. "Ugh. Verse is the *worst.*"

"Well. That answers my next question," Reid says.

The *Melted* script is already in Mrs. Mulaney's inbox ahead of our deadline because we want to cast as soon as possible, but the songs are very much still a work-in-progress. And since there is no way I will direct in a world where Fitz is not playing Adina, we've cut "Keep It In" and are adapting Adina's emotional monologue from the original script into a spoken word poem that I have been trying and failing to write all week. It's the moment Adina learns to trust her powers, decides there is nothing left to salvage, and burns everything to the ground. It has a rhythm but it isn't musical. And there's nothing even close to a rhyme. So how do I translate this moment into something resembling a poem?

"Want to work on it?"

I frown. "You're going to help me write something you are adamantly against?"

"Yeah. Happy birthday?" As soon as the words are out, Reid's expression twists like he wishes he could take them back. "Sorry. You should get back to . . . whatever is happening out there. We can work on this tomorrow. Maybe."

I consider Reid's offer. Fitz is stress baking—and this is *without* knowing Henry's tongue is in Danica's mouth. The thespians took over my speakers and are staging a full performance to songs I will have to pretend I know, otherwise they'll smell weakness. Nothing is worse for a director than a cast who thinks they're in control. I don't really want to deal with any of it.

And . . . truces with Reid are so rare. I can't lose that advantage.

I finish my drink and slap the empty cup on top of the piano. "Not wasting a truce. Sorry."

Reid nods and pulls up the Adina monologue on his phone, explaining his songwriting process to me. "You already did the hard part, Nat. But poetry and songs are all about minimal words, maximum impact. So it's more about stripping the excess and fine-tuning the rhythm."

"What if there is no excess?" I ask, rereading my words.

Reid shakes his head. "You're still thinking of it as a script. Maybe first think of it as a beat?"

Then Reid begins to tap on the side of the piano in rhythm, a half note followed by two quarter notes. I rework the monologue, attempting to stay on beat, but don't even make it two lines before I start laughing, unable to control the giggling that bubbles up from my stomach.

This is so ridiculous. We are so ridiculous. I am so not sober.

"We tried. Insert dramatic sigh here."

"We are not Lin-Manuel Miranda," Reid admits. "Which is why I got something for you."

"What?"

"A peace offering. For your birthday."

He pulls an envelope out of his jacket pocket.

I shake my head. "No."

Reid scrunches his eyebrows. "No?"

"I didn't even invite you to my party," I say.

Reid and I don't do this. We don't exchange gifts. Friends exchange gifts, and though we're not mortal enemies at the moment, it's only because of the musical. When the collaboration is over, when Dad's job is secure, we will snap back into being competitive and insufferable Natalie and Reid, business as usual. Not people who give birthday presents to each other.

"Nat, take it," Reid says.

Despite every fiber of my being screaming *resist*, my curiosity is too much. So I do. I take it. Inside the envelope, I exhale because there is no card, thank God. It's two tickets to a production of *The Lion King* that's running in Boston, for the matinee performance next Saturday. They're paper-clipped together with a passive-aggressive Post-it note that makes me laugh.

Might help the adaptation process. We're on a deadline, no pressure. —Reid.

Then I see the price on the tickets.

"Reid, I can't take these," I say.

"You're welcome."

"It's too much. How did you even—?"

His face flushes. "They're comp seats. Selina's dad works for—"

"Selina?"

"—a friend from All-States. Her dad plays trombone in the pit. I asked, and she pulled a few strings."

I bite my lip, trying to think of how this could be a prank, what other motives he might have, but nothing comes. "Why?"

"I wanted to. You need to see a musical before you can codirect a musical. Plus, it's like the ultimate adaptation. A musical adapted from a movie adapted from *Hamlet*!"

His arm brushes against mine and I'm *definitely* more buzzed than I thought because the space between us is, well, nonexistent. I focus on the piano keys, on middle C, because it's either that or looking at Reid's stupid earnest face and the out-of-place curl that has flopped in front of his eyes.

"Thank you," I say.

"You're welcome."

My phone buzzes on the piano with a string of Very Concerned texts.

Fitz (Not Ava)
natalie where are you? so help me god if YOU FLED YOUR OWN PARTY!!! I made cookies.
10:37 PM

my heart is dkfdlsjfoisdjfejeofjlkefjjdlsk
10:37 PM

dani + chao, sitting in a tree (well on ur stairs UGH)
10:37 PM

Shit. I stand, smoothing down the fabric of the floral sleeveless jumpsuit I'm wearing, an *If the Shoe Fitz* original. "I've been beckoned by Fitz."

Reid stands and takes a step backward. "I should probably get going too."

"Thanks for the birthday truce," I say. I twist the doorknob so the lock pops. "I'm sure my dad will drive us to the train, but I'll double-check."

Reid coughs. "Oh. No. I mean, those are for you. Not, like, for *us*."

My hand drops from the door and my cheeks flush, embarrassed I even thought otherwise. "Oh. Right."

I blame the shitty vodka. Shit.

"You should take Chao," Reid says.

"Maybe. Henry barely cares about *our* musical though," I say.

"It's so good though! He'd be missing out."

"Oh. Have you seen it before?"

"I mean, on YouTube."

"Reid. *Come on*." I take the extra ticket out of the envelope and hold it out to him. My own peace offering. As weird as this sounds, maybe this is exactly what Reid and I need. To get on the same page, to start acting like codirectors, to stop self-sabotaging *Melted*.

Reid considers my invitation just a beat too short to make me believe he's *actually* reluctant, before nodding. "Okay. But Nat-a-lie . . ." Reid drops his voice low, my name spilling out in three awkward syllables. "Our parents are going to think it's a date."

I laugh. "Don't be stupid."

"Well. Thanks," Reid says, his expression unreadable.

"I mean, it's *us*," I say. "We'll call it a research trip, *codirector*."

It's the first time I've called him that. We hold each other's gaze twelve beats too long. Until I recover motor function and pull the door open, only to run right into Fitz. Mascara is smudged onto her cheeks and her bloodshot eyes shift from me to Reid, widening.

"Reid? Hey! I didn't know Natalie invited you."

Reid shakes his head. "She didn't—"

"Hey! We're in a basement full of theater folk!" Fitz says, her voice kicking up an octave too high. "Everyone in this room is going to audition. You should preview some songs for us!"

Fitz grabs Reid's hand and I am immobile. Reid looks like a deer caught in headlights and he's shaking his head, like, *hell no.* But Fitz's grip is strong and her mission is relentless.

"Please," she says. "Otherwise I'll start crying again. *Please please please please.*"

Fitz wipes her eyes before dragging Reid to the other room and pulling the speaker plug, cutting the music before Reid can even say no.

"Hey, friends! Look who has graced us with his presence. None other than Reid Callahan, *codirector* and composer of *Melted: The Musical,* along with the birthday girl herself. After an admittedly bumpy start, its development is coming along quite *swell,* and Reid is going to give us a preview of some of the songs."

Danica's head snaps away from Henry's so fast it takes him a second to realize they aren't kissing anymore. Everyone claps and nods, totally down. It's like their audition brains click on and sober them up and they're ready for any hint of what they'll be auditioning for. Henry's head nod is smaller than the rest. His arm is still wrapped around Danica's waist and Fitz is *not* looking in their direction.

"I'm not singing both parts of 'For the Last Time Ever,'" Reid says in my ear.

I consider it. Singing. In front of everyone. With Reid.

I can't let Reid take all the credit and glory for *Melted*.

"I'm not singing the soprano," I say.

So the party concludes with twenty-five musical theater students I barely know sitting on the floor of Dad's studio, in a semicircle around the piano, while Reid plays and we sing the rough draft. Our performance ends with roaring applause and for the first time I see a universe where *Melted: The Musical* works.

And plot twist: I don't hate it.

"It's becoming too, I don't know. Jazzy?" Henry says the next morning, making exaggerated jazz hands over his cereal bowl.

"It's a *musical*, Hen," I say, popping two ibuprofens. "It's supposed to be a little jazzy."

The house, miraculously, does not look like every standard teen comedy shot of a post-party home. But earlier, Mom texted me that she and Dad would be back by early afternoon, which gives me not enough hours to transform myself into a not-hungover disaster.

"I know. It just, I don't know—doesn't it seem silly to

you? Dancing dragons, power ballads, *tap*," Henry says.

"It *is* silly. But that's what makes it work." Henry's words sting. If he wanted to contribute, he could've joined *any* writing session. Considering he's been invited to all of them.

Henry looks wounded. "Since when are you into this?"

"Since when is your tongue down Dani's throat?" Fitz counters.

Henry chokes on his cereal. "I don't even know. But she's going to friend-zone me anyway, if it makes you feel better." Henry's shoulders slump forward. "I can feel it in my bones."

I hate witnessing shifting friendship dynamics in real time. There is no way this ends well.

"Well, *I* like the songs, Nat. Who's playing Adina?"

"You are," I say.

She narrows her eyes at me, "I can't sing."

"Adina doesn't sing. She's a *poet*."

I leave out that we're still figuring out how that's going to work, but it's a worthwhile pursuit for the look on Fitz's face alone as she throws her arms around me.

"You fought for me!"

"Of course," I say. "You *are* Adina."

"Huh. You and Callahan. Suddenly compromising. Not trying to kill each other," Henry interrupts.

Apparently Henry will not be distracted.

"What choice do I have? I'm hanging out with Reid so much because I *have* to, because we have a musical to pull off."

"Are you even capable of that? Because I really don't

want to stick around and watch you direct this show into the ground any more than you already have!"

Wow.

Henry and I get frustrated with each other, but fights are rare. When one happens, this is how it goes. It's like he's incapable of telling me how he feels *when* he feels it. Nope. He prefers to bottle it up and internalize until it all tumbles out in a heated moment.

And he knows how to hit where it hurts.

I blink. "Henry. What are you *talking* about?"

Henry throws his hands in the air. "I don't want to fight."

"Clearly you do," I say.

"It's her *birthday*, you fart face," Fitz says.

"Do not backpedal." Now that it's out in the open I can't just swallow it down anymore.

Henry pushes his glasses up, his eyebrows pinched. "*Melted* was fun to write—even though you only ever half-listened to my notes. HAVE A HE(ART) was cool, getting behind a cause and rallying the other arts clubs. But then somehow it transformed into a *Natalie vs. Reid* situation. We could've had *Melted.* It could've been the play it was supposed to be. But once again, a prank war blew up in your face. Not just your face—all of our faces. Like I said it would. But you don't listen. Like. Ever. You just *do.* And you're *still* doing it and acting like you're the victim."

I blink back tears.

Where is this coming from?

"It's just . . . it's not what I wanted, Natalie. You know?"

"Henry, I know—"

He shakes his head. "You don't. You never ask what I'm okay with. Not with *Melted*. Not with *anything*. When we started this together, it was supposed to be a reprieve from senior year stuff . . . and now it's just more stress. You don't even realize it, either. You just direct, like we're all side characters in your story helping you get what you want."

Do I have strong opinions? Yeah. I'm the one who's been trying to protect what we both wanted, at least as much as possible. But I listen to his notes! The Moritz compromise was his suggestion! All I wanted was for Henry to be a part of this, to still have our last show together.

He's the one who's walking away.

"It feels like you're calling Natalie selfish and that's pretty ironic," Fitz snaps in my defense. "You totally dumped us for Dani! Knowing how I felt—*feel*—about her. You're kind of an asshole, Chao."

"You don't even know Dani," Henry says.

"I know how she makes me *feel*," Fitz says.

"We can't read your mind, Henry," I say. "So the sudden abandonment? It *sucked*."

Henry scoffs. "You can't read minds? You don't *listen*. I just. I cannot."

Henry ties his Adidas, eyebrows scrunched, his lips pressed together in a thin line, and I blink and he's out the back door, just, like, *gone*. Bye!

With his dramatic storm out of the room accomplished, I turn to unpack it with Fitz. But her eyes fill with fresh tears and she storms off in the opposite direction, toward the living room. I run my hand through my hair, frustrated, and pick up my phone to read my missed texts.

Reid Callahan

last night was weird

9:37 AM

Attached is a video Fitz took on Reid's phone of him and me, singing "For the Last Time Ever." I don't click on it. The still image is the side of Reid's face, with the hint of a smile. My face is flushed pink, probably from the applause we got for the previous song. Or the vodka.

but not bad weird?

9:38 AM

We look like a team, Reid and me. We look like we've been doing this forever—and in what world is this my life?

In what world is Reid the only person who *isn't* stressing me out?

The Prank War

A prank war is way less fun when there are actual *stakes* attached to it. When we were kids, pranks were an easy way to antagonize Reid. I liked outsmarting him. Seeing the look on his face when I got him. Waiting to see how he'd prank back. It was a never-ending battle of wits. Nothing more than a way to channel my annoyance.

But this time, the prank war had to end in a breakup.

Maybe a clarinet breakup too, if I was lucky. But I had to start small.

Since band was the last class of the day, everyone dropped off their instruments in Mrs. Sullivan's classroom in the morning. Reid's clarinet was always one of the first in its cubby. One morning, I took advantage of that. Checking over my shoulder first, I unzipped the front pocket of Reid's clarinet case and pulled out his reeds, rubbing each one with a garlic clove I swiped from the pantry that morning, until I was certain that the garlic clung to the wood.

That afternoon, I could smell a hint of garlic *the moment* Reid unzipped his case.

He slid a reed out of its case, his face twisting in disgust when he brought it to his lips.

"Gross," Reid muttered.

He kept five broken-in reeds on him at any one time, so he reached for another one.

It didn't matter.

They were all garlic reeds.

His head snapped to face me. *"Natalie."*

Loosening the ligature on my mouthpiece, I couldn't not crack a smile.

"You won—" Reid said, his voice flat "—and you're *still* starting a prank war?"

I shrugged.

Reid sighed and raised his hand. "Mrs. Sullivan, can I have an extra reed?"

Mrs. Sullivan nodded. "Sure, Reid. But it's important to be prepared."

Huh. I didn't anticipate *that.* Double win.

"Seriously, Natalie?" Madeline's voice asked behind me.

I swear, I could *hear* her eye roll. Madeline didn't get it now, but she would. Reid returned from the supply closet with a new reed, narrowing his eyes at me like *it's on.* I basked in the reality that he'd sound fifty percent less perfect today with a new reed that hadn't been broken in.

So the seventh-grade prank wars began with garlic reeds, a prank I am proud of to this day.

The rest? Not so much.

Reid retaliated with a prank that got zero points for creativity but maximum disgustingness points. The Saturday following garlic reeds, I came downstairs to scrambled eggs and a glass of orange juice set at my place at the table. Reid was already seated, scrolling through his phone after his morning clarinet lesson.

Without thinking twice, I reached for the orange juice and took a generous sip.

It was a mistake.

Immediately, I gagged, spitting up orange all over myself, and Reid was laughing in his hands. Because orange juice, it was not. Nope. Reid dissolved a mac-n-cheese packet into a glass of water and I hated how brilliant it was—how *effortlessly* he got me.

I haven't looked at orange juice the same ever since.

The pranks escalated as the humidity faded and the fall air turned crisp.

We enlisted the help of the sisters in one round. Hannah hid every pair of Reid's shoes hours before he was supposed to meet Madeline at the roller rink. Reid is extremely meticulous about his belongings, so this one messed with him in the best way. A few days later, pieces I hadn't committed to memory yet were missing from my music folder.

Mrs. Sullivan called me out and my ears felt hot with embarrassment.

"You two are *so* juvenile," Madeline declared after class, while packing up her saxophone.

The more pranks that unfolded, the more frustrated Madeline became. Exactly as I planned.

"Sorry Madi." I shook my head. "We won't stop until there is a victor."

Madeline rolled her eyes. But then they left class together hand in hand, and an impending breakup still seemed pretty unlikely. Reid's prank had lit a fire under me though. It was a reminder that the prank war was serious to Reid. To him, it was all about the clarinet.

I watched Madeline and Reid walk away and suddenly, I knew how to use that against him.

"Natalie. That is a *terrible* idea."

Henry stared at me, his eyes wide, as I unveiled my master plan in the only logical place to reveal a master plan: the too-small tree house in my backyard. Our backs pressed against opposite walls, our arms wrapped around legs too long to stretch out straight.

I frowned. "I need the truth. Reid asked her out *after* chairs were decided. It's sketchy!"

Henry's eyes met mine. "Come on, Natalie. Not everything Reid does is a reaction to you. Even if it is . . . let it blow up in Reid's face on its own. Be there for Madeline in the aftermath. It's a better look."

"So I'm supposed to sit around and let my friend get hurt because of me?"

"In this specific instance? *Yes.*"

"No!"

Henry didn't have classes with Reid and Madeline. He

couldn't see what was happening to her—how she cancelled plans with me *every* week to spend more time with Reid. Them walking in and out of the band room hand in hand became the worst part of my day. Every class, I caught Reid's eyes on *me*. As if he was waiting for a reaction. It felt like validation. This wasn't all in my head.

Henry didn't understand, but he could ruin my plan.

So I pretended *I* understood. "Okay."

He raised his eyebrows. "Okay?"

Shifting to my knees, I crawled toward the winding slide that was the tree house's best exit.

"You're right. Madi needs to come to her own conclusion about Reid."

The words were not even a lie, but I propelled myself down the slide before Henry could see the omission written all over my face.

CHAPTER FIFTEEN

Reid and I are *color-coordinated* and I hate everything.

I'm sitting in one of the structured metal chairs in the waiting area of the train station, earbuds blasting Taylor Swift because I just cannot. I look up after liking Fitz's latest *If the Shoe Fitz* post on Instagram and Reid is walking toward me, returning from the vending machines with two bags of pretzels. When he sits next to me I remove my earbuds because the car ride here might have been a total disaster, but it wasn't exactly Reid's fault.

Reid hands me one of the pretzel bags. "That was the worst thirty minutes of my life. I don't even think I'm exaggerating."

"Dad is the most Extra," I say.

"He's never going to let this go, is he?"

The automated *train approaching* announcement for the purple line plays through the speakers, indicating that Reid and I should move to the platform. I stand, tossing my city purse—a small, black crossbody—over my shoulder, and sigh. "Definitely not."

I regretted asking Dad to drive us to the train station

the moment Reid got in the back seat. Reid would have looked okay, I guess, in his deep red button-down shirt and black pants. If it weren't for the fact that I'm in a black Peter Pan collar dress with tights, red ankle boots I borrowed from Fitz, and lipstick the same shade as his shirt. It looks like we planned this.

It was a rookie mistake, honestly, asking Dad. But I didn't want to interrupt Mom's writing day. Mom would've made polite conversation and hummed along to her favorite Spotify playlist and ignored it. Mom is chill.

Dad is, well, not.

"Look at you, codirectors. Dressing the part! Maybe you'll start acting like it too?"

The pretty much matching outfits were too much for Aaron Jacobson.

The train pulls up and I slide into a window seat for the ride to North Station. I open Spotify on my phone and begin to play *The Lion King*. Of course I know the music, but I want to listen to the Broadway version to get pumped up.

"What are you doing?" Reid asks. He takes my phone out of my hand and presses pause before the opening number even starts. "*Natalie.* Listening to the OBC album right before seeing a show will ruin the live theater experience. This is basic!"

I frown. "OBC?"

"Original Broadway Cast? Come on, Nat."

His expression is so stern, so *serious,* I can't help but laugh. "Reid, it's *The Lion King.*"

My phone buzzes in Reid's hand. It's just a spam email. Not a text from Henry. I grab my phone and drop it in my purse, disappointed. Henry and I have been in a standoff since my birthday. I'm not texting first. No way. Henry blew up at me, out of nowhere, on my birthday! Acted as if I haven't been doing everything I can to protect our vision of *Melted*. All on my own. Since he walked away.

Ugh.

I push away my Henry feelings because I want today to be good. I want to get lost in research. I want to be inspired to go home and write. I want to emerge from this experience as someone qualified to direct a musical.

Codirect. Whatever.

Henry Chao ruined my birthday. He doesn't get to ruin this day too.

Reid slides into the seat next to me. "What's the deal with you and Chao?"

I frown. Is Reid a mind reader now?

"It's none of your business," I snap.

"Right."

Of course, Reid backing off makes me want to talk about it.

"It's just . . . *Melted* was supposed to be ours. Henry's and mine. One last thing we made together before he left for college. And now I don't know what it is, or whose it is, but it definitely doesn't feel like ours. He doesn't come to our writing sessions. He trashes the songs. And then he has the audacity to comment about how much time we spend together, as if we have a choice."

Reid frowns. "He doesn't like the songs?"

"He said I'm directing *Melted* into the ground."

"Wow," Reid says. "I know it's been a rough start . . . but that's not true."

I shrug. "I don't know. Maybe it's all too jazzy."

Reid's eyebrows rise. "Everyone at your party loved the music."

"I know. I just . . . feel kind of like Delia and Hannah right now."

The sisters are as rocky as ever and our valiant attempt to intervene did not help much. Delia vented to Reid. Upset that The Monicas did not get invited to Delia's bat mitzvah, Hannah iced Delia. I tried to talk to her, but mid-conversation, before I could even start to question her about her relationship with The Monicas, she pulled out her phone and opened TikTok. The ultimate dismissal.

Reid sighs. "I cannot explain Hannah's life choices."

"She's twelve. That is the explanation."

Reid pushes his glasses up the bridge of his nose. He's been wearing them more, I notice. "They'll figure it out. You and Chao will too. You're lucky to have a person like that."

I don't know how to respond to that, so I don't. Reid flushes and starts playing matching games on his phone. I try listening to a podcast for the rest of the ride, but I can't focus. I guess I never really thought about it, what Reid said. I mean, he has plenty of friends. At school, he's with The First Chairs. And the underclassmen look up to him. He's their fearless leader.

Reid has his instrument. Reid has lessons with Dad.

Reid has a competitor-turned-temporary-collaborator. Me.

But he's never had a person.

Reid taps his knee to the beat of the music for the entire first act and it's so distracting, but I know, without a doubt, bringing him was the right decision.

Our seats are in the mezzanine, second row, with a perfect view to take in the artistry and choreography of the animal puppets and the set design. The show is incredible. I tear up pretty much the moment the music starts. "The Circle of Life" is an intense emotional experience live, okay! There is so much to take in . . . but I'm having fun watching Reid. I've never seen him so absorbed in a moment. He even sheds a tear when Mufasa dies, and doesn't try to hide it. Then he dances in his chair during "Hakuna Matata"—when he knows I'm never going to let him live it down. Reid is . . . having fun?

It's shocking.

At intermission Reid excuses himself in the name of overpriced M&M's and I try to reconcile this musical theater–obsessed Reid with the serious *clarinet is my life* person in my kitchen every morning. I try scrolling through my phone but the service is spotty this high up, so I drop it back into my purse and take a sip of water. The lady sitting next to me makes eye contact and smiles. She's grandma age and wearing a statement glam necklace.

"How long have you been together?"

I choke on water. Full-on spit up all over my dress.

"We're not," I cough.

"Sure, sweets. *Sure.*"

I blame the matching outfits. But luckily Reid returns, and we all stand so he can squeeze by, ending the conversation with Glam Necklace. Reid's arm brushes against mine when he takes his seat. He doesn't shift, just stays like that, like it's normal for our arms to touch. I don't pull away. If I do, that'll mean I think this is a *thing*. It is not a thing.

Glam Necklace is making me overthink everything.

Reid holds the M&Ms out to me as the lights dim. I shake my head because Glam Necklace is throwing some major side-eye in my peripheral vision. Reid dumps the contents of the M&M's box into his palm, so his arm is no longer pressed against mine and I can relax again.

Except *The Lion King* is based on a goddamn tragedy!

Reid repeatedly tears up during act two. So do I. It's ridiculous. I have seen this movie countless times! (The animated version, of course. In my house, we pretend the live action one doesn't exist.) And *Hamlet* is one of the most heavily adapted Shakespeare plays of all time. Both the movie and the musical require suspension of disbelief, but in the theater the stakes somehow feel higher. The moment when Simba reunites with Mufasa's spirit just hits *different* onstage.

It reminds me of the power in live theater that I love so much. Why I love *Melted* so much.

The show ends with a standing ovation and we both leap to our feet.

This might've been the best birthday present ever.

Reid is, like, full-out cheeky smiling as we exit the theater and walk around the corner to Thinking Cup, home of the best hot chocolate in the city. It's Reid's idea—our train is in an hour and the November air has fully transitioned from fall to winter.

I sip on my hot chocolate while we babble on about the show.

"What was your favorite part?" Reid asks.

I wrap my hands around the paper cup. The heat warms my freezing fingers. "Everything?"

Reid laughs. "That's a nonanswer."

"Okay. Well, the overture made me cry."

"It's a great overture." Reid smiles. "The narrative changes, the choices in direction, they're all so good! Like the scene when Timon almost drowns? How *scared* Simba is in this moment. It's so powerful. I'm also such a sucker for 'Hakuna Matata'—the transition from young Simba to adult Simba? I love that."

"Totally." I smile back.

Reid's sip of hot chocolate leaves foam above his lip.

"You know, I've been so focused on the music. But it's more than the music—it's performances, costumes, the set. The direction. We need to think about everything that comes next *while* we're writing."

"It's hard. It's like, I direct at school. I write at home. I've never let myself think beyond the script, before working on *Melted.* The separation is easier."

The words tumble out before I can take them back.

Reid wipes the foam away. "You write? Beyond *Melted*?"

"It's no big deal."

"Natalie 'I Don't Art' Jacobson is a writer?"

Of course Reid thinks it's a big deal.

I swallow a long sip. "I write for fun. It's not serious."

"Something can be fun *and* serious. It doesn't have to be an either/or thing."

"Maybe at first, but don't you think the seriousness will eventually suck out the fun?"

Reid shakes his head. "Not if you love it enough."

I don't agree. Not at all. I roll my eyes at Reid, who quickly reverts to the serious clarinet version of himself. I'd rather hang out with fun, musical theater Reid today. I don't want to lose this creative high. So I circle back to his initial comment. "You didn't mention the dancing. A pivotal part of any musical."

Reid laughs. "*One* musical and you're an expert? You know I'm staging a tap number."

"I'm pretty sure we need to put Danica in charge of choreography."

"You want to put Danica in charge of something?" Reid looks skeptical. "Is this growth?"

I choke on my hot chocolate. "More like fear that she'll mutiny again if we don't."

Reid nods. "A real low point. *Codirectors, pull it together!*" He drops his voice in a terribly gruff impression of my dad and I laugh, loud.

"I think . . . we're starting to? Pull it together."

"Me too," Reid says.

Reid and I can't stop talking about the show on our walk back to North Station. We dissect the perfection of the performances and the emotional resonance in the second act, the narrative choices the musical made that were absent from the movie—and we both come to the same conclusion.

Every lyric in *The Lion King* is necessary. Propulsive.

Melted has great moments—but some of the songs are so obviously filler. I imagine the moments that could exist if I stop holding on to monologues from the play and let them become songs that move the plot forward.

"Not to ruin the mood, but I think we need to do another pass on the second act."

"It's not there yet," I agree.

"It's unbalanced," Reid says. "Our showstoppers are all in act one."

"I don't think it's about showstoppers, necessarily," I counter, looping my infinity scarf around my neck one more time. "It's about tension—and balancing the showstoppers with the quiet, emotional moments. We've been so focused on big *Broadway* numbers . . . but maybe not everything has to be a big Broadway number."

Reid considers this and I am prepared for the counterargument.

Instead, he simply says, "You're not wrong."

Holy shit! Did Reid just say I'm right? I pull out my phone because I need to get a statement like this on the record, to have in my back pocket for the inevitable creative arguments future us are bound to have when the magic of *The Lion King* fades and we stop pretending we're capable of getting along.

I open my camera and press record. "So I'm right."

Reid covers the camera with his hand. "Is this necessary?"

I pull my phone back and refocus on his profile. "It is."

Reid rolls his eyes and bites down on his lip like he's trying not to laugh. "Yes, Natalie."

"*Yes, Natalie* what?" I prompt.

"You're not wrong," Reid repeats, crumpling his hot chocolate cup and throwing it in the trash. I stop the recording and slide my phone into my purse, already looking forward to a future where I can pull this clip out again.

"I just want a second act—"

"—that's better than the first."

My eyes meet his. "Exactly."

I swallow my last lukewarm sip of hot chocolate to keep my face from reacting. Because Reid finished my sentence. But I don't think he's talking about *Melted* anymore.

And I don't know what to do with that.

Thankfully, that's when we arrive at the station. We have ten minutes to spare, but the train is already waiting for us, since Boston is its origin. I slide into a seat, pull my hair back into a messy bun, and Reid slides in next to me. He posts the picture he made me take of him outside the theater, pointing at the marquee with the silliest openmouthed smile on his face, on Instagram. His toes are tapping, which means he's listening to the—*ahem*—OBC album, something that is for sure allowed after a live theater experience, when you can't, and don't want to, get the music out of your head.

I definitely don't.

But I resist the urge to play it too and I open the notes app on my phone, inspired to start brainstorming Adina's monologue and reframe it as a quiet moment for our second act—but then my phone vibrates in my hand.

Henry Chao
Hi. I came over after my shift to talk, but Delia said you're at The Lion King with Reid??
5:45 PM
Wow. Are you friends now?? Am *I* being pranked?
5:46 PM

This is . . . not an apology.

In fact, it feels like an accusation.

"My friends are confused too," Reid says, his voice pulling me out of my phone spiral. I lock my screen and toss my phone in my purse. "Sorry! I saw my name and couldn't look away."

"I get it," I say. To the rest of the world, Reid and me doing something, going somewhere, together, seems like a big deal. But it's for *Melted.* So what if I had more fun than I'd ever admit out loud? It doesn't suddenly *mean* anything.

"They're not over *Star Wars,*" Reid confesses. "Or that I started the prank war that resulted in a musical."

"Relatable. Pretty sure my friends blame me for losing a play we never had in the first place. I know Henry does."

Reid chooses this moment to offer me an earbud. We're not headphone sharers, so this is the cherry on top of this bizarre twilight zone of a day. Matching outfits. Noncombative conversations. Now headphone sharing. *Who are we?*

"This feels like a truce," I say, taking Reid's earbud.

"Can it be?" Reid asks. "Temporarily, of course."

"Obviously." I keep my expression neutral, but the disappointment I feel is another level of confusing. "Do we agree to extend the truce clause? Pause *Natalie vs. Reid* until opening night?"

I almost mention Dad, but I don't want to bring those stakes into it.

Reid nods. "That seems mutually beneficial."

"I think so too," I say.

Because truces are agreed on with a double pinky swear, Reid's pinkies wrap around mine and I don't know how his skin is so warm or how mine is so cold when I'm the one who is wearing fingerless gloves. After a beat, our pinkies untangle and this temporary truce feels like a weight off my shoulders.

We're quiet for the remainder of the ride, listening to *The Lion King* through one pair of earbuds. I close my eyes and let tonight's performance replay in my memory—excited to return to the pages of *Melted*, to review it with fresh eyes and let it be a musical instead of resisting it.

I guess I never paid attention to musicals in the first place because of Reid.

It reminds me of fourth grade, when Reid created a *Survivor* draft system so intense I gave up watching entirely. I've been unable to listen to "Rhapsody in Blue" since he perfected the clarinet solo in sixth grade. Also, there's a reason my clarinet has been untouched since the conclusion of the seventh-grade prank wars. Why I don't play anymore, not even for fun.

Because if Reid likes something, it's easier if I just don't.

At least, that's what I've subscribed to. But maybe I've been missing out.

Maybe rejecting something solely based on Reid's enthusiasm is on me.

I hand him back his earbud as we approach our stop and are nearly back to reality.

"Thanks for inviting me," Reid says. "I'm really glad I came."

"Even though you're with me?"

"Yeah. Spending time with you isn't the worst. Who knew?"

I feel the tips of my ears get hot. "It's still a little bad, right?"

He smiles. "A little."

My heart does this pitter-patter thing that I one hundred percent do not understand as we pull into the station, and there's a small part of me that wants to turn around and go right back to Boston. I can't remember the last time I had so much fun or felt so inspired and I'm not sure what that means. I do know that Classical Clarinet Reid will always be The Worst. But . . . the Reid I spent today with?

He might not be.

CHAPTER SIXTEEN

I laugh at past Natalie and her confidence in her lyricism—and her ability to do it solo.

I am a playwright, not a poet.

Also, I have so much to learn about musicals. I started a list of movie musicals and I am determined to watch as many as I can before rehearsals start. Directing a musical *is* going to be different than a play. I can't downplay that reality anymore.

I almost text Henry the list.

Research is his favorite part of the writing/directing process.

But then I remember that I never answered his text and we sre still very much not talking.

Like he-stopped-coming-to-*Melted*-meetings not talking.

And we-avoid-each-other-during-school not talking.

Pretty much we're-both-waiting-for-the-other-person-to-apologize not talking.

So that's not really an option right now.

At least . . . I have Reid? In the week since *The Lion King*, we've spent every day after school together, reworking act two and polishing my rough draft lyrics.

And all that's left is Adina's monologue.

I have no idea where to start, so I take a leap and knock on Mom's office door, hoping her newfound creative energy will rub off on me in the form of a brainstorm session. But when I swing the door open, Mom isn't behind the screen working on her next bestseller—she's reading creative writing assignments.

"Hey, Lee," Mom says. "Working on *Melted*?"

I take my spot on the futon. "Trying."

"Same." Mom's chuckle is half-hearted and I mirror it, trying to hide my disappointment. I want it to be like old times, when *The Lola Diaries* was at the height of its success and Mom was cruising through a book a year.

I miss my mother's words. Her energy when inspired was contagious.

Now I sit next to her and type and delete and type and delete.

A couplet.

A sonnet.

Even just a line.

Nothing is landing. Frustrated, I open the original script in the shared doc because maybe I'll be, I don't know, inspired by the brilliance of our creation.

When I'm not, I pull out my phone and text Reid.

how do i verse???

6:21 PM

Reid Callahan

What do you have so far?

6:22 PM

NOTHING

6:22 PM

Ok so first you open Word

6:23 PM

Then you type words

6:23 PM

Maybe, if you're feeling crazy, they'll rhyme????

6:23 PM

I close out of our messages. Reid is useless. I don't know why I expected more from him. We called a truce. But still. One great afternoon away from *Natalie vs. Reid* doesn't erase the reality that Reid is still . . . *Reid.*

"You okay?" Mom asks.

I close my laptop screen halfway. "How does one verse?"

Mom laughs. "I'm a novelist for a reason."

I brush my hair out of my face. "Fair."

"You already wrote this, Lee. The bones are there. Trust yourself."

I close my laptop and flail my limbs across the futon. "How's the romcom coming?"

Mom sighs. "I don't know. I'm grading during writing time. So."

"Not today?"

Mom shakes her head. "Not today."

I am also an unproductive potato and the minutes become hours, staring at a blank screen while Mom is going to town with her red pen. The major poem isn't happening. Not today. I should call it and study for any one of the three tests I have tomorrow.

I stand.

"Leaving already?" Mom asks. "Can I help? Brainstorm session?"

I shake my head. "Not today."

Mom nods. "That happens. And it's okay. There's always tomorrow."

I'm struck by the optimism in Mom's voice. Even when writer's block stretches from days to weeks to months to years . . . there's always tomorrow. It came in the form of a grad school romcom inspired by her students. Instead of letting the block defeat her, she insists it's temporary. It always is.

But I'm still not sure the lows are worth the fleeting moments of inspiration.

"Thanks, Mom."

Upstairs, I flop onto my bed and my phone buzzes on

my stomach with a new text from Reid. I click it, expecting more snark. But it's not words, it's a beat—steady, constant. I close my eyes and imagine Fitz, center stage as Adina, scared and exhausted. The beat accelerates—and it is Adina, finding her voice. Accepting her powers. Acknowledging that in some cases it is better to burn it all down and start over.

My phone buzzes again.

Reid Callahan

I've said it before, but you can't think of it as a monologue.

10:21 PM

It's still a song-ish. You have to feel it. It needs a beat.

10:21 PM

I know I'm attached to Keep It In the same way you're attached to Moritz . . . but maybe there is something in the rhythm of the song we can salvage.

10:22 PM

It might be easier than starting from scratch.

10:22 PM

I consider Reid's idea.

For the first time, I *see* the poem.

And I FaceTime Reid.

"Natalie?" He answers on the second ring, my name a question mark in his voice.

I immediately hang up.

Shit. What is wrong with me? Reid and I don't FaceTime! Casual texting is new enough! Seeing him on my screen, sitting on his bed, his curls out-of-the-shower damp—it's a new level to this truce I'm not sure I'm ready for. But we're collaborators. And I can't convey over text what I'm feeling when I hear his beat.

It's *Melted*. It wasn't even weird . . . until I panic hung up and made it weird.

My phone starts vibrating.

He's calling back.

I check my hair in the mirror. I cannot explain why.

"Hey," I answer. "What's up?"

Reid's eyebrows raise in amusement. "I don't know. *You* called *me*."

"Right."

Cue a too-long beat of silence.

"Natalie?" Reid asks. "Did I freeze?"

"The beat," I say. "I think I know what our quiet act two moment needs to be."

"You had a breakthrough! Okay. Give me a second."

Reid is in motion, off his bed and moving to his desk. It takes more than a second to get the setup right. I reach for my laptop while I'm pretty sure Reid is trying to balance me on a stack of books. The screen keeps going black with a flop. But after a measure, I'm set up to see Reid's profile, his keyboard in the background.

"Okay. Hit me with the vision," Reid says.

"'Keep It In,'" I say. "Can we strip it down?"

Reid stops typing and looks at me. "Wait. Really?"

I nod. "I never considered reworking your lyrics because I always pictured a showstopper. Maybe it's *not.* Maybe it's the quiet, powerful moment *Melted* needs. Not sung. *Spoken.*"

Reid considers. "But . . . you're so attached to the monologue."

"I still am," I continue. "It has everything I want to say—about Adina's relationship with her powers, about the fear and anger that comes with reckoning with a climate crisis that no one else recognizes. But it doesn't fit. Not anymore. So maybe we use the monologue as inspiration to rewrite it. Your music. My monologue-turned-lyrics."

Another beat of silence.

"So what you're saying—" Reid begins, a smirk tugging at the corner of his mouth "—is that you don't think we should . . . *let it go.*"

I hang up.

Reid calls back immediately.

"I hate you," I answer.

"Come on! You set me up for that," Reid says, laughing. "It's a great idea. A true collaboration."

He shares a Google doc with me titled KEEP IT IN—REDUX.

I click into the file and watch Reid type in real time.

"I'm thinking we keep the accompaniment super simple," I say.

"Agree. We have to be careful. It can be done right, or it can be the *Les Mis* movie."

"I don't know what that means," I say.

Reid sends me a link to "Valjean's Soliloquy" in which Hugh Jackman is speaking? Singing? I'm not quite sure what this is supposed to be. I make it thirty seconds into the clip before I exit out because Reid made his point. "Keep It In" can't be . . . whatever this is.

"That's just *one* example," Reid says.

"Understood. And crossing *Les Mis* off my list."

I don't mean to say the second part out loud.

"What list?" Reid asks.

"Oh, I'm watching musicals," I say. "To prepare."

Reid fights to hide the surprise on his face. "Don't cross it off! Watch the tenth anniversary concert instead."

"Noted."

Reid pastes his lyrics to "Keep It In" and the original monologue into the document side by side and we spend hours rewriting the lyrics, transforming a fully orchestrated song into a more personal emotional moment for Adina. We experiment with the accompanying music, play with the tempo and volume and how much we can pare back. It feels like a *real* partnership, a true collaboration that hasn't felt this easy since Henry and I wrote the opening scene of *Melted* during the summer that now feels like a lifetime ago.

By the time we come out of our creative zone it is almost two a.m.

I blink. How?

"I am supposed to be at your house in five hours," Reid says.

"I have three tests tomorrow," I say.

"Well, at least *Melted* is done." Reid closes his laptop and moves back to his bed, the screen going dark for a moment as he flips off the overhead lights and turns on the lamp on his nightstand that only hits half his face. "It *is* done, right?"

"It is," I agree. "But the real work is just beginning. Codirector."

"Right. Ugh. I'm not even tired."

"Me either," I admit. "The regret will hit by second period."

"No regrets." Reid shakes his head. "This means I can dedicate some real time to my Albany submission this week. Before casting starts next week. How are we at this point already?"

"It's a ridiculous schedule," I say. "How is it going? The Albany stuff?"

Reid is speechless for a beat.

So am I. When our conversations stray from *Melted*, it's never toward the clarinet.

"It's not due until mid-December," Reid says. "I still have time. It needs to be perfect. I need to . . ."

The sentence trails off, unfinished.

"What?" I ask.

"There's just a lot on the line—a leg up on conservatory applications, potential scholarships, signaling to my parents that this isn't just some hobby. I know I'm good enough."

"Confident," I say.

Reid smirks. "Always."

I roll my eyes, an action that feels normal.

But the smirk disappears. Reid sighs. "They don't even know I'm applying."

"To Albany?"

Reid nods. "It's a long shot, so why start anything? My parents are pushing the traditional route *hard.* My dad says he won't partially finance a *useless art degree.* It's like my parents forget there are people behind the art they love to consume. People like me. It's not even about the money. I'd have loans either way. It's more like . . ." Reid trails off again. "I'm sorry. I don't know why I'm telling you this."

Me either.

Reid venting in the middle of the night is the opposite of normal. I mean, I've known things with his parents were tense re: conservatory. I've always appreciated Rebecca and Leonard's pragmatism. But listening to Reid talk about *experiencing* it . . . I'm not sure I do anymore. It's, like, no wonder he's so intense about music.

He has something to prove.

"Anyway, you're lucky," Reid continues, filling the silence. "Your parents are the best. I don't know what I'd do without your dad."

And there it is. Why I don't lean into clarinet conversations. I wait for the flood of angst and animosity to come. The typical reaction to push away that I am so accustomed to. But it doesn't. Maybe I'm overtired. Maybe *The Lion King* epiphany had more of an impact than I thought. Maybe it's just nice talking to Reid without having to think about how it could be used against me.

"Yeah, I am. But you are too."

There's a pause.

It's late.

I should say goodnight.

"Well—"

Reid cuts me off. "Can I ask you something? Now that I bared my soul."

My heart beats in double time. "Maybe."

"We *collaborated*," Reid says. "Like, all week."

"That's not a question."

"I know." Reid runs his hand through his hair and bites his lower lip. "Sorry. I'm still processing. I don't know. I'm still me. You're still you. Except, you're serious. It's more than the truce and it's more than saving your club. What changed? Besides 'Hakuna Matata.'"

I process Reid's question and the *earnestness* in his voice.

It takes everything in me to not panic disconnect. Because this feels intimate. Our faces may be on screens, but they're closer than they've ever been. Every expression is on display—the quirk of Reid's eyebrow, the intensity in the way his eyes hold mine.

There is nowhere to hide.

Nothing to stop me from admitting to myself that Reid's face is . . . not a bad-looking face.

Objectively.

Oh my God.

I have never wished harder for the ability to delete a thought.

So I pivot to a distraction. The truth.

"I overheard my parents talking a few weeks ago. About potential layoffs."

Even in the dark, I see the color drain from Reid's face. "Shit."

"It sounds like a rumor. But it scared me—" almost as much as this word vomit confession is scaring me "—so if I seem more serious, it's because I *am.* I will compromise, direct a musical, and put our history aside for the duration of our truce."

"Shit," Reid repeats. "Sorry. I wasn't expecting that."

"I know. The stakes already felt high," I say.

"Uncle Aaron can't seriously be on the chopping block," Reid says.

"I don't know. But if he is, it's my fault, so we have to

do this right, Reid. We need to *be* codirectors."

"We will."

I believe him.

"A weird note to end on, but we should—"

Reid cuts me off. "Yeah. Goodnight, Natalie."

"Night."

I hang up, this time for real.

But sleep is impossible—my mind is racing, this entire week of conversations on a loop. Tonight's collaboration. Last week's gushing over the magic of *The Lion King*. Tonight's two a.m. confession. There is one line I'm stuck on.

I wasn't expecting that.

So what did Reid expect me to say when he asked what changed?

I don't know.

I do know it's a relief—sharing the weight of the stakes with someone else.

Even if that someone is Reid.

The next day is the *most* Monday.

The highlight of my morning? Mrs. Westfield is out, so we watch Baz Luhrmann's *The Great Gatsby* in AP Language. I take it as a cue to catch up on some sleep before my psych quiz and feel zero percent guilty that I don't even make it to Gatsby's first party before my eyes close.

"Natalie," Fitz says with a gentle shoulder nudge.

My eyes snap open. Class is over. "Thanks."

In the hallway after, Fitz is on a mission.

"I saw Reid overfill his water bottle," Fitz says. "*His eye bags have bags too.*"

"Okay," I say.

It's not that I'm *not* going to tell Fitz about last night. I will. Once I figure out how. Because *Reid and I FaceTimed until two a.m.* is a sentence that is still impossible to process. Fitz will overanalyze. Convince me it means something. And it doesn't.

We turn the corner, making our way toward the stairs up to the social sciences classrooms, when I see Henry approaching us from the other end of the hallway. He's supposed to be heading to AP Spanish with Danica. This route is out of his way. Fitz and I look at each other, like, *Is he trying to intercept us?*

No way. We are not having this conversation at school.

Luckily, Fitz agrees.

She grabs my hand and we dip into the girl's bathroom.

"Not to be basic," Fitz says, reapplying her lipstick in the mirror. "But I still just cannot."

"Same," I say. "It's been *two weeks.* He's ready to talk now? Well, maybe I'm not."

"He should've apologized to us *the next day,*" Fitz insists.

You just direct, like we're all side characters in your story.

I can't unhear how *harsh* it was.

How *over it* Henry sounded.

Over *Melted.*

Over me.

And I just want to cry.

If we didn't duck into the bathroom, if we let Henry come and talk to us and say I don't even know what—I'm not sure how it would go. I don't know what a conversation with Henry looks like right now. Awkward at best. Confrontational at worst.

I hate that.

So I avoid it entirely. We hang out in the bathroom until the bell rings, choosing to be late for our next class instead. Then we book it.

I'm running on empty the next three periods. My three test periods.

So that's great.

Thankfully, study is next. In the library, I claim a table by the window and shuffle through my planner. Most days, I dedicate this forty-five-minute period to powering through as much homework as possible, so nights can be more or less dedicated to *Melted.* But today? I spend half the period answering one math problem and fighting my eyelids.

"Zombie solidarity."

Reid stands over me, a chai latte in hand.

"So. Many. Regrets."

"Logan and I did a Kiskadee run during lunch," Reid says as he places the chai on the table because *oh . . .* it's for me. I must be making a strange expression, or maybe it occurs to Reid how truly out of character this is for us, because he takes a step backward and clarifies. "It's not—I just thought you might need this as badly as I do. Codirector."

I pick up the paper cup and its warmth radiates to my fingers. "Thanks."

Reid nods once before exiting the library without another word, his cheeks tinted pink. Huh. Yesterday, I FaceTimed Reid out of the blue. Today, Reid brings me a chai unprompted.

At least this truce is doing strange things to both of us.

CHAPTER SEVENTEEN

We've worked so hard on *Melted*'s script—and finally it's time for our true debut as codirectors.

Auditions are crammed into the half week of school before Thanksgiving break, with rehearsals set to start the week after. HAVE A HE(ART) meetings are also scheduled to reconvene, with Makayla and Cherish in charge of organizing the art auction that we still very much intend to have and rallying the rest of the groups. Because even though it feels like the whole world revolves around *Melted*, there is, of course, still a bigger picture.

But casting! Reid and I are in charge and Danica is onstage, teaching a dozen thespians the tap dance she threw together last night, like it's easy. I watch her move through the piece step by step, shuffling and—okay, so "shuffle" is the only tap word I know. How so many Lincoln students have tap shoes, I have no idea.

Henry is standing in the wings because apparently this show only matters now when Danica is involved. He avoids eye contact. Obviously. Overlapping shifts at Chao Down have been a new form of misery. Casting is a major milestone, a step toward making *Melted* real. We should be celebrating.

Instead, we're both too stubborn to concede an apology standoff.

Dad is here too, grading AP Music Theory papers in the back of the auditorium. With Delia's bat mitzvah only weeks away, term grade deadlines approaching, finding a new gig for Lincoln Street Blues, and the vague threat of layoffs—it seems like he's happy to defer this process to Reid and me. I guess us getting along probably helps.

It's the last day of auditions, and so far it has been nothing short of a smooth, *collaborative* process. I picked out the monologues last week and chose a flashback of the first time Adina used her powers. Reid chose the songs, a mix of contemporary show tunes that best reflect the style of *Melted*. The dancing is all Danica, as I can't even pretend I know how to choreograph anything. Most days, I can barely choreograph *myself*, like, walking down the street.

"What are we going to do about Fitz?" Reid asks.

So much for smooth.

Fitz is currently onstage in the back row winging this routine because, like me, she has never shuffle-hop-whatevered before. Fitz is one million percent the best actress we auditioned. I'm not saying it because she's one of my best friends. I'm saying it because when she reads scenes, they make me feel exactly how I wanted the audience to feel when I wrote them.

But the dancing . . .

"It wasn't *that* bad," I whisper, as if it's possible for Fitz to hear us over the music.

"Natalie."

"Okay! It was bad. I don't know what happened?"

Fitz restarted twice but sort of kept up with the musical theater people during the jazz routine. Tap though has been an implosion. In all fairness, one cannot exactly learn how to tap dance overnight.

"If we need a backup plan, I think Emerson is a solid alternative to play Adina," Reid says.

"Emerson is a *freshman*," I say, my mouth practically dropping open.

Everyone likes to pretend the audition process is blind and not biased. But there is a hierarchy at work here. One in which freshmen rarely, if ever, get cast as leads. It's not their time.

"Plus, Emerson can sing!" Reid says.

"But we spent so much time reworking 'Keep It In.'"

"You were humming the melody during breakfast," Reid says.

I shake my head. "I was not."

"You were!"

No way. "I don't sing. Not at breakfast. Not in front of you."

"You were *humming*. Whatever. The point is the stripped-down version we wrote is great. Fitz would monologue the hell out of it. But I'm still imagining it as a song. I think you are too."

I sigh. "You're wrong."

As if on cue, Fitz slips and falls on her ass midsong.

"I'm okay!" she yells over the music.

"Ugh." I groan into my hands.

To cut one of my best friends for a better show . . . or cast someone who can't sing and has no rhythm in a leading role in a muscical?

Okay. When I put it like that, the choice *sounds* obvious.

But it's an impossible decision.

"It's not personal," Reid says. "It's an audition."

Danica, satisfied everyone sans Fitz knows the steps as well as they can, jumps off the stage, jogs over to us, and takes her seat with the judges. It's unfair how good she looks in MC Hammer pants and a loose crop top tank, her dark hair pulled back in a wavy ponytail, a black baseball hat on her head. She collapses into the seat next to me with a loud *exhale.*

"Cue music," Danica yells.

Makayla, who in addition to being an incredible artist is also a secret tech wizard, has been commanding the sound booth with Arjun. Music fills the auditorium, an upbeat Bruno Mars song, and the tappers are tapping. It is . . . interesting? The sounds are not all in sync, arms are flailing, and it's kind of a mess. But there is potential, I think. Emerson is annoyingly great. Toby, a junior who is the top contender to play Moritz, doesn't fall on his face. Everyone miraculously ends on the same beat. I start to actually get excited about it.

"Again," Danica yells. "It's shuffle hop step *toe toe heel heel*! Not *toe heel toe heel*!"

It takes three more rounds for almost everyone to nail the basic choreography. Then Danica breaks the dancers into smaller groups so we can assess each individually. This goes on for about an hour, until Danica is satisfied. Thirty minutes or so into it, Henry steps away from the wings, joining us in the audience and taking the empty seat on the other side of Danica.

Danica is *literally* between us.

The metaphor is not lost on me, but I avoid eye contact through the rest of the tap routine.

Finally, when everyone has gone, we move on to chemistry reads, the last piece of the puzzle. It is always my and Henry's favorite part of auditions because it is the first time we see the character interactions that make the words in a script come off the page. At this point, we already have our top contenders. The chemistry reads are to seal the deal, to make sure our actors can work together and their energy feels organic, which is why we do them last. We call front-runners and backup contenders to read. I cross my fingers behind my back, wishing all goes smoothly with my favorites. Mainly, that Fitz knocks it out so hard that it removes the memory of her disastrous tap from everyone's memory.

Danica says, voice low, "What are we going to do about Fitz?"

So much for that. Reid's eyebrows rise, like he's been vindicated.

"Fitz has been Adina from the start," Henry says.

Oh my God.

He speaks!

To Danica. Not me. But it *is* a defense of our vision of *Melted.*

"I mean, she said she couldn't sing. But I assumed . . . she was being dramatic," Danica says.

I shake my head. "Fitz has two months to figure it out. She *will.* We just have to be really great directors and help her."

"Can I just try something?" Reid asks before standing and turning around to face the chemistry read hopefuls. "Emerson Roper?"

Emerson stands and smooths her skirt, her brown eyes wide and nervous. "Yeah?"

"Can you read scene three with Danica?" Reid asks.

Emerson frowns. "But we've both been reading for Emma?"

"You'll read Adina," Reid says.

Emerson's mouth practically drops open. "Really?"

"Really."

Wow. So much for collaboration! The first opportunity Reid has to undermine me in front of the future cast of our musical . . . and he does it. I know I said I would compromise. Codirect a musical. Put our history aside.

I look over at my dad grading papers in the balcony, and remember why.

But Reid can't just steamroll me!

He has to be willing to compromise too.

"Fine," I whisper to Reid. "But Fitz needs to remain an option."

Henry's expression is incredulous.

Fitz and I lock eyes from her spot in the wings, where she is sitting with her arms wrapped around her knees. She mouths, *What the hell?* and I mouth, *I don't know,* and it's not even a lie. Danica and Emerson stand center stage. Emerson adjusts the hem of her T-shirt. She's also so *young,* she looks better suited to be onstage opposite Delia and Hannah, especially next to Danica.

"Emerson looks like a fetus," Henry says, like he read my mind.

It makes me miss him and how we're always on the same page. But it also feels like he's only here to support Danica and make things hard for me.

"Since when do you even care?"

Henry frowns. "Since when don't *you*?"

I cannot even.

"Let me help you," Danica reads. "Please, Adina. Just let me in."

Emerson shakes her head. "No."

It's one syllable, but the break in her voice is devastating.

"I can't do this," Emerson continues. "This crown? This kingdom? I don't want it."

Danica takes a step toward Emerson. "The people of

Infernodelle need you. Now more than ever. The fires, Adina. They're out of control."

"And I could just make them worse!" Emerson cries. "I make *everything* worse."

It . . . actually feels like I'm watching siblings bickering. Not two people who could start making out at any moment. Danica and Emerson's back-and-forth is natural. It works.

I don't want to admit it, but while Emerson may be a freshman, she is a *talented* freshman.

The scene ends, Reid thanks Emerson, and she shuffles back to her seat—her face pink and her long red hair knotted from nervous twirling.

Fitz texts me.

Fitz (Not Ava)
oh to be an OLD upstaged by a FRESHMAN
4:45 PM

don't stress out!! we're just testing some combinations, I swear. please don't hate me—i can only handle so much friendship angst!
4:45 PM

omg natalie
4:45 PM

i love you but don't worry on my behalf

4:46 PM

I FELL. it's ok to be objective.

4:46 PM

as long as i'm still designing the costumes

4:46 PM

I exhale.

The best part about Fitz is she wears her emotions on her sleeve.

Total opposite of Henry.

I don't have to read between the lines—or worry that she doesn't mean it. But even so, it doesn't make the decision any easier. I mean, we already wrote an entire musical around Fitz's inability to sing. Because Adina has *always* been Fitz.

I don't know if I'm ready to let her go.

I wrestle with the idea for the remainder of chemistry reads, until the future cast of *Melted: The Musical* is dismissed, leaving Reid and me to finalize the list with my dad. Fitz wraps me in a hug on her way out. Danica and Henry leave together and I cannot even process that the first real conversation Henry and I have had since my birthday was him accusing me of dumping Fitz. Especially when Fitz is more okay with dumping Fitz than I am!

It is beyond frustrating.

"What a week!" Dad exclaims as soon as everyone leaves, using his teacher voice. "Your show is going to—"

"Emerson should play Adina," Reid says.

Wow. Doesn't even let Dad finish his sentence!

Even if I almost agree, the way he approaches this reignites the *Natalie vs. Reid* in me.

"Fitz can do it," I counter. "If we're good directors, we can help her do it."

"We're already on a ridiculous deadline, Natalie. Why would we make any part of the process harder for ourselves?" Reid asks.

"Because we put in the work! We stripped down a song for Fitz! I . . . thought we were on the same page."

"We *were.* But it's hard to be now, when Emerson is right in front of us."

Dad raises his hands and shoots me a *hear me out* look. "Look, Natalie. I know you're invested in Fitz. It's understandable."

"She's one of the best actresses we have," I insist. "This isn't friendship bias!"

"But this is show business and also school committee business, and if you want to be taken seriously . . . Fitz isn't strong enough to lead a musical," Dad says.

There is it. The word. *Serious.*

And okay. I know *I've* said it. But it hits different, hearing it from Dad.

So far, taking the musical seriously has meant losing Henry as a codirector and putting our friendship in the worst place it's ever been. Now it means dropping Fitz. I hate that there are stakes. That I'm helming a *serious* production without my favorite people—the exact opposite of why we fought so hard for drama club.

This is not why I Art.

But right now, it's how I *need* to Art if I ever want to be able to do it that way again.

If a casting error—if my stubbornness—ruins next year's art programming for an entire student body, I will never be able to show my face at LHS again.

I don't even let the other worst-case scenario become a thought.

"You're not wrong," I say. "But I have conditions."

I don't know who looks more shocked.

"Really?" Reid asks.

"You're . . . not going to fight this?" Dad asks.

I shake my head. "I want to keep stripped-down 'Keep It In.' We can write a simple melody for Emerson, but we're not reverting. She'll be a great Adina. And if that gets us the funding, I can write something great for Fitz next year."

"Deal," Reid says.

"Fitz is also Emerson's understudy," I say.

Reid nods. "Fine. But no pranking Emerson out of the show."

"I would never!"

Reid looks at me like, *really though?*

Dad is stunned silent for a beat, before he pulls it together. Of course it stings, the way Dad was so obviously taking Reid's side. The way Dad *always* takes Reid's side. But I swallow it. For now, I am a professional. I am putting the future of the arts ahead of my own issues. It's called growth.

"Great!" Dad says. "Huh. Maybe we *won't* be here all night."

Adina was the only role up for debate and the rest of the cast list comes together with little fanfare. Everyone who auditioned will get a role in the ensemble, of course. Outside of the main cast there are featured roles, principal dancers, and key solos to cast, but we mostly agree. When we don't, Reid concedes to me because we have an Adina who can sing.

"We did it," Reid says. "We have a cast."

I review the typed, final list.

MELTED: THE MUSICAL—THE CAST

Adina: Emerson Roper

Emma: Danica Martinez

Moritz: Toby Daniels

Kris: Kevin McGuire

Featured roles, ensemble, and orchestra members are listed below. Please initial after your name to confirm your participation in Melted: The Musical.

The rehearsal schedule has already been confirmed and approved. Please do stop by Mr. Jacobson's classroom to pick up a copy. The first rehearsal is Tuesday, December 1st @ 2:30 p.m. in the music room. We are so excited to begin!

Sincerely,

Natalie Jacobson and Reid Callahan
Codirectors of Melted: The Musical

I can't lie. I feel Fitz's loss—seeing her name in the ensemble.

But excitement is there too.

Because next week, I get to direct.

Well, *co*direct.

The Setup

"Reid asked me if I wanted to get *sundaes on Sunday*. I mean, what a dork, right?"

I gripped my phone so tight the joints in my fingers turned white. It had been one month and Madeline was *still* swooning over Reid via FaceTime. *Swooning*. Our friendship had strained in an excruciating way, with Reid now in the middle of it—his *dorkiness* consuming much of Madeline's thoughts. Every time Madeline came over for a movie night or to paint each other's nails or whatever, she'd ask for Reid. If he'd be around, practicing the clarinet. If the answer was yes—she'd leave me midactivity to go knock on Dad's studio door and say hi.

Seriously. One time she left me with an unpainted thumb, distracted by Reid's texts.

In retrospect, our friendship was failing the Bechdel test *hard.*

It had been building, a slow crescendo over the past thirty days. And I was tired of waiting. I had to take matters into my own hands.

"Madi, I think . . . you like Reid too much."

Madeline frowned, confused. "He's my boyfriend, Natalie."

"It's only been, like, a month," I say. "You don't know—"

Madeline shook her head. "Look, it's not that your feelings aren't valid! But the prank wars drama is *your* thing. *Yours.*"

"Reid doesn't *like* you! He's *using* you! To mess with me! How is that not obvious?"

The silence that followed extended so long, I thought we'd maybe disconnected.

"That's . . . really mean." Madeline's eyebrows pinched together, like she was trying not to cry.

"You've been around all summer. Don't you think it's weird that the first time Reid asked you out was after he lost first chair?"

Madeline's nose scrunched.

After another painful silence she asked, "Are you *jealous*?"

I blinked, horrified by the insinuation. "Madeline. Are you *serious*? No! Gross! I'm *worried.* You don't understand. *Reid broke my arm because of the clarinet.* Well, that sounds violent. But the obstacle course *he* set up broke my arm! I wouldn't put anything past him, honestly. I'm sorry, but that's the—"

"Natalie. *Stop.*"

But I couldn't stop. "I don't want you to get hurt. Look, I know you're opposed to pranks—but what about a test?"

I unveiled the details of my setup proposal and Madeline's reaction was . . . not to hang up.

She raised her eyebrows. "And then what?"

I shrugged. "If I'm wrong, my best friend and my arch-nemesis live happily ever after."

"You *are* wrong," Madeline said before disconnecting.

• • •

I entered Dad's studio on the day of the setup, walking down the basement stairs with Madeline as my dad was heading up, shifting gears from music dad to soccer dad. Mom used to handle soccer with Delia, but her weekends had become dedicated to fighting through the pressure of producing a new novel. I'd never seen her blocked like that. That was the first year I ever saw her finish an apple. While obsessing over Reid and Madeline was the A story in my life—worrying over Mom was the B story fighting for attention.

But back to the A story.

I walked downstairs beyond excited. I was finally about to get my best friend back. Reid was packing up his clarinet as I entered the studio. Madeline stayed behind, taking a seat on the second to last step and wrapping her arms around her knees. She rolled her eyes, annoyed at this whole situation. Resolute in her feelings that I was wrong. Reid liked her. She listed things they had in common—music and Marvel movies and *Survivor*. What else could you need?

But Madeline Park did not know the Reid Callahan I did.

"Hey," I said.

Reid nodded. "Fancy seeing you here."

"In my own house?"

"In the studio. You know what I mean."

I stopped myself from devolving into meaningless bickering. I was here on a mission.

"I'm here with purpose. I have a proposition."

"Okay?"

"First chair. It's yours," I said.

Reid raised his eyebrows, shocked. "What?"

"You can have it," I continued. "Just break up with Madi. Stop messing with her. *Please.*"

Reid was stunned silent. "What are you *talking* about?"

"You win. It worked. You can stop leading on my best friend."

"Natalie. You are *so* off base. I . . ." Reid's cheeks flushed in frustration. He zipped his clarinet case and stood. "I don't even know what to say. But *no.* I don't want a chair I didn't earn. Also, I *like* Madeline. That's not a prank."

Reid pushed past me on his way out of the studio.

Of course, he ran into Madeline on the stairs. He looked between the two of us, stunned.

"Natalie. Your *face.* Is it that surprising? That Reid would like me?" Madeline said, looking right at me.

"Mads . . ." My voice trailed off because, honestly, I was still processing.

"A real friend wouldn't think someone dating me is a *prank.* Reid likes me. I like him too. The only person I don't like right now is you."

My eyes stung like I'd been slapped.

She hugged Reid and they exited scene together as I stayed frozen in the studio, processing the reality that . . . I was wrong. It still felt *so* impossible. But I was, and Madeline left without saying goodbye, without looking back. My stomach dropped because in an attempt to expose Reid's relationship, all I did was sabotage *mine.*

That moment, the curtain closed on my best friendship with Madeline Park for good.

CHAPTER EIGHTEEN

We dive into rehearsals head first, and it feels *so* good being back in the director's chair. I armored up with a musical movie marathon over Thanksgiving. Highlights include the staged recordings of *Hamilton*, *Rent*, and yes, the tenth anniversary *Les Mis* concert. I took meticulous notes and I'm riding the high from the study session into our first week of rehearsals. Sure, the production schedule is tight, requiring daily rehearsals. Yes, the stakes are high. But when I'm following along during the first table read with the cast of *Melted: The Musical*, marking up a script with a number two pencil, I feel like I'm exactly where I'm supposed to be.

Sans the codirector who has always been by my side.

The first few rehearsals are introductory, filled with team building exercises to foster trust among the cast.

By the end of the week, it's is all about the music, the eleven songs that make up *Melted: The Musical*. Today, we are working on "For the Last Time Ever" and "Hate Is a Closed Window" with Danica, Emerson, and Toby. Dad should be behind the piano, but a faculty meeting takes precedence, so he is going to be running late.

But I mean, who isn't running late at the moment?

"Hey, Natalie."

Danica is the first to arrive, her Doc Martens clomping against the linoleum as she crosses the band room and sets up at one of the chairs by the piano.

"Hi," I say.

I attempt to project leadership and confidence in one syllable, but the delivery falls flat. It's awkward. *I'm* awkward—because as thrilled as I am to have someone as talented as Danica to direct, I can't just forget how vocal she has been *against* me and Reid as codirectors. Or how she became the person in the middle.

Of Henry and Fitz.

Of Henry and *me*.

"Question." Danica flips her hair in front of her head, bunching it in a messy topknot, then reaches into her backpack for her script and a pencil. "Me. Asking Fitz out. How would that go?"

Holy shit. I was expecting a *Melted* question!

Now *I* have so many questions.

"You and Henry—?"

"Are *friends.* I swear! One drunk kiss does not make a relationship."

I frown, confused. "Does Henry know that?"

Even though we're fighting, I can't help feeling protective.

"Yes! Trust me, I am *so* not the reason Henry is miserable

right now." Danica takes a seat and flips through her script as I try to form a response other than *ouch.* "Never mind. I'm sorry I asked. I really don't need the judgment that's all over your face. You don't know me, Natalie."

Danica's tough exterior cracks. It is a shock to see a single tear slide down her cheek.

Shit. Rehearsal hasn't even started . . . and the talent is already crying?

I take a seat next to Danica. "You're right. I don't."

Danica wipes her cheek. "Sorry. For the record, the passing judgment is very mutual."

The laugh that escapes me is a surprise. "I noticed."

"Maybe we can stop that."

"I wouldn't hate that."

Danica nods. "Henry's, like, the best person I know. He will literally do *anything* for you—and sometimes you take that for granted. It sucks to watch. People Pleaser tendencies should *not* apply to friendships."

I want to retort.

But *People Pleaser* reverberates in my ears.

I think of every Henry note I've argued against—from directorial cues to prank wars. When Henry and I collaborated, I always thought the decisions were mutual. What if Danica has a point? What if Henry was just letting me win? What if we've never been on the same page?

Oh my God.

I cover my face with my hands. "I didn't see it that way at all. Not even when he *told* me."

Danica shakes her head. "No. Henry can also be a shit communicator."

I nod. "He really is."

"Yeah. So now that your flaws have been exposed, why not just apologize? Life is short. The planet is dying. You both are too stubborn."

"Both?"

"Don't fish. Obviously, I've been telling him to get his act together too."

I laugh. "Fair enough."

"Text him," Danica says.

"I will," I promise. "So. Fitz."

Danica blushes. Blushes!

"I've . . . kind of had a crush on her since we first read together. But I didn't know she was bi until she mentioned Luna—and I didn't want to assume. I am too. Biromantic, at least. I'm still figuring out my labels."

Oh my God. All this time Fitz's pining has been mutual.

"We didn't want to assume either. About your identity. You should absolutely ask Fitz out."

Before Danica can respond, the door swings open, Reid and my dad interrupting our pre-rehearsal heart-to-heart. As Dad plays scales at the piano and Reid adds to my agenda on the board, I take a moment to pull out my phone and text

Henry. Because Danica is right, life's too short and the planet is dying and I miss him and I'm sorry.

hi! i think this is the longest we've not talked . . . ever?
2:30 PM

i am not a fan.
2:30 PM

i'm sorry. for more than melted.
2:30 PM

delia's bat mitzvah is saturday. of course, you know that. i really hope you're still coming.
2:31 PM

When I look up from my phone, Danica's eyes meet mine and I nod. Up until this point, it has felt like my friendship issues have multiplied with Danica in the picture. And maybe there's some truth to that. But the issues themselves?

They're not *on* Danica.

And honestly? I could use another no-bullshit friend in my life.

Our first musical bump happens twenty-four hours later, ending what was already a shit day.

First, I had to ask Ms. Santiago for extra credit after bombing a molarity vs. molality quiz.

Then, I had an existential crisis in my guidance counselor's office.

Also, Henry never texted back.

And now, Emerson can't hit the final note of "For the Last Time Ever."

"Let's move on," Reid says after attempt number ten, and I am incredulous.

Reid has *the* highest standards of perfection.

How is he so chill about this?

"Em's still flat," I say.

Emerson's entire baby face is red. "I'm sorry."

Danica shakes her head. "Don't apologize."

"You're doing great," Reid assures her.

"Doing great would be hitting the note. Are you even a soprano?" I ask.

"This isn't as simple as line memorization, Natalie. Maybe we take the time to let our cast learn the songs," Reid says.

Emerson ties her hair in a messy bun, takes a sip of water, and tries her verse again from the top. It's even shakier than the last time and it's like, *Come on, girl.* You are filling the shoes of the one and only Ava Fitzgerald, get it together. This is why we don't cast freshmen in leading roles. It's not just about the fairness of seniority, it's because underclassmen are known to fall apart in the presence of upperclassmen. I did. Freshmen year, my very first show, I shadowed the student director, Lionel Goldstein. Lionel put me in charge of the curtain. A task that is virtually *impossible* to mess up.

The cords caught and tangled together and I delayed the play fifteen minutes because the curtain *wouldn't open.*

I ran across the stage to find Lionel, tripped, ate shit, and my earpiece cracked against the ground and made a horrendous screeching noise that I still have nightmares about to this day. I wanted to *die,* or at the very least, quit. Lionel wouldn't let me. *Freshman fumbles, Jacobson. They happen to the best of us.*

Emerson is eating shit all over this high note, her freshman fumble. But unlike me, the entire future of the arts at LHS rests on her not fumbling.

"You're going to have to drop the harmony down an octave," I say to Reid.

I don't think so," Reid says, lips pursed, like, *Maybe let's not have this conversation in front of the actors?* Danica's arms are crossed. Emerson's face is almost purple.

"We're learning," Danica says. "I've messed up too."

"The rest of the song sounds great," Toby says.

He's been so quiet, I forgot he was here, to be honest. Toby Daniels, a short white boy, is the only guy at LHS on the dance team, which gave him the edge for the part. Yes, there is still a dance team—it's a sport, not part of the arts department.

"I'll get it," Emerson says, her voice straining toward confidence, but her eyes fill with tears and for the first time this week, I remember how young she is. I take a step back because I'm intense. I *know* I'm intense, and stressed, and frustrated.

But taking it out on my cast makes me the opposite of a good director.

"I'm sorry, Em," I say. "I just want us to get this right."

She wipes her eyes. "Can I take five?"

"I think we should all take five," I say.

I push through the music room doors toward the hallway, toward air. After refilling my water bottle, I take a long sip. I wipe the sweat from my eyebrows and check my phone, even though Henry and I are still broken and Fitz knows better than to text during rehearsals.

"Hey," Reid says, meeting me at the bubbler. "What's going on?"

"I'm fine," I say.

"That . . . wasn't fine," Reid says.

Wow. Is Reid insinuating that I am . . . too *serious*?

I exhale. "Rehearsals just make everything feel more real. Mrs. Mulaney has made it sound like everything will go back to almost normal next year if we can fill the seats and convince the school committee. I want that."

"Me too."

I want a world where Dad's job is secure and I am directing not-serious plays, the senior in charge. A world where Reid is wrapped up in band activities and conservatory auditions and we don't have to keep renegotiating the terms of interacting with each other.

"I never thought I'd be the serious codirector," I say.

"Natalie, this music is new to everyone except us. Learning it is supposed to be fun."

"You're . . . not wrong."

Through the door window, I see everyone is back from break, so Reid and I should probably be back too. We walk toward the music room and Danica, Emerson, and Toby are sitting on the choir bleachers, Toby twisted around, his back to us, waving his arms animatedly.

Reid pushes the door to the music room open.

"—but Natalie doesn't have to be such a Nazi about it."

I blink, the shock of Toby's words sending me backward. Toby is the quietest cast member. Toby doesn't speak unless it's a line. Toby . . . is a total asshole.

Reid slams the door closed behind us. "Excuse me?"

Toby whips around so fast his glasses fly off his face, landing on the chair he was previously kneeling on. His cheeks are flushed, embarrassed. "Um, I—" he stutters.

"What did you just say?" Reid asks.

"I, um. I understand that we're on a tight turnaround. But I just think—" Toby inhales "—Natalie doesn't have to be such a, um, Nazi about it."

I am on fire. "Really, Toby? You're going to call me, your Jewish director, a Nazi?"

"That's fucked up, Toby," Danica says, crossing her arms in my defense.

"I didn't mean it like that," Toby says dismissively. "It's

a figure of speech. You're intense. You knew what I meant."

"Just a figure of speech," I say, turning toward the piano. "That doesn't make it okay."

It's another casual Nazi reference in colloquial conversation, like words don't matter. Nothing new in America, a country that has, you know, *actual Nazis.* I hate it. When you're a Jewish person in America, when you have a name that identifies you as such, you listen to a lot of ignorant, triggering bullshit that no one even thinks twice about. I cringe every time a Twitter mutual casually refers to themselves as a *grammar Nazi.* No. Killing a comma does *not* equate to fascism and genocide.

Toby opens his mouth and . . . does not apologize.

He says, "Chill, Natalie."

Yeah. No. I can't do this right now.

I turn for the door but Reid is already there. He twists the handle so it opens. "Get out."

Toby swallows. "Like—rehearsal is over?"

"No. Like, you're out of the show, asshole," Reid says.

"Reid," I say, turning around in surprise. Do I want to permanently kick Toby out? Of course. But we are a week into rehearsals. Next week we already start blocking. Yeah, it's nine weeks until show night, but we have a two-week hiatus during winter break since so many people are traveling and celebrating the holidays. Opening night will be here before we know it. "I'll be fine."

Reid shakes his head. "I won't. I'm not working with someone who doubles down on fascism."

Oh my God. Toby stares at him, jaw slack, waiting for him to say *never mind.* But Reid points toward the door, emphasizing the exit. Without quite thinking about it, I put my hand on his arm and it is *tense.* I don't think I've ever seen Reid *angry.* Upset? Yes. Annoyed? Absolutely. Reid's anger manifests in passive-aggressive quips, never like this.

"Is Natalie intense? Yeah. But it's because she cares about this show *so much.* Probably more than everyone in this room combined. I already have a short list of five replacement options for you. But no one could replace her."

Honestly, I expected Reid would get pissed too. But Reid's anger *on my behalf*—Reid *defending me*—is so unexpected, let me tell you. I look down at my hand and realize it is still on Reid's arm and *shit,* I drop it to my side.

"I can go to Mulaney," Toby says, trying to bluster.

Reid laughs, the sound sharp. "And tell her what? That you casually referred to your director as a Nazi? Because that will go over well."

"Well—" Toby starts, but he's flailing.

"It's over," Danica says.

"Apologize and leave," Emerson says.

I flip through my brain, trying to remember the Moritz auditions, and almost regret fighting so hard to keep this character in the script. But Toby isn't the *only* option. Reid is right—we don't have to work with him.

I don't want to.

I mimic Reid's stance, pointing toward the door. "You're out."

Toby rolls his eyes. "Whatever. At least I'm getting out before this shit show goes down in flames." He throws his backpack over his shoulder and pushes past us out the door. I step back so I'm not whacked with his Herschel and bump into Reid.

"Um . . . let's pick it up on Monday?" I say.

Danica and Emerson exhale, relieved that this mess of a rehearsal is over. On their way out, Danica stops at the door and swivels back to face us. "Callahan, you are *savage.* Damn."

"Toby's a jerk," Emerson says. "Good riddance."

"I'm a jerk too," I say. "To you, at least. I'm sorry."

Emerson shrugs. "It's cool. Reid said it wasn't about me."

"It wasn't."

Emerson nods before exiting behind Danica. Reid and I are now alone in the music room, straightening sheet music and rolling the piano back to its place, and I want to be, like, what was *that*? I mean, it was awesome. But the Reid Callahan I know is not, um, *awesome.*

"You didn't have to do that for me," I say.

"I didn't do it for you," Reid says. "I found Hannah sobbing in her room the other night. I think because The Monicas aren't invited to Delia's bat mitzvah so they want her not to go. And I just . . . I comforted Hannah. Because it seemed easier than making her more upset. But it feels like such a fail. This shit is so insidious. If Hannah heard Toby, she wouldn't even be upset."

I reach for the eraser to wipe this afternoon's schedule off the whiteboard. "Middle school is a casual antisemitism cesspool. You let things slide, you tell yourself it's a joke. In sixth grade, I was partnered with Lacey for an art project where we had to trace each other's profiles—" I apply pressure to the words that seems to have dried to the board "—and Lacey overdrew my nose. Instead of speaking up? I *laughed.*"

I swallow. I cannot believe I just told Reid that. I never told anyone that.

"Band Lacey?" Reid's eyebrows furrow. "We're friends. I never knew—"

I shake my head and brush off Reid. "How could you? We don't talk about these things."

"So why are you telling me now?"

Because there are so few people in this town who would react that way to antisemitism.

I didn't even react that way and I have been leading the anti-Monicas charge all year. Reid is right. This shit *is* insidious, and every time we let it go, it signals that it's okay.

It's never okay.

"Because it's *Hannah,*" I say instead. "Don't be too hard on her—" this is the point where my mouth should stop moving, but for whatever reason, it doesn't "—or yourself. I'd comfort Hannah too, because at the end of the day she needs to work through these feelings on her own."

Reid nods. "I wish I knew about Lacey."

I shrug. "It's always the quiet ones."

Reid's expression softens. He opens his mouth like he has something else to say, but then he turns away and starts wiping down the other side of the whiteboard. We finish cleaning up quietly. I try not to stress about the fact that today was a nightmare, swallow down the worry Emerson will never hit the high note, and we're now temporarily down a cast member.

Instead, I can't stop replaying the Toby scene in my head.

And how Reid backed me up when it mattered.

CHAPTER NINETEEN

Reid in a well-fitting suit is a personal attack.

"Reid. *Come on.* You know the drill. Move closer to Natalie," Aunt Jenn says, posing us for yet another photo. Aunt Jenn—a travel photographer and Mom's best friend since the beginning of time—flew in from London for Delia's bat mitzvah and jet lag is definitely real. The service begins in an hour, at nine-thirty sharp. Mom demanded that family arrive early for photos, because what is an event without professional photos to commemorate it?

Reid moves a half step closer to me on the bima step that we are being posed on. In my heels, Reid and I are the same height and the tallest, so we are supposed to split center in this photo with our sisters on each side of us.

I smooth down my dress for the morning service—a simple deep purple maxi dress with long sleeves and an empire waist—and focus on the lens of Aunt Jenn's camera, pasting a plastic smile on my face. If I look at Reid, I will fixate on his deep blue suit, on the paisley print bow tie around his neck that the sisters insisted he wear, on the suspenders. I didn't know I could have *feelings* about suspenders until today—much less, *Reid* in suspenders.

This is mortifying.

You hate *him*.

The truce is temporary.

These two sentences loop in my brain—as if they will stop it from short-circuiting. That is clearly what's happening. Reid shutting down antisemitism in such a badass way less than twenty-four hours before a full day of Jewish feelings broke me. It's the only explanation.

"You are wasting my talent!" Aunt Jenn groans, pressing her lips together.

"People are going to start arriving soon," Delia says. "I need to get in the zone."

"I mean, can we just wrap this?" I ask. "There has to be *one* decent photo."

Aunt Jenn must've already taken at least a million photos in every variation and combination. Delia alone. Delia with my parents. Delia with me. The four of us. Photos with cousins and grandparents and all the extended family in town to celebrate Delia's day. Reid's family. Do we really need to dwell on this?

"It's a miracle you got them this close," Dad jokes.

"Oh my God." Hannah pushes Reid closer to me. If anyone wants to be here less than Reid right now, it's Hannah. Which sucks because Delia needs Hannah in full best friend mode today. "Can you just put your arm around Natalie so we can make this stop?"

Hannah's attitude snaps my priorities back into focus.

Today is not about how good Reid looks in a suit! It's about Delia, about a day that she's spent an entire year working toward. It's about making sure everything is perfect for her today—yes, even this photo!

I cross the electric fence between us, until my arm is just barely touching his. Reid swallows and stiffens and I'm pretty sure this is worse.

"Reid," I say, my voice low, "pretend you don't hate me for thirty seconds. For Delia?"

"I can only handle twenty," he counters, but he's smiling and his shoulders relax, and suddenly I'm smiling too.

"Deal."

His eyes meet mine and I notice that one of his curls is out of place. Without thinking about it, I reach to smooth it down. I mean, if we can only handle twenty seconds of this without self-destructing, at least the photo better look good.

"Natalie, you read my mind," Aunt Jenn says, breaking the tension.

Then Reid's hand is on the small of my back, and for twenty seconds we pretend not to hate each other. Honestly, it's not that hard to pretend right now. Because in this moment—and this is something I will deny until the end of time—I don't feel like hating Reid. At all.

"Wrapped!" Aunt Jenn exclaims, and it breaks the truce.

I sidestep out of the pose and Reid's hand recoils so fast—and just like that, the electric fence is back up between us. I exhale, relieved the torture that is posed photographs is over. But then it is on to the next task on Mom's extremely detailed to-do list. Delia disappears with Mom to "get in the zone," Reid and my dad double-check that the sound system is good to go, and I am on greet-the-guests duty.

"Natalie!" I'd been so fixated on the picture scene, I didn't even notice my people have arrived and slipped into the back row. Fitz beckons me and I don't know what's more shocking—that Fitz is *early* for something or that Henry is *here.* Henry's eyes meet mine and anxiety bubbles in my stomach because he never answered my texts and I've been in my feelings all morning about how he's not going to be here.

But he *is* here.

And . . . I miss him.

"You came." I slide into the bench next to Fitz and wow I hate that this feels like a surprise, not a given. I miss the three of us in the same place. "You're here. Together."

I didn't know Henry and Fitz were back on speaking terms, never mind carpool terms.

"It's Delia's bat mitzvah," Henry says simply.

Fitz nods. "And we're very much over the standoff!"

"Danica?" I ask.

"We're just friends," Henry says.

"We're . . . going out next Saturday," Fitz says.

"Which I support. Fully," Henry says.

I don't know how to process this. "You're here."

"Yes. That has been established," Henry says with a hesitant smile.

I check my phone for the time. "The service is about to start. Can we talk later? For real."

Henry nods. "I'd like to."

Without overthinking it, I reach across for a hug because at the end of the day, Henry is my person, he is here, and I don't want to be mad at him anymore. As much as the distance sucked—Danica was right, Henry *did* have a right to be mad at me too.

But an apology deserves its own scene.

Not to be rushed in the minutes before Delia's moment.

"Are you okay?" Fitz asks. "We know about Toby."

"Right. Danica witnessed that mess."

"You could've called," Fitz says. "I'm so sorry you have to deal with that shit."

I shrug. "It's not like casual antisemitism is a great conversation-starter."

"I always thought he was a bigoted shit," Henry says.

"We need a new Moritz, stat," I say.

"I'll network the other choices," Fitz assures me. "But Natalie. Come on! Please don't bury the lede. You and Reid certainly looked . . . *comfortable* posing together," Fitz says, gesturing toward the bima.

I snort. "You must've caught the last twenty seconds. Literally. Delia and Hannah can confirm. Actually, ask Aunt Jenn. Pretty sure we made her wish she missed her flight—"

I snap my mouth shut. I am babbling.

"I didn't realize Reid's family was included in the photo session," Fitz says.

"Yeah. I guess it's, like, how often does my family get professional pictures? Mom milks it when she can. And the Callahans count as family. So . . ."

My voice trails off.

I don't know if I like thinking of Reid as family. I don't think I like that at all.

Eight hours later, Delia is the star of her party.

The music is loud, the food is yum, and the challah is aplenty. Delia killed her Torah and haftarah readings this morning, just like I told her she would. Reid tried to convince her that she's secretly musical at heart—her voice is a lot prettier than she'd ever give herself credit for. Delia said this was a onetime performance and her singing will henceforth remain exclusively in the shower, thank you very much.

I haven't seen my parents all night; they're too busy mixing and mingling and being hosts. Everything came together—from the purple and gold mini-basketball centerpieces to the emotional slideshow that I was up until two a.m. finishing last night, to the speeches that every member of my family delivered to the hundred or so guests scattered throughout Rosario's ballroom. Dad's whole family came up from Connecticut and Mom's flew in from Florida earlier this week. Then you have the assortment of cousins who only manifest at bat mitzvahs and weddings, the family friends my parents couldn't *not* invite, and Delia's friends because it is in fact her party—despite what all the adults in the room indicate.

Now everyone dances.

I will too, after I talk to Henry.

I pull him away from the commotion of the ballroom, toward a sitting area in the hallway.

"It means a lot. That you still came. Despite . . . everything," I say, fidgeting with the tulle fabric of my dress. "I'm so sorry I made it feel like our *Melted* didn't matter—or if I made *you* feel like you didn't matter. All I wanted was to share this show with you. I hate how that got lost in translation . . . and execution."

"I . . . am not the best at expressing myself," Henry admits. "Your birthday was not my finest moment. Things have been *a lot.* Pressure at the restaurant, pressure with all the college stuff. I keep retaking the SATs, as if my mediocre math score isn't my fate. When *Melted* became something musical and stressful I just . . . didn't want to deal with it. But I didn't want to lose it entirely either. And I threw that on you. I'm sorry too."

I shake my head. "I didn't know."

"I don't love talking about it. My anxiety," Henry says with a shrug. His leg bounces and he pushes his glasses up the bridge of his nose. "Danica has anxiety too. We talk about it, and it's not because I don't want to talk to you. It's just easier to talk to someone who understands. But you're right, you're not a mind reader."

I nod, appreciating the new piece of Henry and Danica's friendship he shares with me.

"Still, I didn't listen about *Melted.* Or the prank wars."

Henry's laugh is sharp. "You really did not."

"I don't think I knew how to be a codirector."

"You seem to be getting the hang of it with Callahan," Henry says.

"I know. It's *bizarre,*" I say.

"I'm glad," Henry says, to my surprise. "I want it to be great."

He stands and holds his hand out to me, pulling me up to my feet. I wrap Henry in a hug—a *real* hug because the shift in our conversation feels like a step closer to being okay again. Blowups between us are rare, but they make us stronger because at the end of the day, Henry will always be here. And I know I've been consumed by all the things we usually shy away from. But I don't want to lose sight of what matters about *this* year.

Or the reason *Melted* even exists in the first place.

With the drama over, now I can spend the rest of the night dancing and laughing with Henry and Fitz. I'm so glad they're here, we're reunited, and that they can distract me from all things Reid and his suit, because ugh, it's way worse now that the jacket is off and I can really see the suspenders. Why can't he just be Hot Guy in a Suit? Reid has to be *Reid.*

After the Cupid Shuffle—because one cannot hear

"Cupid Shuffle" and not do the Cupid Shuffle—Fitz grabs my hands and pulls me away from the dancing tweens. "What's up?"

"Hmm?" I ask, tugging at the hem of my party dress. Because while the purple halter pocket dress felt perfect when shopping for it October, it's a lot of exposed leg for a Massachusetts December—even with tights.

"Do you know how many times you've looked at Reid's butt tonight?" Fitz asks. "Too many times! I know the guy has a great Suit Butt—but pull it together!"

I frown. "Suit Butt?"

"It's a thing," Fitz says.

I sip on water until I can come up with a sufficient rebuttal regarding Reid's, um, Suit Butt that is not *actually, it's his shoulders in suspenders, thanks.* Someone taps on my shoulder and I exhale with relief because all my possible responses are terrible. I turn around and it's my cousin Molly and her boyfriend, Sawyer.

Molly wraps me in a hug, already talking. "So, update time. Have you and Callahan finally gotten your shit together?"

"Translation: Have you boned yet?" Sawyer asks.

I cover my face with my hands and I hate my life. So much for saved by the interruption. Molly subscribes to the belief that Reid and I are inevitable—and it's only gotten worse since she declared a double major in neurobiology and psychology at Amherst College. She's all, *I've been watching you two at family parties my whole life, you are destined to have hot sex someday.* Which is obviously mortifying.

"They're codirectors," Fitz says, before making a break for the dessert table.

Sawyer wiggles his eyebrows suggestively—I can't help but laugh. Sawyer is a freshman baseball recruit at UConn. I've always been jealous of Molly—not of *Sawyer,* but of how she found her perfect person. We're both high-strung, type A Jacobsons. Sawyer balances her out well with his relaxed demeanor and goofy smile.

Reid might be more type A than I am . . . so I don't know what she's thinking.

"We're working together because we have to," I explain. "It's a whole spiel."

Molly pulls out the chair next to me. Ties her dark ringlets into a ponytail. "I have time."

She's going to psychoanalyze me. I know she's going to psychoanalyze me.

Still, I tell her everything.

First words out of her mouth? "Fuck Toby."

"Yeah. Pretty much."

But then Molly smiles and I can see the wheels turning in her head, like her hypothesis is correct. "This is the best development in, like, two years."

"Yeah. Okay. So, tell me about Amherst," I say.

"You are not deflecting!" Molly laughs.

"Absolutely not!" Fitz says, returning with a plate full of pastries.

"What aren't we deflecting?" Henry asks, sitting down in the chair next to Molly.

"The Natareid situation," Molly says.

"The what situation?" Henry asks.

"It's their ship name," Sawyer explains.

"Nat-a-reid," Fitz says, slowly.

My favorite cousin has been demoted tonight, oh my God. Her boyfriend too. Break up tomorrow, for all I care! I stand up, because if I can't deflect, I'm going to flee for the bathroom.

"Natalie," Reid says after I've taken maybe three steps. He's at the table two over from the one I just left, with the rest of my cousins, who are all older and real adults. "Can we talk?"

Why did Fitz and Molly have to make this such a thing tonight? Now *can we talk* feels so intense. "Yeah, sure. Let's just—"

Reid stands, takes my hand, and pulls me toward the dance floor. For someone who could barely deal with putting his arm around me for twenty seconds literal hours ago, he grabs my hand with a confidence I cannot comprehend. Out of the corner of my eye, I see the table I left behind, where Henry looks confused, Fitz looks mildly amused, and Molly is pumping her fist in the air.

"You know everyone is watching us, right?"

"Why do you think we're not going off alone?" Reid answers.

Delia bumps my hip as she dances past me, totally living her best life because she's dancing with Hannah. I have no idea what happened between the photos this morning and now, but I also have no idea what happened between Reid and me between then and now, so who am I to ask questions? I will get the full story from my sister at a later point in time.

Standing on the dance floor, it occurs to me that we should, I don't know. Dance? I'm not a self-conscious dancer, until I'm dancing with Reid. Well, not *with* Reid. I sway to the beat of whatever top forty song is currently playing. Reid mirrors my sway. We're just . . . swaying.

"I could be this awkward all night, I swear. But you wanted to talk?"

"Right," Reid says. "Well—"

The music cuts to a slow song and everyone pairs up in three seconds as if they discussed it ahead of time. Even my eight-year-old cousin, who promised he'd save a slow dance for me, bails for Hannah. Reid and I look at each other. I'm about to say *let's ditch*, but before I get the chance to speak, before I get the chance to breathe, Reid's arms are around my waist and my hands are around his neck and . . . well. Reid can dance. We're dancing.

"Molly is going to lose her shit," I whisper. "She's calling us Natareid."

Reid snort-laughs. "That is the most disgusting thing I have ever heard."

"Right?"

Reid twirls me. "May as well give her a show. Before I squirt ketchup on your dress."

I fake-gasp. "You wouldn't."

"Alas, I'm not seven. My pranks are civilized now. I won't reveal my plan."

I nod along. "Civilized. Right."

His expression changes and I remember there's a reason we're dancing.

"So. Toby's friends are boycotting *Melted*," Reid says.

I frown. "Okay?"

"It means every plausible Moritz replacement is out."

Oh. Up until this moment, *Melted* was the last thing on my mind.

I stop swaying. "Your timing is impeccable. I really want to be stressed out about *Melted* right now."

"I'm sorry! Tomorrow I'm spending all day finalizing my Albany submission and then it's Monday and we don't have a lead. It's only fair we panic together. Codirector solidarity, right?"

I shake my head. "At Delia's bat mitzvah?"

"I know," Reid says, looking down.

I stare at my feet, too annoyed to dance with Reid, to dance with anyone. Without a Moritz, we have to stall production for a script overhaul, to consider cutting the character all together. The character *I* fought hard to keep. But we cannot stall production. So we need someone fast.

My eyes snap up to meet Reid's. "You can do it."

"Do what?" Reid asks.

"Moritz," I say. "You already know the part. And your voice isn't shit. So . . ."

"*Isn't shit?* What an endorsement," Reid says.

"This is coming from *me.* Scale it appropriately," I say.

Reid presses his lips together in a thin line. "I don't know."

"Reid. *Please.*"

Reid looks at me, contemplating. "Codirecting and starring. Isn't that a little—extra?"

"Please. Danica and Emerson are the stars," I say.

"You'll have to direct my scenes," Reid says.

"You'll have to *let me* direct your scenes," I say.

Reid nods. "I will. Maybe. Hey, Nat?"

"Yeah?" I ask. *What now?*

"You look really pretty tonight."

I hate how those words—*Reid's* words—suddenly have the ability to speed my heart.

"Sucking up to your director already? Bold move."

Reid's laugh helps my heart return to a normal rate. We dance to the rest of the slow song, Reid and me, and I keep wondering when the dynamics between us will stop changing. It used to be so clear. Reid's always in my space, finding ways to compete, sharing things with my dad I probably never will. Reid pranks me, I prank back, Reid challenges me, I challenge back.

Problem-solving with Reid is weird because Reid has always been the problem. It throws our entire trajectory out of orbit. It makes me admit to myself how cute he looks in his suit. How cool he was telling Toby Daniels to get out of our show. Everything is confusing, and I can't put us in a box right now and it's the worst because who is Reid Callahan to me if he's not my problem?

Right now we're so close I can smell the lingering scent of his cologne. So close I can see the tiny freckle under his eye. So close I could stand on my toes and my mouth would press against his and I would change everything about us. I almost want to.

Luckily, the song ends. The moment is over, and we're supposed to break apart.

We don't.

Not right away, anyway.

When we do, Reid lets go first.

My face is hot, the idea of Reid's mouth on mine lingering. What the—?

Blame the Suit Butt.

"Are you around tomorrow?" Reid asks.

I swallow. "Yeah."

"I'm recording my submission at your house."

I nod, because this is not exactly news.

"Could you let me know what you think of my piece? Honestly?" Reid asks.

I scrunch my nose, confused. "Why?"

"You're still a musician, Nat. The *Melted* music is better for your notes."

"But my dad should—"

"I want you."

"Oh. Okay. I mean, yeah. Sure." The way he says *want* sends me backward.

I need to walk away. Right now. So I make my move, going left through the dancing circle of Delia's jumping friends. I emerge from the dance floor, hot, my feet burning, and I succumb to the inevitable fact that these heels must be removed immediately.

Back at the table, Molly gives me her most satisfied smirk.

Fitz and Sawyer wiggle their eyebrows in unison.

Henry shrugs like *How ridiculous are they?* and I exhale because we're on the same page.

But I can't stop thinking about the last words Reid said to me. *I want you.* Like, Reid meant my opinion, right? Obviously. He did not lower his voice. Did not chew on his lip. It's just the suit. Everyone looks better in a suit. It's a fact. Tomorrow Reid will be normal Reid and I will be normal Natalie and our relationship will be us on a truce until *Melted* is over.

That's all this is. Just a truce.

Except I can't shake the image of us dancing and laughing, of how close we were. Of how close we've *been.* Working on music until the middle of the night. Sharing a piano bench. I don't know if we can just wipe that away when the time expires—or if I even want to.

Reid has always been in my space, but for the first time in our entire lives, I don't think I want him to go away.

CHAPTER TWENTY

Delia, Hannah, and Henry beat me to the leftover cupcakes the next morning. They beat Fitz, too, technically—but that's less of a surprise, as she's still snoring on the air mattress in my room. Henry and Fitz both slept over last night, coming back to the Jacobson residence for what was a truly wild after-party. By which I mean we drank a bottle of Manischewitz left over from the Kiddush and watched Netflix romcoms until Henry fell asleep on the couch and Fitz and I relocated to my room, per house sleepover rules. For the first time in a month, we didn't mention *Melted* or Danica or Henry's impending college decisions—we were just *us*.

I enter the kitchen as Delia and Hannah explain how Animal Crossing works to Henry.

"Turnips are a scam but we love a good con," Hannah explains.

Henry frowns. "And you need turnips because . . . ?"

"For the bells, Henry!" Delia exclaims. "To pay off our housing loan! Keep up."

I need to get up to speed with the sisters—better to focus

on their drama, or sudden lack thereof, than my own.

"Hey, Natalie," Hannah says. "I need all the details."

I reach for a glass of water. "Details?"

"On Reid's acting debut!" Delia says.

Henry is confused. "Wait. Callahan is now an actor?"

Oh. Right. Post-apology, we explicitly did *not* talk about *Melted*. "Yeah. There isn't really another choice. We've been blacklisted. Toby told everyone I'm a nightmare to work with. We are hemorrhaging the talent we already had."

"What the hell? Don't they know what's at stake?" Fitz asks.

"They don't care," I say. "We don't *need* a big ensemble—but we do need a Moritz."

"Reid wants to do it?" Henry asks, his mouth full of cupcake.

"*Wants to* is an overstatement," Hannah says.

"But he will," I say.

Henry considers this. "I guess his voice isn't shit."

I grin. "My thought exactly."

"So." Henry pauses, like he has a question he's considering how to phrase. "Do you need help? Now that Reid is in the cast?"

It's the last thing I expect Henry to say. "Really?"

"Not as a codirector," Henry clarifies. "More as like . . . an assistant to the codirector?"

"Henry, I would love literally nothing more. But you cannot be my assistant!"

"Part-time partner, then? Resident blocking expert?"

I laugh. "We'll work on the title. Wait. So, you're really back?"

Henry nods. "I want to see this through. Plus, my college apps are all in . . . so there is nothing left to do but wait. What could be a better distraction?"

"I could *not* agree more. I promise that there will be no more pranking involved in the making of *Melted.* I cannot, however, promise I won't torture Reid with directorial notes."

"I'd expect nothing less," Henry says before stuffing a second cupcake in his mouth.

With Henry back on board, it feels like all the pieces are falling into place.

Mom emerges from her office and sees the cupcake breakfast already in progress. "I don't condone this," she says, before participating in the narrative by reaching for a lemon meringue.

"Devil's food cupcakes should be illegal," Henry adds.

Mom plucks a napkin from the table and holds her cupcake in her hand. "I know."

It's a throwaway line, and just like that I know her mind is still with her manuscript. I'm right, because her cameo appearance ends as quickly as it began and she retreats to finalize the synopsis and partial sample for *Guy in Your MFA* before her call tomorrow with Anna, her agent. I get to proofread it before she sends it off to Anna's inbox, something she promised just as she was crossing over from wine-tipsy to wine-drunk last night. She even signed a napkin that says, "Natalie Jacobson has the exclusive right to proofread Michelle Leigh Jacobson's undisclosed proposal." I wrote it with the Sharpie everyone used to sign Delia's giant card. It's basically a contract.

Part of me won't get my hopes up, but most of me can't wait to read new Mom words.

"Pay up, Chao," Fitz says, emerging from her slumber in fleece pajama pants and my oversized Charlie Brown shirt, her phone queued up with a saved Snap from Molly, a video of Reid and me awkward-dancing last night with the caption *Natareid 4 Life*!!!

Oh my God. I'm going to kill her.

Hannah holds out her hand too.

Henry rolls his eyes. "Thanks, Nat." He slaps a twenty in each of their palms.

"We bet on whether you and Reid would dance together," Delia explains. "Group dancing didn't count; you had to be, like, holding hands. It was very specific. I thought you'd be stronger."

"Henry acted like he didn't see it but boom—here is proof! I knew Queen Molly would come through. I'm changing her name in my phone to that. Queen Molly." Fitz pumps her fist, validated. "Never underestimate the power of a good suit."

"It wasn't like, um . . ." Why I feel the need to explain myself, I don't know. Why my best friends and the sisters are betting on me and Reid, I'll never know. "We just talked about *Melted*."

"The why is irrelevant," Hannah says.

"Right," Fitz confirms. "It happened."

It happened. Fitz and Hannah and Delia spew Team Natareid shit at me for way longer than acceptable. Henry rolls his eyes at his phone. I check his screen out in my peripheral vision—he's texting Danica. To my right, Fitz is . . . also texting Danica.

Hannah tries to hide her smile. "You know, Reid is downstairs."

Delia raises her eyebrows. "He said you can come down *whenever*."

"We're specifically supposed to tell you that." Hannah licks frosting off her fingers. "On our way over, he was like, *I'll be in the studio all day. Tell Natalie she can come down whenever*."

"*Whenever*," Fitz emphasizes.

I bite into my cupcake I don't even want to eat. "I get it. *Whenever*," I say.

Hannah and Delia raise their eyebrows in unison and it's, like, stop it, you are twelve.

Henry looks at me, confused. "Why are you going downstairs, um, *whenever*?"

"Reid's Albany submission is due tomorrow," I say.

"Okay." Henry's fingers drum his water glass. "Shouldn't your dad help with that?"

"Dad is back-to-back booked today with LSB," Delia says.

"The hustle never stops. Besides, Reid asked for Nat. Specifically."

"He asked if I could listen before he sends it," I say. "It's whatever."

Henry raises his eyebrows. "Okay, Natareid."

Fitz, Hannah, and Delia laugh as I kick Henry's foot under the table.

Henry throws his hands up in the air. "Kidding. Kidding. I truly cannot even imagine that."

I exhale because okay, bless, Henry finds the thought of Natareid as ludicrous as I do.

"So how're you going to mess with him?" Henry asks.

My eyes flicker to the door that leads down to the basement. "Oh . . . I'm not."

Reid has put so much work into *Melted.* The time he should've been spending perfecting his audition pieces, he's spent writing show tunes and going to musicals and codirecting. The old Reid would've had his recording finalized weeks ago, but instead he's doing it last minute. It doesn't even occur to me to mess with Reid—and I'm not sure who's more surprised by my response.

Henry. Or *me.*

As soon as Henry and Fitz leave, I decide it is officially whenever.

Reid is sitting at the desk, his laptop open to Pro Tools. I scan his computer screen, trying to decipher the piece based on the splices and edits. Post-production is my favorite—I mastered Pro Tools and Adobe Audition before I knew how to use Excel. It's like, for some people, listening to music is magical, right? But understanding the music, how it is layers and layers of sound waves intricately positioned and exported—that's the real magic to me.

"Hey," Reid says, pulling the over-ear studio headphones down so they're around his neck. He stares at an open notebook and chews on a pencil eraser, his curls mussed.

I hold out the cupcake box and Reid plucks a vanilla with chocolate frosting that he eats in two bites. "Thanks."

I put the box down on the built-in shelf above me. "How's it going?"

"I'm almost done, I think." Reid takes off the headphones and hands them to me. "I don't know. There are two components to the audition—the mandatory Mendelssohn piece everyone is required to send in, but also an original composition, since that'd be my concentration. Listen."

Reid presses play, and I almost fall backward from the force of the music, our music, *Melted,* playing in my ears. It's the first time I'm hearing our show orchestrated, the first time it's not only Reid on a piano. *Melted* is alive, with the cadence and nuance only a full orchestra can deliver. It's more perfect than I could've imagined. I close my eyes and I see the script through the music, hearing how the orchestration will take the words we wrote to the next level. The piece feels too short, even though it's just under six minutes.

I sense the end coming with the decrescendo, with the forte that fades to pianissimo, but I want it to keep going forever.

When the final note fades, I open my eyes.

Reid's eyes are waiting for mine, wide and anxious. "What do you think? I was going to write something new, something classical. But I can't get *Melted* out of my head. I didn't want to use our music unless you knew. But it's good, right? Part of me thinks I should take the string section down a notch. I'm not sure. I've never arranged a full orchestra before. . . ."

His voice trails off and silence settles between us.

I'm supposed to say something, but if I speak I will gush. And I do not gush. Not to Reid. Not about Reid. Seriously, I don't know how to tell him that it is perfect, strings and all, and I feel the sort of calm I haven't felt since rehearsals started because *we have music.*

"Reid," I start, hoping words will come.

"You hate it," he says, his voice flat. He starts scrolling in the Pro Tools file. "Okay, so. Okay. I'll pull back the strings. And, hmm—" he highlights a section in the middle "—maybe add some more snare here? Does that even make sense? I've been working on the arrangement all week and I've made so many minor tweaks my brain is kind of like, *What's a triangle?* at this point. I . . . thought I had it. Shit. Okay, I'll figure it out. I'll—"

"Reid," I repeat.

He stands and runs a hand through his curls, like he's ready to start pacing, but I reach for his hand, as if it can steady him. As if *I* can steady him. That's not what we do though. We push, we don't hold. Reid is competition. Reid is opposition.

But.

Reid never complains that it's too late to create. Reid is the guy who says *Zombie Solidarity*, when we are sleep-deprived and spend half of our AP Study period answering one math problem. Reid takes the show as seriously as I do.

And he called it *our* music.

"It's perfect, Reid. It's—"

I don't know what I'm going to say next but I don't need to because Reid's mouth is on mine and my brain short-circuits. Like, holy shit, I actually might be dead? Did I choke on a cupcake? Is Reid trying to, I don't know, revive me? He'd be the first suspect if I randomly died.

But Reid pulls me closer to him and his hands are on my hips. My arms wrap around his neck and my hands are in his hair and it's soft, so soft, and nope, okay, I am definitely not dead. His lips are rough against mine and I feel the impulsiveness of the kiss, the recklessness of this moment, and oh my God I want it. We move together, a step backward, and Reid lifts me so I'm sitting on the desk. He teeth brush against my lower lip and it's *hot.* Reid is hot.

He pulls back. "Is this okay?"

I nod even as my mouth is saying, "This is a bad idea."

"Probably."

Reid smirks the smirk I hate so much. I've wanted to

wipe it off his face a million times and this time I do. I pull Reid's lips to mine. Reid opens his mouth and I sigh into it. He pulls back, only to inhale a sharp laugh. I say, "Shut up," and Reid says, "Gladly," and we're kissing like it's just what we do, no big deal. I haven't kissed anyone since summer camp, freshman year, the last year my parents could afford it. Jacob Simon was cute and knew who August Wilson was, but the kissing was sloppy—neither of us knew what we were doing.

Reid knows what he's doing.

My heart is hammering against my chest, my hands are clammy, my cheeks are on fire. I'm wearing leggings and an oversized blue T-shirt knotted at my waist. But kissing Reid, Reid kissing me, I feel sexy. He kisses my neck and oh my God. I lean back on the heels of my hands for support, but my left hand connects with the keyboard, pressing down on some keys. I move my hand back up to his cheek but Reid breaks the kiss, looking past me to the computer screen. "Pause." He reaches for the mouse and I twist to see what's going on—and what's going on is the screen is blank. Like, just the desktop. Like, I must've exited out of Pro Tools.

"You saved it before we, um—"

"I think so," Reid says.

But the speed with which he reopens it does not portray the same confidence.

When he hits play on the recovered file, it's only half-finished.

"Shit," Reid breathes. He starts to pace, then he stops and looks at me. "Did you—?"

"Did I what?"

Reid is quiet. But I heard it, the accusation in his voice.

"Say it."

"Did you delete it?"

I stand up. "Yes, Reid. You've been the best thing to happen to our show, so I am showing my appreciation by hatching a plot to sabotage your Albany submission. Which makes total sense since *you* kissed *me*."

Reid kissed me and then accused me of deleting his audition, as if I did this on purpose—and the worst part is I can't even be *that* mad, not really, because one kiss does not erase a decade of prank wars and sabotage.

"I know. I'm sorry. I'm just . . . it's ruined."

"It's not ruined! It's—" I glance at the clock "—still early. We have all night."

"Until eleven."

"We have until eleven!" I correct myself.

I'll be up all night working on a take-home pre-calc exam after, but it's fine.

Reid raises his eyebrows, but he does not look convinced.

"We'll redo it. It's only the back half, anyways. Maybe you did need less strings," I tease.

"Ha," Reid says, glaring.

"Kidding. Or am I?"

Reid opens a new file in Pro Tools. "You're the worst."

This time I smirk at him. "I know."

I chew on my lip. It tastes like chocolate frosting. It tastes like Reid. I don't even have time to process what happens next or what this means or how much I wish we weren't interrupted by technology, or how bad I want to kiss Reid again. We have to get to work.

Reid uploads each file and I splice. Every so often my hand skims against his, or he readjusts my glasses when they slide too far down my nose and it's not even weird. It's okay. It's almost like music, a rhythm all our own.

We work on the medley through dinner, and we don't have to talk about what this is, what we're doing, what happens next. For the tiniest moment in the universe nothing exists except Reid, the music, and me.

Aaron Jacobson's Protégé

The setup only brought Reid and Madeline closer. An all-around catastrophic fail.

Band became the worst part of my day. At the time, it was easier to blame these feelings on Reid and Madeline than to acknowledge the truth.

Rehearsals were a slog. Practicing? My least favorite thing in the universe.

However, one silver lining in the mess I made was the lessons I reinstated with my dad. Reid slightly toned down his rigorous lesson schedule to be a *boyfriend*, or whatever. So the empty slots in my dad's schedule became mine solo, and working with him, spending *time* with him again, was exactly what I'd hoped, what I'd wanted since Reid butted in.

"I knew you had it in you, kiddo," Dad said the first time I nailed "The Tempest." I would play eighteen measures of A any day to see the pride on his face like that.

Muscle memory pulled Madeline up on my phone. All I wanted was to text her.

Except she had never answered my last text. Begging her to hear me out. To let me apologize.

I couldn't text her. So I put my phone away, deconstructed the clarinet, and exited my dad's studio, hyped to celebrate my accomplishment with Dad's special chocolate chip peanut butter pancakes. Maybe I'd lost Madeline, but at least today's lesson felt like the old days, before the clarinet became synonymous with Reid. Now, *I* could be his protégé.

Except at the top of the basement stairs, I heard the sound of my father's voice.

"It's okay to wallow, but chin up, Reid. There's always next year."

My clarinet case slipped out of my hand, falling down the stairs and landing with a thud. Tears sprang to my eyes as my dad's words reverberated in my eardrums. *There's . . . always next year? No.* I beat Reid. It was supposed to be my moment. But of course, it was never over. As long as Reid and I were in contention for the same chair, it would always be like this.

I won, but it suddenly didn't feel like it. I looked at my clarinet on the basement floor, tears streaming down my cheeks, and it hit me all at once. Nothing changed. I would never be my dad's first choice. And . . . it was suddenly so clear to me, the thing I had never let myself admit: I didn't even like the clarinet! I just didn't know how to have a relationship with my dad *without* it. So I practiced, alone and in tears, until my blisters had blisters.

But for what?

I would never be Aaron Jacobson's protégé.

And from that moment on I knew . . . I'd never love the clarinet, either.

CHAPTER TWENTY-ONE

I stir my straw in my root beer absentmindedly, watching Reid behind the piano as tonight's stand-in for Lincoln Street Blues. We haven't kissed since the Oops-I-Deleted-Your-Audition-Tape-in-a-Moment-of-Passion fiasco, haven't even mentioned it, and *okay yeah*, it's only been four days—but it's been four *long* days full of no sleep, rehearsals, studying for midterms, and being professional in front of the cast.

It's like, sometimes I almost forget the kiss even happened.

I hate how much I don't want to forget.

Mom, Delia, and I are sitting with the Callahans at a corner booth at Olive & Twist, the restaurant where Lincoln Street Blues has a new regular gig. Charlie's sub, Tony, called in this morning with the flu because Lincoln Street Blues has had the worst luck with pianists lately. This isn't the first time Reid has subbed in for the band in a time of need.

It *is* the first time his parents have been here for it though, thanks to Chanukah. It's been tradition for as long as I can remember, the Callahans and Jacobsons in a jazz bar on the first night of Chanukah, listening to the mellow tunes of Lincoln Street Blues before everyone comes back to our house for latkes and a small gift exchange.

Hannah laughs. "The fedora looks ridiculous."

Delia shrugs. "He sounds good, at least."

I roll my eyes in an attempt to act bored—to act like myself. As if anyone is paying attention. Mom and Reid's parents aren't even listening to the music or watching Reid in his element. Instead, they're chatting a million miles a minute about how the Fisches—a family from Temple Beth Elohim—got a bernedoodle puppy. Granted, that puppy is adorable, but they need to chill with the cooing and creating the false sense of hope that maybe Delia and I will be able to convince Mom to get us a dog.

Meanwhile, Delia and Hannah catch me up on the latest seventh-grade drama.

The Monicas are yesterday's news, because they tried to crash Delia's bat mitzvah. They wanted Hannah in on the plan, but in a best friend power move, she pulled my mom away from the party to intercept The Monicas' drop-off. It sounded like Mom was a *boss.* Hannah told them off too. I don't know how I missed it in the moment!

I blame Reid's Suit Butt.

"I've been iced from the gossip circle at dance," Hannah says. "But those conversations were, like, way mean anyways."

"You need to start a friendship circle," Delia says. "Open to anyone who has been personally victimized by The Monicas!"

"I wish," Hannah says. "I can't believe I was a part of that."

Delia swallows a sip of her Shirley Temple. "Popularity is alluring."

It's surprising how easily Delia and Hannah snap back to themselves, post-Monicas. When I asked Delia about this the other night, while we were eating the last of the bat mitzvah cupcakes, she shrugged.

"She stuck up for my bat mitzvah and called out The Monicas. What am I supposed to do, stay mad? She's my best friend."

My gut says *yes. Stay mad. At least for a little bit longer! Your best friend has been treating you like trash for months!*

I almost wonder how we're related.

I definitely wish I was more like her.

Lincoln Street Blues is deep into their set when Leonard's attention shifts to me. "How're rehearsals going? I mean, *codirectors.* Who'd have thought?"

I chew on the inside of my cheek, focus on the swirling motion of the straw in my cup. How *are* rehearsals going? Well. This week we've been blocking the opening number, Reid onstage as Moritz. I can't give him a note without thinking about his hands on my hips, his mouth on my neck—and thinking about the next time we can be alone.

Because the only directorial note I want to give Reid is, *Again. Do that again.*

"We haven't killed each other yet," I answer instead.

The joke falls as flat as my root beer is going be if I keep stirring it.

"I mean, if you were able to convince him to sing in public, maybe you can talk some sense into him about—" Leonard gestures to the stage "—all of this?"

"That is more credit than I deserve."

Leonard shakes his head and takes a sip of his beer. "You're thinking seriously about what's next. That's smart, Natalie. My son wants to throw away his future on a pipe dream, make a career out of a hobby. At the end of the day, that's what it is. A hobby. Not a life. I mean, not even Aaron made it to the symphony, and he's the best musician I know."

I nod, only so this conversation will stop. I'm not ready to admit out loud that *Melted* is more than a hobby. But somewhere between the formation of HAVE A HE(ART) and sitting at the piano next to Reid—*Melted* kind of became everything to me. I can push these feelings aside, keep using the budget cuts, the fear of more layoffs, and my desire to have one final show with Henry to justify just how serious *Melted* has become to me.

Or I can be honest.

I'm not smart. I'm scared.

I wish I believed in my art the way my parents believe in theirs. The way Reid believes in his. I don't. I can't. Because I can't believe in something with no guarantees. If I had a magic mirror that showed me my future and revealed, *Natalie Jacobson, you will write a Tony Award–winning script*—I wouldn't hesitate. But not even my high school drama club has a guaranteed future! Never mind anything bigger. I've seen what art has put my parents through. *Is* putting my parents through.

My dad has a job that is not guaranteed.

Mom is late sending the sample of *Guy in Your MFA*, the romcom that she promised her agent.

Her next book—even when inspired—is also not guaranteed.

I can't live like that.

I'd rather be scared. Because I'll never know what pursuing theater could have been.

But at least I will always love it.

Avoiding Leonard's gaze, my eyes flicker toward the stage. I want to be, like, *Watch him!* Because as much as I doubt my own art, I don't doubt Reid's. His specialty is clarinet, but over the course of the *Melted* process I've loved watching him play the piano. His fingers move with such ease, his shoulders bouncing to the beat of the percussion. He chews on his lower lip every time he flips to a new page, not that he even needs music.

"Natalie." Delia waves her hand in front of my face.

I blink, wondering how many times she's said my name.

She hands me her phone and asks if I'll take a non-selfie of her and Hannah. Leonard pretends to be offended Delia doesn't ask him, but he always cuts off the tops of our heads or covers part of the camera with his thumb like a tech-dumb dad.

I take the photo as the music fades with the soft crash of cymbals. Polite applause fills the lounge and I watch my dad bask in it, in his element. Lately, Dad has been consumed by *Melted* in his own way—and as much as I resisted his involvement, it has brought us closer together, too. He spends afterschool rehearsals dedicated to the band and making sure the music sounds nothing less than perfect. And at home, we recap our progress from the day and discuss what's next. If Dad has questions about the songs, he even comes to me, not Reid.

It almost feels like how the clarinet used to feel, but better, since . . . I actually like this. And that has been the best surprise.

Delia and I applaud with loud woots, yelling, "Aaron!" because it's the only time we get away with calling Dad by his first name. And though he pretends to hate it, we all know that's the furthest thing from the truth. Mom smiles her most toothy grin when she looks at Dad. I hope I look at someone someday the way that Mom looks at Dad when he plays the clarinet. I think maybe it's easier to Art, to pursue dreams that feel impossible, when someone believes in you the way my parents believe in each other.

Dad and Reid join us after the closing notes of their set, as we're gathering our coats and hats. I for onc am so ready for the latke portion of the evening.

"Nice set, Reid," Dad claps Reid on the back, pride radiating in his voice. "Maybe your best yet. What did you think, Leo?"

"He's okay, I guess." Leonard laughs, like he's just teasing, but he doesn't look up from his phone and I can see Reid's face fall as he starts making his way to the exit. I hurry out after him, slinging my scarf around my neck.

"*Okay, I guess* is a glowing review," Reid says before I can say anything. We stop in the parking lot under a streetlamp and I wrap my coat around me tight, holding it in place because the zipper broke last week. "He didn't even watch, did he?"

I shrug. "I'm sorry."

Reid sighs and covers half of his face with the fedora. "You'd think I'd stop giving two shits by now. Why do I care?"

I lift the rim of the hat and place it back on his head properly. "Because he's your dad."

It hits me like a punch in the stomach, the fact that Reid has Dad Feelings too.

"I watched," I say. "You're more than okay, I guess."

Reid blushes.

"How are you . . . ?" My voice trails off before I finish the question. "How do you know that conservatory is your path? Why not also consider liberal arts schools with great music programs, like your parents want? I mean, it would make everything easier. How can you . . ." Reid takes a step back, his face scrunched, and I pivot because I'm doing this wrong. I don't mean he *shouldn't,* I don't mean that at all. "How are you brave enough to pursue *maybe*?"

Reid frowns. "It's my life, Nat. Music is hard, I'm not stupid. But for me it's not *maybe* or *if.* I don't practice and write for hours every day for a *maybe*, you know? It's *when*."

I press my lips together to keep my teeth from chattering. "I know that."

Reid looks confused. "Yeah?"

"For you. It's just kind of amazing that *you* know. I wish I knew myself like that."

Reid's hand brushes against mine. "Natalie, despite being told there is no money, having to change the entire type of show, and *literally every odd*, *Melted* is happening. Were questionable methods involved? Definitely. But *you* didn't give up. *You* brought the arts clubs together. *You* write the kind of shows that could be on real stages. You do know yourself like that."

I shiver, but even though December in Massachusetts is no joke—like holy shit why are we still outside?—it's not from the cold.

"Maybe it's not about knowing. I know that I like this, that I'm not bad at it," I say. "But I've only ever seen it as a hobby. Maybe it's more about . . . believing."

"I believe in you," Reid says. Even in the shadows, I see his breath in the air. "I kind of always have."

In any play, this moment would be the perfect END SCENE. Reid would press his lips against mine and I would throw my arms around his neck and the world would fade to black. In this moment, though, Delia and Hannah barge in, horrified that Reid and I are even standing outside when the car is *um, right there.* Hannah pesters Reid until he hands over the keys so the sisters can dash inside for warmth.

Then Reid looks back at me. And the way he looks at me?

I can't help but hope that this isn't end scene—just intermission.

Post-jazz Chanukah dinner is too-loud parents, too much food, and too many missed opportunities.

Okay, so I got Reid a present this year. I don't know why. Fine, I know why. Fitz, the enabler, is why. When I go to Fitz for advice, ninety percent of the time it's because I want her to talk me *out* of something. One hundred percent of the time, she talks me *into* something else.

Fitz (Not Ava)
did u give it to him yet
8:37 PM

does he love it
8:37 PM

are u not answering because 🙃
8:38 PM

u totally are!!!
8:41 PM

your ship name is now neid, by the way
8:44 PM

because u neid each other. get it?
8:44 PM

molly supports it.
8:45 PM

she called me a punmaster.
8:45 PM

you're welcome.
8:46 PM

These are Fitz's texts *and she doesn't even know we kissed.*

Also, I don't support Molly and Fitz texting each other. Nope.

But no, I haven't given Reid his present yet. Reid and I barely sign our names on the family cards! Mom had to sign my name for me for three years. The idea of walking up to Reid with a present in hand, from me and *me alone*, is so embarrassing. Plus, we've been good tonight. Why would I screw it up with a *present*? Especially because he most definitely doesn't have one for me, so that'll just be awkward.

I shake off Fitz's texts as Reid dips his last piece of latke into applesauce like a weirdo. I think the history of us never agreeing on anything begins with latke toppings. Sour cream for life.

"Can I show you something? Downstairs?" Reid asks. "*Melted* related."

Dad overhears and inserts himself into the conversation at the worst possible time. "We're in a good spot. It's okay to take the night off. It's a holiday!"

Mom hits my dad's shoulder. "Like that has ever stopped you!"

"*Never,*" Leonard reiterates.

"Can't you show everyone?" Delia asks.

"I'm not confident enough in my tap dance abilities yet," Reid says without missing a beat.

Hannah raises her eyebrows. "You need to practice a tap routine? *Now?*"

I nod. "Considering the first thing on tomorrow's schedule is a full run-through of 'In Winter,' it's incomprehensible that Reid is even at this table eating latkes tonight. Speaking as his director."

Fully aware that we are acting sketchy as hell, we bolt. Reid closes the basement door behind him and starts laughing and we are close, *so close.* His hair is flat from the fedora and it takes everything not to run my hands through it, not to ruffle it back to its curly norm.

"I got you something," Reid says, after the laughter subsides. "For Chanukah."

"Oh?" I fall backward onto the couch and raise my eyebrows

because I was hoping *go downstairs* was code for, um, *let's make out.* I don't know what's more surprising—the fact that we're not making out right now, or that *Reid got me a present too.*

"It's not a big deal," Reid says. "I know we don't do this. I didn't want the parents—or Hannah and Delia for that matter—to see and make this something that it isn't."

"What isn't it?"

"A big deal," Reid reiterates.

I smile. "You like me."

Reid shakes his head, but he's smiling. "I really don't."

"Where's my present?"

Reid rolls his eyes. "Shut up."

He tosses me a small box wrapped in blue menorah paper. It is jewelry box–size, which unleashes a sort of panic I've never quite felt before. To distract myself I reach into my oversized sweater pocket and pull out my small gift.

"You have a present too. From me."

Reid starts laughing. "Wait, seriously? I've been so stressed out that this is weird."

"I mean . . . it *is* weird."

Reid opens his present first, a customized reed case that I found during one of my more pathetic Etsy spirals. It says REID'S REEDS on the back because, well, I write, I can't resist wordplay. Standing here, watching him open it, seeing his face—like he's shocked that I'm capable of being thoughtful.

He smiles so big. "I love it. Thanks. Open yours."

My present is *not* jewelry, thank God. It's a key chain with two enamel charms—a flame and a director's slate. They're metal and flat, both engraved on the back. MELTED: THE MUSICAL on the flame charm and the date of opening night on the back of the slate. I'm probably making the same face as Reid right now, because it's somehow perfect.

I wrap my arms around my knees. "Thank you."

"You could do it," Reid says. "Write and direct, for real. If you want to."

My heart swells. My parents have told me this for years, but in a very *wish upon a star and dreams can come true* way. When Reid says it, I believe I can do it, for real. Reid doesn't speak words he doesn't mean, at least not to me. He never could.

I open my mouth to say something, but instead of speaking words my mouth is on his mouth, oops. Except it doesn't *feel* like an oops, like our first kiss. This kiss is softer, intentional—his hand cups my cheek, and mine are in his hair, *finally*. Kissing Reid feels so good it's, like, why did we spend all these years fighting when we could've been doing *this*?

It's probably *Melted* brain, most likely the rush from a week of great rehearsals and seeing our show come to life for the first time that's stirring all these feelings up out of nowhere. I've been convinced that after it's over, things will go back to the way they were. It's *why* we've been doing the work—so

Reid can have his band back and I can direct non-musical dramas and we never have to work together again.

But . . . I think I'm going to miss it. I think I'm going to miss him.

CHAPTER TWENTY-TWO

After the two-week intermission that is winter break, the countdown to *Melted* is on.

Up until this point, Reid, Henry, and I have been consumed by getting everyone off book, blocking choreography, and ensuring the ensemble harmonizes in perfect pitch. Now it is time to cue the second act in the theater production process—to bring the entire cast together, to build sets, to finalize the costume designs. Full cast rehearsals bring Arjun back into the fold and I am so happy to have a stage manager and tech crew, I could cry. Makayla and Cherish manage to convince Mrs. DiCarlo to let a handful of students paint the sets during class as an art project on modern impressionism. Fitz and Danica plan to scour thrift stores next weekend for all the metallics they can find for Fitz's costume vision.

Slowly, the details start to come together, transforming the auditorium into Infernodelle.

The auditorium we need to sell out to impress the school committee.

It's the final piece to focus on—and the one aspect of

Melted that makes my stomach twist with uncertainty. I'm not worried about our ability to execute an incredible performance. I am *terrified* no one will come to see it. Tickets go on sale in two weeks. We need a strategy to get the community involved in *Melted* and show up the way they do for band events.

At least, we connect with an organizer at The Sunshine Project. Fifty percent of *Melted*'s ticket sales go to their organization, and in return they promise to blast out the details of *Melted* across their social channels.

So maybe that will help.

But of course, the group with the following and reputation to fill seats are the least engaged.

"It's going to be awkward at first," Reid admitted over break while we were watching *Newsies* in my basement. Yes. *Actually* watching. Research musical weekends are serious occasions! "There is still . . . um . . . Nationals angst. Most of the band doesn't *want* to be a part of this."

I paused the musical. "No one is forcing them to participate. It's optional."

Reid shrugged. "Not really. It's the musical . . . or *no music*. And we always played for the musicals anyway. So it's not like that's the issue. It's more like . . . the *why we're here* piece."

Reid and I sat on opposite ends of the couch for the rest of the movie.

The band entering the picture affects our dynamic as

codirectors. It reminds me that Reid will always be loyal to them first and he's only doing *Melted* because—like his friends—he has to. Not because he *wants* to. The reality check stings more than I expect it to. And it lasts, resulting in a rough week.

Monday, Reid and Henry had different visions for blocking Moritz's death scene.

I voted Henry's direction.

Tuesday, Reid was a rogue actor, performing Moritz's death his way.

Wednesday, Dad suggested a key change for "In Winter" that felt unnecessary.

Reid agreed with Dad.

Thursday, Reid and I argued over whether to order Thai food or pizza for a rehearsal dinner.

I cannot explain that one.

Finally, it's Friday but also the first full run-through of act one, a somewhat momentous occasion because from this point forward, the band will be at every rehearsal. It's supposed to be a major moment, but it's kind of tarnished by the *entire* band icing me upon their arrival. Even Lacey and Logan! They set up their instruments without so much as a glance in my direction. I'm sitting in the second row with Henry, staring at Logan as if I can *will* a reaction, because if I can't get a smile from him it's, like, am I a monster? Reid is backstage with the cast and I know it must be weird for him—being onstage and not in his chair.

"Predict this rehearsal's trajectory on a scale of one to mess," Henry says.

"It's going to sound amazing," I answer. I believe that. Because even if the band is pissed, every member strives for validation from my dad. "But awkwardness? *Mess.*"

Dad raises his hand and cues the overture.

I just hope I'm right.

Outside of the context of *Melted,* Reid and I have zero clue how to behave in front of other people—something that becomes obvious the moment I walk into Lincoln Skating Rink on Saturday night for a *Melted* group hang—a necessary morale boost after a bumpy week. As predicted, the band's love of Aaron Jacobson rallied them to sound every bit the award-winning group they are. But directorially, I still have a lot of notes for the cast.

It's all very much a work in progress.

So when Reid says he thinks everyone needs to bond outside of rehearsals, I suggest ice skating because it ties to our *Frozen* roots.

And here we are.

Reid is hanging out by the snack bar with Logan, Makayla, and Arjun when I arrive with Henry, Fitz, and Danica. Otherwise, band members still seem to be socializing in their own circles, but for what it's worth, they are *here.* Reid is noticeably shorter than everyone else, due to the fact that he is not wearing skates.

"They're eating cheese fries," Fitz comments. "I want cheese fries!"

But first, we need skates.

Reid doesn't even so much as *glance in my direction* when Arjun yells my name and okay, so this is how tonight is going to be. I understand wanting to keep things on the down low since we have had literally no conversations about what we are doing. Trust me, I have no intention of shouting *I am kissing Reid Callahan!* from the rooftops any time soon. But is it really just secret making out?

Danica picks her skates up off the counter as I try to shake these thoughts.

"You know we know, right?"

My ears heat. Know *what*, exactly? They couldn't. I don't even know!

Danica laces her fingers between Fitz's because now that Henry promised he is one thousand percent okay, he swears, and dates one and two went well, Fitz and Danica are public and adorable. "You're a great director, but you're a terrible actress, Natalie."

"It's painful to watch," Fitz says.

It's even more painful to experience, so I pick up skates for Reid too and march over to the snack bar, because this needs to be a bonding night so the awkwardness needs to stop *right now.*

He has the audacity to *not* take the skates. "You know my size?"

"Everyone knows," I say, ignoring the fact that *yes* I do know that Reid wears a size ten and *no* I have no idea at what point I obtained this information. "So we can just, like, I don't know. Skate?"

Reid's shoulders relax. "Everyone?"

Logan caps his bottle of Gatorade and rolls his eyes. "It's pretty obvious."

Makayla and Arjun nod, double confirmation.

Reid flushes but takes the skates and we sit side by side, lacing them. I pull the laces tight, working my way from the top of my foot to my ankle. Out of the corner of my eye, I watch Reid watching me and attempting to mimic my motions.

I frown. "Have you not—?"

Reid shakes his head.

I double knot my right skate and move on to the left. "Never?"

Reid exhales a shaky laugh. "Nope."

My eyebrows arch. "And you weren't going to say anything?"

Reid stands. "The original plan was to hang out by the snack bar all night. Now I'm hoping that I'm secretly a skating prodigy."

He's wobbling in his skates and we're not even on the ice yet.

"Sit down."

Because the pressure is off, I retie Reid's skates for him.

There's so much slack on the laces, he'd roll his ankle, no doubt—and that is the *last* thing *Melted* needs. My phone buzzes in my back pocket as I finish Reid's skates. It's Fitz, demanding that we find them on the ice, with way too many wink emojis.

"You could have told me you don't skate before we made this a *Melted* activity," I say on our slow and wobbly walk toward the ice, where some of the cast and the band are mingling. A small victory. I spot Fitz and Danica skating in circles, hand in hand. Henry is also on the ice, catching up with Makayla and chatting with Logan and Lacey.

Reid pulls down on the green beanie he's wearing, so it covers his ears. "I appreciate the irony. And you seemed excited. I'll be fine. It'll be fun."

"Natalie!" Fitz yells with a big wave as we reach the edge of the rink.

But Reid can barely walk in skates, never mind *skate* in skates. His eyes go wide as soon as his feet touch the ice, like, *What is this witchcraft and why are all these twelve-year-olds so good at it?* He tries to take one step and when he almost goes down hard, decides he won't let go of the side of the rink.

He's not going anywhere any time soon, so I skate over to say hi to everyone at the opposite end of the rink.

"Reid's having a blast," Lacey says.

I roll my eyes. "I didn't know he's an ice virgin."

Makayla laughs. "I'd say go put him out of his misery, but this is fun to watch."

"*This* is fun," Logan admits, gesturing at the glory that is theater and band intermingling on the ice. "We were going to skip for a movie night. I'm glad Reid brought us."

"Really?"

Huh. Reid told me this afternoon that the band was all in.

Lacey nods. "We're masters of holding a grudge."

"I didn't mean to ruin the Harvest Festival. I'm really sorry about that. And Nationals—"

Lacey cuts me off. "You couldn't have known that would happen. Honestly, the school could've found another reason to not send us. It's been easier to blame you for the band's problems than reckon with our own entitlement."

"We're not better than anyone else," Logan adds. "We can act that way. I'm sorry too."

This is not the direction I thought this conversation would go. The whole reason I have waited so long to approach the band is because their frustration is valid. I mean, Reid and I derailed their year with a prank war that got out of control.

"You're not supposed to be apologizing right now!"

Lacey shrugs. "We just want *Melted* to be great. For everyone."

"Does the rest of the band feel that way?" Henry asks.

"They will," Logan says. "We're the first chairs. They'll follow our lead."

"Thanks," I say.

"Thank Reid. He's the one who called us out," Lacey says.

I look back at Reid as he lets go of the wall, takes two steps forward, and falls back on his ass. Henry and Makayla double over laughing. The instinct is there, like muscle memory, but I don't, because Reid is trying something new—without the guarantee that he'll be *good*—just because I *seemed excited.* Also, he got the band here! I skate over to him, and his butt is still firmly planted on the ice when I get there. I hold out my hands and he takes them.

"So, definitely not a prodigy," Reid says.

I laugh. "We can't have it all."

The rest of the night, Reid won't let go of my hand. If we're on the ice, our fingers are twined together, his palm pressed against mine. It takes a lot of coaxing for Reid to let go of the wall. I promise him I don't fall, so *we* won't fall.

"Okay, but if I do you're going down with me," Reid says.

"If you fall, I will probably deserve that."

He lets go so slowly you would not believe it. I turn so I'm skating backward and reach for his newly free hand, pulling him forward as I glide back. Reid squeezes his eyes shut every time we go a speed he deems *too fast* and it feels good, being out in the world with Reid, not talking about *Melted* or music, but also not just kissing.

Reid opens his eyes when we slow down to an appropriate speed.

"This almost feels like a date," Reid says. "If, you know, our cast and band weren't here."

"And watching," I add. "Thanks to you."

Reid shrugs. "Oh. I mean. I just—"

"—got the band to take *Melted* seriously."

"It *is* serious," Reid says. "As is my request that an actual date be less dangerous."

I roll my eyes. *Dangerous* is a bit dramatic but that doesn't stop my stomach from swooping. "Actual date?"

Reid blushes. "I mean, if you want to. I do."

"Me too," I admit.

Reid and I skate in circles and our hands don't separate, not even once.

Every time I kiss Reid Callahan I wonder why I wasn't *always* kissing Reid Callahan.

We're in my basement, post–skate date, our noses and fingertips still defrosting from the hours at the rink. Delia is at Reid's house and my parents are in Connecticut tonight for a gig, and for the first time, we don't have to worry about someone walking in or pretending we're just working together or keeping our voices low. We can *be* whoever we want.

I want.

We barely make it to the couch before I unzip Reid's sweatshirt. His breath hitches because this is new, but he shrugs the sweatshirt off and it falls to the floor. Reid sits, and I move onto his lap, my legs wrapped around his waist. I pull his T-shirt over his head between kissing his mouth, his jaw, his neck. My lips press against his pulse and Reid moans softly. I don't even have time to get lost in it because before

I know it Reid wraps his arms around me and flips me so my back is pressed against the couch. I pull my sweater over my head, revealing my black camisole.

Reid pulls back, brushing my hair out of my eyes.

"You're so beautiful, Nat."

I roll my eyes. "Shut up."

Reid shakes his head and before any more mush comes out of his mouth I pull him back to me because I don't want to have any questions right now, don't want to think, I just want to feel. Reid's hands move down my body. His lips follow. Reid kisses *my* jaw, *my* neck—

The door swings open, the light switches on, and Reid falls on the floor.

I blink, my eyes readjusting to the light.

"Oh." My dad's face is fifty shades of mortified, but Reid has him beat. I'm pretty sure Reid wishes he could melt into the floor and disappear. I know I do. "Um."

"How was Connecticut?" I ask, because maybe if I pretend this is normal, no big deal, Reid is not shirtless on the floor, *nope*, my dad will leave quietly and we can talk about it in the morning. If we have to talk about it. I'd prefer to never talk about it, thanks.

"Fine. Uncle Adam, um, has the flu so we didn't . . ." Dad pauses. Inhales. "You know what? I can't do this right now. I just have to ask—are you being safe?"

"Oh my God," Reid says.

"Dad," I say.

"We're not . . . we haven't—"

Dad holds up his hand, cutting Reid off, whose shirt is now on inside out. "Spare me the details. I am—" Dad looks back and forth between us, swallows "—going to walk away now."

Dad backs up, closing the door behind him.

Shit.

Reid and I sit shoulder to shoulder, in silence, stewing in embarrassment. Reid worries my dad hates him now and he'll stop teaching him. I talk him down because that is *impossible.* Dad's temporarily traumatized, sure. Do I wish my parents texted me a heads-up that they were coming home tonight? Of course. But the biggest thing is . . .

"How long until my parents know?" Reid asks.

I sigh. "I'd guess they already do."

"Ugh." Reid's cheeks are so red they're almost purple. I'm not sure they'll ever return to a normal hue. He zips his sweatshirt and swipes his keys from the end table. "I'm just going to, like, go home and pretend the last ten minutes never happened?"

"Yeah," I say. "The before, though? Pretty okay."

Reid smirks. "Yeah. Pretty okay."

Reid kisses me once more and then he leaves out the side door. I curl up on the basement couch, watching my favorite episodes of *Parks and Rec* until I'm certain my parents are asleep. I don't want to talk about what this means. Dad's face, seeing Reid and me partially clothed on his couch, screamed,

Shit, I wish they still hated each other oh my God it was better that way!

I don't know how Reid and I will be after the musical is over.

I don't know what the school committee's verdict is going to do to us.

I *do* know, though, that when I don't waste so much energy convincing myself I hate Reid—I like him. A lot.

CHAPTER TWENTY-THREE

Reid's Albany Institute fate is in my hands.

I am holding a large envelope addressed to Reid, sealed with a fancy embossed sticker. Inside is the answer to whether Reid has been accepted to audition in person. He asked me to be on the lookout for the letter, since his parents don't even know he applied and the Albany Institute is archaic in their devotion to sending news via the mail.

Reid has been so hyped for *Melted*, he hasn't mentioned the Albany Institute much. Every time I bring it up, he shrugs it off. Then he kisses me and I forget what we were even talking about. It's getting more . . . normal, us dating. Last week, high on a great rehearsal, I posted on Instagram a candid Fitz took of Reid and me laughing between scenes and Molly lost her shit. So regarding of the status of us, I guess we're Post-Pictures-Together-on-Instagram official. Also, there are rules now when Reid comes over. The main one? No more closed doors.

I told my dad it only happened because we thought no one was home but he just covered his ears, all *la la la*. Reid told me that my dad tried to have *the talk* with him before their Monday morning lesson and it was by far the worst five minutes of his life.

"He asked me what my *intentions* are. Then asked if I needed condoms. And I died."

"He did *not*," I said. We were watching a movie in my basement, like *actually* watching it because, you know, open door policy and all.

Reid arched one eyebrow. "Because we're apparently having, you know, *so much sex*."

I threw popcorn at him. "Obviously."

Reid laughed and kissed the tip of my nose. And that's when I found out we're both virgins—which is somehow surprising, but not. I don't know, it's not like I thought much about Reid's sex life until I factored into it. But after we kissed for the first time, I assumed he was more experienced. Band camp and all. He laughed, *loud*, when I asked him straight up.

So in reality, my parents have built up a whole lot of nothing in their heads. Yes, Reid and I have super hot make-out sessions in my basement, in his car, and pretty much anywhere we can be alone. No, it has not progressed beyond second base. It's not for lack of wanting to, at least on my end. Sometimes I get so lost in kissing Reid, *I'm* the one pushing the boundaries. Last night, Reid unhooked my bra for the first time in the back of his car, but not before asking, *Is this okay?* I nodded and kissed him, because consent is sexy. Reid's always checking in like that and it's kind of adorable.

But he's also always the first to pull apart.

Before I get lost in that memory again, I palm the envelope in my hand. It's big, like *acceptance letter big*, and I am dying to know.

I should not open Reid's mail.

Absolutely not.

I open Reid's mail.

Carefully peeling back the gold sticker, I split the envelope slowly, meticulously, so I can re-glue the seal. Reid is at a rehearsal for Districts—a regional audition-only festival—and he's coming over tonight, but I can't wait until tonight. I'm too excited and I need to *know*.

I pull the letter out of the envelope. It begins with *Congratulations*, and I pump my fist in the air because Reid did it, *we did it*. The invitation to audition is personalized, noting the *unique strength* of the composition portion of Reid's application. The *Melted* portion. And I am just so happy for Reid I want to call him and scream, but I can't because he's in a closed rehearsal. He also probably wouldn't love that I opened his mail before him. But he'll forgive me, for sure. Because Reid *got in*. Well, okay, he got an audition. But he's *going to get in*. He's—

My eyes pause on the last line of the letter.

> Your audition slot is Saturday, February 6th
> at 3:30 p.m.
> Please RSVP no later than Wednesday,
> January 20th.

I'm confused. *So* confused.

Because February sixth is *Melted.* Reid wouldn't choose an audition slot that weekend.

This must be a mistake.

Unless it's the *only* weekend.

I pull my phone out of my back pocket and Google the Albany Institute's audition calendar.

It's bold on the home page:

ALBANY, NY, AUDITIONS: FEB 6–7

I click into the FAQ.

Time slots will be mailed to accepted students. Based on the volume of auditions, we cannot accommodate individual requests.

No.

But Reid took on the role of Moritz, knowing we don't have an understudy. He *said* he'd do it. He made a commitment to the show, a commitment to act and deliver a performance, to be more than my codirector. He *has* been delivering. Rehearsals have been on the upswing. Reid nails every scene. Reid listens to my notes. But why, if he was totally prepared to screw this show, *our show,* over?

It makes sense now. His hesitation before agreeing to play Moritz. The evasiveness every time I tried to talk about the Albany Institute. I *asked him,* explicitly, when the in-person auditions would be. He said, *I don't know.* Why would he say that unless he knew that if he had an audition, it would conflict with *Melted*? He knew! He *knew* and he didn't care. He didn't—

My phone buzzes.

Reid Callahan
and break! any mail today? 🙏
3:22 PM

I ignore it because my thoughts are spiraling.

And they land on this: Reid never cared if *Melted* happened. He used my play as a muse to create great music, *amazing* music for his Albany audition. I helped him get here. He acted like he cared about something other than clarinet, but he was just . . . using me and *Melted.* But . . . I'm stuck on the band piece, the music stakes, my dad. Does all of that mean nothing to Reid? So long as he sets *himself* up for musical success?

I think of Reid and Madeline, not caring that he ruined our friendship in the process. Dad telling Reid there's always next year, even though that would mean unseating me. All these buried memories resurface and—

I am so stupid.

And now—what about *Melted*? The show is in three weeks! Tickets are on sale! It's too late to do anything except let Reid ruin us.

Tears spring to my eyes and *shit,* I hate how much this hurts.

I hate that I've given him the ability to hurt me.

I rip the letter in half.

Rip the halves in half.

Stuff the quarters of Reid's future back into its envelope. Then rip the envelope in half for good measure. I run upstairs to my room, taking the pieces of Reid's future and burying them at the bottom of my desk drawer, where Reid will never find them.

Only then do I text him back.

nope
2:27 PM

I have worked too hard on this musical.

The entire future of the arts at LHS depends on this musical.

Reid would bail on *Melted* for this audition. I know he would. It's a spot at one of the most prestigious summer programs. His conservatory application with Albany on his resume would be a lock. It'd be a no-brainer.

How could I ever think Reid and me could be more than the rivals we always were? I knew the rules and I ignored them because I guess I thought we could change. But apparently nothing about us has changed.

So the truce is over. And this time I'm making the first move.

Reid's Albany Institute fate is in my hands.

I have the ability to hurt him too.

Anything But Music

It turned out, my friendship with Madeline Park was nothing more than a brief interlude.

At the end of seventh grade, Madeline and her family moved to Wichita.

She and Reid ended in a no-drama mutual breakup the week before she left.

She and I ended without saying goodbye, without fixing anything.

The summer afternoon that the moving truck pulled away, I set my clarinet down after a solo bedroom practice and went downstairs—extremely in my feelings—to find Reid, in the kitchen, making an epic sundae. Mint chip ice cream with chocolate sauce, more whipped cream than ice cream, and two maraschino cherries on top. Maybe not *epic* by everyone's standards, but the perfect sundae to be consumed by one Natalie Jacobson. Two maraschino cherries were Reid's trademark move.

"What are you doing?" I asked.

Reid didn't owe me an ice cream. I'd be the first one to claim it if he did.

Rule nine was specifically prank-related.

Oh my God.

"It was all a prank," I whispered. "I was *right.*"

Reid frowned. "No. That's not . . ."

I waved at the ice cream, the hard evidence. "Rule nine!"

Reid closed the jar of cherries, his neck flushed pink, further evidence. An entire year's prank just because I had beaten him for first chair.

Then it hit me.

It was summer.

We'd be doing the first chair wars *all over again.* Competing with Reid didn't get me anywhere. If anything, my dad paid more attention to Reid *now* than before! It didn't strengthen my friendship with Madeline. And it definitely didn't make me fall in love with the clarinet.

I spent so many hours practicing and crying.

Forcing myself to get a little better at something that just . . . did not come naturally.

For what?

"It doesn't matter. I'm done," I said.

"Done?" Reid asked.

"With the clarinet."

The words spilled out but I didn't want to take them back because it was the truth and it set me free.

"Wait. You're just . . . *quitting*?"

I expected Reid to be thrilled. Wasn't this what he always wanted?

Instead, he was *mad.*

I nodded. "Yeah. You can have the chair. I don't want it."

"I didn't want it like this!"

"I don't want it *at all.* The music, the pranks, *Natalie vs. Reid*? I can't do this anymore. You win."

"What're you going to do?" Reid asked.

"Anything but music," I snapped.

"It doesn't have to be—"

I cut Reid off. Was he *that* desperate to always compete?

"You might want to get back to practice. I hate it and I'm still better than you."

I expected snark. A witty retort. A *Reid* response.

Instead, he placed the bowl of ice cream in front of me and my words sent him away, silent—with an expression on his face that made no sense because it could only be described as "hurt."

But the clarinet weight was off my shoulders. I would never be my dad's first choice—and I had gotten so caught up in the prank wars, I had become the person whose best friend leaves them without saying goodbye. That wasn't going to happen again.

Still the image of Reid's hurt face stayed with me as I sat frozen at the kitchen table and watched my sundae melt into mint chip soup, two Reid-signature maraschino cherries floating on top.

Without the clarinet, I was free from the constant pressure to measure up to Reid.

And I felt *relieved.*

CHAPTER TWENTY-FOUR

I don't tell anyone what I've done. Not until it's too late to fix it.

The week between learning the truth about what Reid did and the RSVP deadline for the Albany Institute audition is spent doubling down on all things *Melted.* We're mere weeks away from opening night and everything begins to snap into focus. I've been so distracted by all things Reid. Not anymore. Henry and I are codirectors again and when Reid asks to hang out after rehearsals, I make excuses. I'm exhausted. I have too much homework. We have a long day tomorrow. It's crunch time. All of which are true—but have *been* true. It's never stopped Reid and me before from lingering after rehearsals.

Every time I look at him, I see who he really is and what he was going to do to us. But then I'll watch him steal the stage, so into *Melted.* Or there's a chai waiting on the kitchen table for me the mornings he has clarinet lessons. And it becomes hard to reconcile again.

I have to give him credit, he's a better actor than I ever would've thought.

But I can't confront him about it until that due date passes.

On Wednesday, Makayla asks Cherish to bring her DSLR to rehearsal during costume fittings and they do a photo shoot of Danica and Emerson in front of a green screen. Cherish and the photography club will create fliers with an illustrated Infernodelle backdrop that markets *Melted*'s partnership with The Sunshine Project.

The closer we get to opening night, the more clubs participate, and it feels so good.

Like a true showcase of why *all* our clubs matter.

As Cherish snaps away, Reid approaches me in a metallic gold vest and gray jeans. The fittings are taking up way more time than they should. It's worth it because Fitz is an incredible designer, but it means Reid has time to come talk to me.

"Hey." Reid sits next to me on the right wing of the stage, our feet dangling over the side. "Are we okay?"

No. "Hmm?"

Reid scratches his elbow. "You're acting weird."

Because you're a manipulative lying liar and I want to kiss your face so bad but I can't because you proved once and for all that you are the worst. "I'm fine." I brush my fingers through my hair. "Stressed. It's all so close, you know?"

Reid nods and looks at me. "I didn't get into Albany."

My breath catches in my throat. "What?"

Reid shrugs, chewing on his bottom lip. "They never contacted me for an audition. They should have by now. Which means I didn't get one."

"That's stupid of them." My voice is barely a whisper.

"It's whatever," Reid says. "I knew it was a long shot. Musicians from all over the country apply. Most have been taking fancy private lessons since they could walk. I don't know. I felt so *good* about the audition when we sent it in, but I guess I'm not Albany material."

You are. I dig my nails into my palms because I should *not* feel guilty.

And yet—

"I'm sorry, Reid," I say.

"I wanted you to know. I thought maybe me keeping it to myself was why we feel off."

"It's just *Melted* stuff. I swear," I say.

Reid nods. "Well, I'm here if you need me."

Fitz, done with the photo shoot, calls Reid over to take more measurements and Reid pushes off the stage with his hands, his feet landing on the ground with a soft thud. Reid knows something's wrong. In spite of everything, I almost want to tell him before it's too late. I can't quite separate that I know how much he wants this. How much I wanted it for him before I knew the truth. But I also know I need *Melted* to happen, and he's the one that kept this from me. He started the secrets. Telling Reid the truth means sacrificing *Melted.* And I can't, I won't.

I don't.

• • •

That night, Henry drives me home from rehearsal, with a much-needed pit stop at Chao Down for dinner. The new year has reset us, I think. Henry's been chill at rehearsals and we're a great team, codirecting the not-musical parts of *Melted.*

"I missed this," Henry says, echoing my own thoughts.

"Me too," I say.

But I can't unsee Reid's face at rehearsal, the way his expression deflated when he told me he didn't get an audition. I can't stop thinking, *Yes, you did, because you're brilliant, okay?* I can't stop thinking that he doesn't know because of me.

"What?" Henry asks.

The expression on his face morphs to genuine concern.

"Natalie. What's wrong?"

And because it's what we do, I tell Henry everything, the truth spilling from my lips before I can take it back. I, Natalie Jacobson, have Reid's dream hidden in pieces at the bottom of my desk drawer. I, Natalie Jacobson, ruined the boy I hate before he could ruin me. Because I, Natalie Jacobson, think the boy I hate might accidentally have become the boy I love, even though it will never work because he'll always love music more.

Henry blinks. "You have to tell him."

"But *Melted.*"

"The Albany Institute is no joke. Uncle Joey already has

Kelli working on her application. She's a freshman! Callahan has no classical training beyond public school band lessons and your dad and—okay, yeah, your dad is pretty great—but the odds were stacked against him from the beginning, *and he got a shot.* You can't take that from him."

I swallow, indignant. "You have to admit that it's messed up he took on Moritz, knowing that his audition will be *Melted* weekend. And he has a history."

Henry shakes his head. "I have to believe there's an explanation."

"Explanation: Screw Natalie over," I say. "It's Madeline Park all over again."

"Okay. In the spirit of communicating better, I, for one, never believed that was a prank. And even if it *was* . . . that's seventh grade bullshit. Reid is *so into you* now, Nat." Henry's expression softens. "I'm your person, right? Do you really think I wouldn't tell you if I thought Reid was screwing with you?"

I look at the floor. "No."

"You need to talk to him," Henry says.

I pull my phone out of my backpack. There are three missed calls. From Reid. And another one comes through.

"Hey, Reid. I'm—"

"Natalie? Can I come over? It's important."

Reid . . . doesn't sound like Reid.

"Is everything okay?" I ask.

"I don't know," Reid says. "Is it?"

The challenge in his voice catches me off-guard.

"Yeah. I'm at Chao Down with Henry. I'll be home in ten."

Reid coughs. "Forget it. Just tell me where my Albany Institute letter is. I need it."

I almost drop the phone, my hand is shaking so hard. "In my desk. Bottom drawer. I—"

The line cuts before I finish my sentence.

I expect him to be gone, but Reid is still at my house when Henry drops me off.

All chatter stops when I enter the living room. Reid's eyes are glued to his laptop, his typing frantic. He doesn't even look up. Mom's eyes are narrowed, glistening with the sheen of disappointment. Delia pushes past me on her way upstairs, muttering *not cool* under her breath. Dad though is on another level. His arms are crossed and I can't look at him right now.

"Hi," I say to the floor.

Dad's face is so red, the vein above his eyebrow makes an appearance. "Is that all you have to say for yourself right now?"

"I know this is bad."

"Do you?" Dad asks. "I don't think you get it. The Albany Institute isn't summer camp. It's not just for fun. It is one of the most competitive preconservatory programs in the country. Do you know how hard it is to get an audition? Ten percent. That is the acceptance rate *just to audition.* Reid got that. Reid *worked* for that—and it's all in jeopardy. Because of *you.*"

"Can I just—" fresh tears start falling down my cheeks, *shit* "—talk to Reid? Alone?"

"Fine. I am so disappointed, Natalie."

Dad retreats through the kitchen and downstairs to his studio to give us space. Mom follows. I curl myself into the chair adjacent to Reid, wrapping my arms around my knees. Every time I wipe my eyes, fresh tears fall because I do feel bad, but this is also the same story of my life. Dad doesn't even think to ask me why. Doesn't even consider that I might not be the only one who betrayed someone in this situation.

"I didn't see until after rehearsal, but I had a missed call from a 518 number. I thought it was spam, but there was a voicemail. From the Albany Institute admissions office. Calling because they didn't receive my RSVP, or the fifty-dollar deposit, and today is the last day to submit it. I thought they must have the wrong number. I didn't get the letter so I didn't get an audition. So I didn't call back right away. But then I realized . . . I did get one. And you knew. You had to." Reid's gaze is still fixated on the screen. "It's why you've been so distant all week."

I nod because I can't form words.

"This isn't some prank, Nat. This is my *life.* My future. We said it in the rules, pranks are funny. This is . . ."

I dig my nails into my skin. "Okay. I should not have ripped up and hidden the letter. But can we at least acknowledge that you were prepared to completely leave me and the entire cast hanging this whole time? The ultimate prank. You cared about the music because it gave you a portfolio. But codirecting? Kicking Toby out? Becoming Moritz—you did all of that when you knew your audition would be the same weekend if you got one. Now everyone is screwed. My senior year will be gutted, and just because I'm not a prodigy like you doesn't mean my art doesn't matter."

Reid stares at me with the most dumbfounded look on his face. "Wow."

My nails leave imprints in the skin on my palms. "There's one piece I don't understand. Hurting *me* is one thing—but screwing over the band is something else entirely. How could you do that? To your friends? To *my dad.* It's not like . . . I told you what I overheard."

He closes his laptop. "First of all, I'm not even going to dignify you bringing Toby into this with a response. Second, you really think I would put *that much* effort into *Melted* just to abandon it? I love this show. I love what we did. Don't put words in my mouth or act like I don't care or try to tell me that I've treated *Melted*—and you—like one big joke. That's bullshit."

"If that's true, why did you agree to do Moritz when *Melted* weekend is the only audition weekend?" I challenge him. "It says right on the website, no individual requests."

"Because it isn't! There's a deferral period for school-related activities. I would have submitted for a deferral and auditioned the makeup weekend. Now I can't. So thanks, Nat. Now it *is* Albany or *Melted.* If they even give my audition slot back to me. By the time I called back, no one even answered."

The air rushes out of me. "Oh. I . . . didn't know that."

It's not like the Albany Institute website said anything about *audition deferral.* I checked the website but—I jumped to the worst conclusion. I didn't think.

I . . . didn't trust him.

Reid's laugh is cold. "No shit."

"But then why didn't you tell me?" I ask.

"Because it was a nonissue! Until you made it an issue."

"I thought . . ." My voice trails off. I am defenseless, but suddenly I'm desperate to make him understand. "Reading that letter was like emotional whiplash, okay? At first I was happy, *so happy.* Then I saw the date. It felt like the punch line in the prank of all pranks. Like everything between us was all a big scheme too and I fell for it. *Ha, you thought you could fall for Reid Callahan? Well, joke's on you!* I'm sorry. I'm really not defending what I did. I know I can't. Only how I felt. Because my feelings for you? They're real. So real, Reid, and the idea that it all could have been a lie? That scared me."

Reid blinks back tears, but when he speaks his voice is fire. "The only person who contrives elaborate schemes is *you,* Natalie! It's always been you. Like with the clarinet. *You* made everything a competition. *You* ruined your friendship with Madeline. *You* quit."

"Because it was never about the clarinet!" The words burst out of me, from a place they've been hidden too long. "Clarinet was the only way I could fit into my dad's world. But then you came along with your perfect technique and passion and my dad chose *you.* Every. Single. Time."

I've never heard silence echo like this.

Reid finally speaks. "Your issues with your dad are not my fault."

And those words shatter me.

Because he's not wrong.

My entire life, I've been mad at the wrong person.

Reid pinches the bridge of his nose and takes a step backward. "Whatever. I just . . . I *cannot* keep talking about you right now. I need to go and, like, figure out how I'm going to beg for my audition back."

"We'll figure it out," I say, reaching for his hand, but he flinches away from it. From me.

"*I'll* figure it out."

Reid exits scene and it hits me that if anyone has ruined *Melted,* ruined *us*—it's me.

CHAPTER TWENTY-FIVE

Reid doesn't show up to rehearsal on Monday.

When he comes over for lessons, he enters and exits through the studio door. No burnt scrambled eggs before school, no chai waiting on the table, no bantering text messages—nothing. In school, we get through an entire chemistry lab *with a Bunsen burner* in silence.

Reid's presence has been a constant in my life that I always wished would go away.

Well. He did.

Now I miss him.

And also. What are we going to do about *Melted*?

Today Emerson and Danica are mic'd for the first time. Arjun is in the sound booth, his voice in my ear apologizing every time there is feedback. It's not his fault—these microphones probably came with the school when it was built. Even when LHS had an arts budget, it never went to upgrading the tech. It makes me want to march into Mrs. Mulaney's office and demand to know what we're even fighting for. It makes me ask myself if this was all even worth it.

But then Emerson takes center stage, in costume, and

recites the lines Henry and I wrote, the words we spent a summer agonizing over—and it is. What we created matters. I take a seat in the second row and switch the volume to low on my headset, absorbing it all. There will only be so many moments like this. If we fail, my brief stint as Natalie Jacobson, student writer-slash-director, will be these short few weeks. If we succeed I'll at least have one more year, but even so, that's not much more.

And any thoughts of success burst with the awkward pause that is Moritz's first entrance.

I blink back to reality, reciting lines I know by heart from my chair. It throws Danica and Emerson, who look at *me* instead of the empty space on the stage where Reid should be standing. And without him halfway through, the blocking is all wrong. They end up mirroring each other's moves, nearly bumping into each other twice, and then *actually* bumping into each other the third time, sending the screech of feedback through the auditorium.

Fitz collapses into the chair beside me. "My ears. Are murdered. You are an ear murderer."

My fingers tap the armrest. "Emerson hit the high note at least."

"Yeah. It triggered these poor senile microphones. Thanks." Fitz pulls on the ends of her hair. "Ear murderers!"

I turn my head toward the stage. "What she means to say is 'good job.'"

Emerson smiles her innocent-freshman-thriving-on-upperclassmen-affirmation smile.

Henry whispers "ear murderers" in my ear. He's backstage helping the crew assemble the set, wearing a matching headset.

"Can we run 'For the Last Time Ever' one more time? From Moritz's entrance."

Danica crosses her arms, the edges of her mouth twisted into a scowl. "Sure. I mean, if only there were a Moritz. To, you know, enter."

"I know, okay?" I snap.

"So what's the plan?" she challenges.

"We're giving him space and hopefully he'll come back." I say.

It's a shit plan.

Reid called the Albany Institute eleven times, according to Delia.

Went straight to voicemail every time, according to Dad.

Emails? No answer.

Reid's silence is so loud, it consumes every non-*Melted*-related thought. At home, I search for reasons to go downstairs and interrupt their lessons, but I come up blank. At night, my phone glows with the messages we've sent, my eyes burning as I scroll all the way back to before—flirting in emojis, making weekend plans, sending links to the best Broadway performances. If it's a really bad night, I scroll even further, to *before* before and the ease of our banter, the cleverness of our quips, the evidence that maybe I never hated him, not really. But I wish I still thought I did. I wish I still resented his talent, his relationship with my dad, his face.

I wish I had a reason to hate him, now that he has a reason to hate me.

"Come on, everyone," Dad says, his voice clear and authoritative from the orchestra pit. "Henry, can you stand in?"

After another slightly less bumpy run-through, I call the rehearsal, cutting it an hour short.

"I think he'll come around," Henry says, his voice low in my ears.

Maybe for *Melted.* But not for me.

The future of the arts at LHS being in Reid's hands once would have been my nightmare, but if he's going to let everything burn to the ground, I can't even be mad because, really, I'm the one who lit it all on fire.

"Reid says stop texting him," Delia says, flopping on my bed belly-first.

I'm scrolling through the home page for the Albany Institute, writing down all emails and phone numbers. Communicating through the sisters is nothing we haven't done before. Except it's not childish rivalries and stupid pranks and being too stubborn to talk to the other person first. This is pointed.

"I'm only trying to figure out who at the Albany Institute Reid has already contacted."

Since he won't answer, I'm cold emailing everyone with an @albanyinstitute.edu address. I attach Reid's audition pieces, which I managed to swipe with a flash drive from Dad's studio computer. Someone will open the email. Someone will know Reid *has* to audition. Someone will have mercy on my stupid heart and give him a second chance.

"Hannah said you wouldn't last a month. I hate that she was right."

"Me too," I say.

"Reid should've had the chance to choose," Delia says. "Fix it."

"I'm trying."

She stands. "Well, maybe don't text him unless you do."

Delia pops bubblegum in my face and disappears back to her room.

I feel like the world's worst director. "Director" is a fancy word for glorified problem-solver. *Melted* has been a special sort of disaster from inception to execution—but even the best productions have roadblocks. A good director—a *great* director—isn't scared of something going wrong. That's inevitable. Something *will* go wrong. A good director is prepared to fix it. I should have been from the start.

I don't know if fixing Reid's problem will fix the bigger problem of us.

Still, I *do* know that I am not a director who takes no

for an answer. If I can make a musical exist, a musical that was supposed to be a play, a play that was shot down before it even had a chance—I can get Reid's audition back. Reid believed in me once. I have to believe now.

He'll get his audition, we'll find a replacement in some form for *Melted*, and . . . maybe he'll still hate me forever.

But I'll know I didn't take away his shot at the thing I'm too scared to try.

I click on the staff directory page and skim each member's bio until my lids are heavy, looking for anything helpful, anything that can—

Jennifer Nelson, Professor of Clarinet
Alma Mater: Berklee College of Music '95

I yell for my dad twice at a volume that probably wakes the entire street up. Adrenaline pumps through my veins, and my heart is loud *so loud* in my ears. I click on the extended bio, which includes the list of Jennifer Nelson's accolades and a personal statement in which she professes how thrilled she is for her first year on faculty for the Summer Institute.

"Dad," I call for the third time.

My door flies open. "This better be good, Natalie."

He doesn't even attempt to hide the annoyance in his voice. In the course of five days, our relationship has devolved beyond passive-aggression into overwhelming silence. I was expecting a confrontation. A punishment. But Mom says he doesn't even know what to say. How I could've done such a thing. She doesn't, either. I want to say I put so much into *Melted* for Dad. *Because* of Dad. But I know that won't be enough.

I press my palms into my thighs. "I have a question."

Dad leans against the doorframe, folding his arms across his chest. "It couldn't wait until the morning?"

"Is Jenny from college, um, Jennifer Nelson?" I ask.

Dad's eyes widen. The Jenny in his stories is a fearless musician, the girl who rivaled Dad every semester for the top spot in their clarinet performance classes. Jenny's clarinet has taken her around the world, to Vienna, Florence, Nice—everywhere. Last Dad heard, she completed a residency with the New York Philharmonic.

"Yes. Why?"

"Are you still in touch?"

"I mean, it's been years, Nat. I haven't heard from her since she was in New York."

"Did you know she's the newest Albany Institute faculty member?"

Dad scratches his beard. "I did not."

"She's heading up the woodwind section for the summer program."

"Oh?"

"Yeah! So I'm wondering if maybe—"

Dad cuts me off. "—I can fix the problem you created?"

I deflate. "Honestly? Yeah."

Dad softens ever so slightly with my admission. "I'll leave

her number on the fridge in the morning. You have to be the one to call her though."

"Thanks," I say. "Dad?"

"Yeah?"

"Is . . . he okay?"

Dad presses his lips together. "How could you do it, Natalie? Seriously? I'm not—I'm trying to understand, I really am. I know things have always been, um, complicated. But I think he's more upset not even about *what* you did, but that *you* did it."

I close my laptop. "I thought he was going to break my heart. I wanted to break his first."

"Well, mission accomplished," Dad says, closing the door behind him on his way out.

Seven voicemails and five emails later, Jenny Nelson finally, *finally* responds.

> Dear Natalie,
> While I am sorry that Reid Callahan missed the RSVP deadline, I am more sorry to inform you that nothing can be done. The institute follows up with each applicant prior to the deadline, to ensure that everyone has been properly notified. Records indicated we did call Reid. If we make an exception for one applicant, the integrity of our entire program is compromised.

Reid is welcome to apply for Winter Institute, a weeklong intensive in February. Applications open this summer.

Send my regards to your father. I hope he still plays.

All the best,

Jenny

After the thirty-five form rejections I've received from various Albany Institute faculty, it was refreshing to open an email that begins *Dear Natalie,* so I was sure this was it. But still, it's a rejection.

Emails are so cold.

I show Dad the email at breakfast, over scrambled eggs.

"What did you say to her?" Dad asks.

"I told her the letter got lost."

Dad looks at me. "That's a nice way to phrase it."

I stab cold eggs with my fork. "I couldn't explain it in a voicemail. I'm sorry. I tried."

"Because it can't be explained. I will never understand you, Natalie."

There it is again. It doesn't matter what I do or how hard I'm trying. It doesn't matter how hard I've worked—*we've* worked—on *Melted.* It doesn't matter even when I do something *right.*

I screwed up Reid's audition. I can't fix it. That's all that matters to Dad.

"You can't say that if you've never even tried. You're so

fixated on Reid. Always. From the time he picked up the clarinet. It became a competition—who could do scales the fastest, who could sight-read a song better, who would be first chair. You're a teacher. You saw Reid's potential. I get it. But you never saw me struggling to measure up. I'm sorry. I know I messed up. I get it. It was one hundred percent wrong. But if you want to understand why, it's because I've been fixated on Reid too—my *whole* life—because of the clarinet. Because of *you*."

A lifetime of complicated Dad Feelings reverberate off the kitchen cabinets.

My heart pounds in my chest.

I can't believe I said all of that out loud. Finally.

Dad frowns, but when he speaks all he says is, "So you're trying to say this is my fault? You never accept responsibility."

I shake my head. Of course he still doesn't get it. But I don't let up.

"This *is* me taking responsibility. For blaming Reid when it was really always about us. I wasted so many hours on an instrument I never loved because I thought it was, like, the key to spending time with you. Music came first. If I played music, I'd come first too. But then Reid started playing and I was no longer worth your time even if I played."

Dad frowns. "That's what you believe? Don't be—"

"Dramatic?" I finish.

"*Ridiculous.* Seriously, Natalie. That's not fair." Dad swallows. "It's different. Music isn't a hobby for Reid. It's his *life.* He wants to make it his life and I'm the only one who wants to make that happen for him. You can't imagine not having a support system. Your mother and I, we've made it clear that we support whatever makes you happy. You don't know what it's like doing it alone. You just don't."

My bottom lip trembles but I will not cry, *I will not.*

"My parents were . . . a lot like Leonard and Rebecca, actually. At least, when it came to me applying to Berklee," Dad says. He rarely talks about his parents, who were both surgeons who passed away when I was too little to remember them. "Same stance. You can do music, but on your own. Even if the intentions are good, it hurts."

"You're still missing the point. You *always* miss the point."

Dad frowns. "Okay. Enlighten me. What is the point?"

"It's *always* about Reid. Even now, when Reid getting the audition back might jeopardize *everything* for our family. I threw myself into making *Melted* serious for you, for your job, because I was *terrified* I ruined so much more than a concert when I messed up the Harvest Festival. I knew the stakes. And I know this is my fault in the end, but even with all that on the line, Reid is the priority! So I get it. I will never be enough for you."

Dad looks at me, so completely taken aback.

Takes a whole note rest.

Then responds. "Natalie, what are you talking about?"

Tears stream down my face. "I overheard you and Mom. Talking about layoffs. And how perfect *Melted* needed to be for you to keep your job."

Dad's expression softens. "*Oh.* That's not . . . Whatever you overheard, you weren't supposed to. I was . . . under a lot of pressure. But we're okay. My job is okay. At least for now. Even if it wasn't, that's not a problem for you to fix. But there *is* a problem to fix. You threw away Reid's chance."

Silence settles between us and the small hope I had burns out. No one wants to fix this for Reid more than me. But Dad brought it back there after everything I said. He will never understand me. When it's clear that I'm not going to respond, Dad resorts to the move he knows best.

Exit scene.

I let the crash of years of feelings unleashed settle for a moment, but it's not as bad as I anticipate. In some ways I feel lighter. Even so, I set aside the rest of my Dad Feelings to process at a later time. Despite what he doesn't get, Dad *is* right about Reid's problem. I wish Jenny had called. Because this isn't a *compromise of the integrity of the program*—not at all. It's punishing Reid for *my* mistake. She'd understand. I know she would.

If only I could talk to her.

I am up and FaceTiming Henry and Fitz in two seconds.

"Hey!" Fitz answers.

Henry yawns. "What's—?"

"How do you feel about Albany?" I ask.

"Um. Cold?" Fitz says.

"Is there any reason either of you need to be at school today?"

Fitz clicks her tongue. "Besides *Melted* and, like, the law . . . no?"

"Would you maybe. I don't know. Go to Albany. With me. Today?"

Before I admit once and for all that I can't fix this, I need to speak to Jenny Nelson. I need to make my case to her, in person. It's easy to say no to an email. It's easy to say no when you don't understand the talent you're losing. She needs to hear his *Melted* composition. If she says no, she needs to say it to my face.

"Skip school?" Henry asks.

"It is the second semester of your senior year, Hen! What even *is* school?" Fitz asks.

"A calc exam, a physics lab, and a Hemingway essay," Henry says. "Sorry, or I would."

I mean, Henry breaking the rules is always a long shot, but I didn't want to not include him.

"If we leave now, we'll make it back in time for rehearsal," I say, directing back to Fitz.

"I've always wanted to go Albany, you know," she says. I can hear the smile in her voice.

"I'll hold down the rehearsal," Henry says.

"I love you both," I say, hanging up the phone before Fitz can change her mind.

She texts that she'll pick me up in ten and I run upstairs in a whirlwind, gathering everything I need for the day. Pack backpack now. Deal with my parents and the consequences of skipping school later. By the time they even know I'm gone, we'll have crossed state lines. It's three hours to Albany. If all goes well, we'll be back by last period.

The chances this will work are slim. I know that.

The chances I get in even more trouble are guaranteed.

But there's a chance that it *will* work. A small chance, but *a* chance.

And I'm taking it.

CHAPTER TWENTY-SIX

As it turns out, the Albany Institute isn't *in* Albany.

It's in this tiny town *outside* of Albany. Important distinction. I tap my fingers against my thighs, staccato. Glance at the dashboard. It's almost ten-thirty. I should be in Chemistry, next to Reid. Lab reports were due today. Or are they due tomorrow? I don't know. Deadlines that aren't *Melted*-related don't stick in my brain anymore—and in my rush to leave this morning, I left my planner on the kitchen table.

The texts from my parents started an hour ago.

Dad

Why did I get an email that you're absent?

8:54 AM

I saw you leave with Fitz this morning. Fitz is also marked absent.

8:57 AM

Dad Voicemail

8:58 AM

Dad (2) Voicemail
9:01 AM

Mom
Natalie Louise—where are you? Where is Fitz? Are you together?
9:04 AM

Dad
Henry's not talking. Reid says he doesn't know either.
9:05 AM

we're in springfield. at the moment.
9:06 AM

a little over an hour away from the albany institute.
9:07 AM

Dad's typing bubble disappears and reappears for ten whole minutes, I swear.

Dad
Natalie, I understand you feel bad, but please just come home.
9:17 AM

Mom
We've never had a kid flee the state before. How does THAT punishment work?
9:18 AM

Dad
I'm sure we'll think of something.
9:19 AM

I tossed my phone in my backpack at that point because I had done my duty, told my parents where I was, and served myself up for certain grounding. I did not need to watch them plot out my punishment in real time, thank you very much.

Fitz takes the exit toward the Albany Institute. "Can I distract you with news?"

"Please," I say.

"On the subject of summer programs . . . I applied for one too! In New York. Not, like, *middle of nowhere, New York,* like this. In *New York, New York.* FIT, specifically. The Fashion Institute of Technology."

"Fitz, that is *amazing.*"

She smiles. "Danica encouraged me to apply! She's doing a summer internship at a theater before starting at NYU."

"Wow. That's serious."

"Seriously perfect. They have the most incredible precollege program. *And* it is the perfect test run to see what college in Manhattan would be like. I used *Melted*'s costumes for my portfolio. I hope between that and *If the Shoe Fitz* it's enough."

"Your costumes and platform are *perfect*, Fitz. Wow. I love all of this for you so much."

I'm quiet for a beat. Everyone in my life is so confident about their path and what's next. Conservatory for Reid. Fashion school for Fitz. Business school for Henry. They're all jumping head first into not just a direction, but their passions. They're not afraid to fall. To fail.

Fitz's GPS alerts us we're entering *not quite Albany*. The neighborhood has the prettiest street signs and snow-dusted lawns. It's honestly an attack. I expected streets and coffee shops and strolling through the downtown shopping center until we found a place to properly caffeinate before the big moment.

"We're here. I think," Fitz says, pulling into guest parking, and we are, in fact, here. The Albany Institute of the Arts in front of us is this gorgeous campus. As Fitz looks for a spot, I marvel at the string of Dutch colonial buildings, at the snow-covered quad, at the fact that the dorms are named for chord progressions and the buildings after composers. Students pass from one building to the next with cellos on their backs and saxophones around their necks and I can already see it: Reid here. Reid thriving. Reid *belonging*.

I open the car door, ready to begin my mission: find Jenny Nelson even without caffeine.

But wow, Fitz is right. Albany *is* cold. As soon as I step out of her car, freezing wind whips my hair. I wrap my scarf around my neck as tight as it will go.

"Okay. What now?" Fitz asks.

I, in fact, have no idea where I'm going. *Get here* is the farthest I got in my plan.

And, well, we are here.

"Excuse me?" I say, inserting myself into the direct path of a guy with ginger hair passing by whose trombone case is dangling by the strap over his shoulder. "Which way is woodwinds?"

Trombone raises his eyebrows. "New students?"

"Prospective," Fitz says. "Natalie here plays a mean clarinet."

"Cool." Trombone smiles. "Woodwinds are in Mozart."

Of course. He points us in the direction of the building and we're on our way toward Mozart, toward Jenny Nelson, toward the chance of fixing my massive mistake.

I knock on the door to Jenny's office once, twice, three times.

I close my eyes and inhale because *this is it.* Jenny Nelson is not an easy person to get in front of, let me tell you. I had to convince the receptionist at the front desk that I had an appointment.

"Jenny's first appointment is at eleven," the receptionist said.

"Right. It was last minute. Jenny is good friends with my

dad. She's giving me a tour. I play clarinet, like Jenny. Like my dad."

The receptionist tried to call Jenny, at which point I pulled out my phone and said, "I have her number. See? I can call her but she's expecting me, so . . ."

This earned a reluctant okay and a point in the right direction, toward the door with the plaque that reads JENNIFER NELSON, M.F.A.

I twist the knob and push the door open to Jenny's office. It's the sort of office that screams *academia* in a way that surprises me, with a huge wooden desk in the center, bookshelf walls, and a set of two mahogany chairs facing Jenny's desk. Her blonde hair is parted down the center, brown eyes sit behind clear plastic glasses, and she wears a cherry-patterned dress I swear I've seen on ModCloth. She doesn't look up from her computer screen.

I clear my throat.

"Office hours are tomorrow," Jenny says. When she does glance up from her screen she blinks, clearly taken aback. I hope the surprise is an advantage, not another thing counting against Reid. "You're not my student."

I shake my head. "My dad says hi."

"Natalie?" Jenny removes her glasses. "Wow, I haven't seen you since—wow. Is Aaron here? I'd love to catch up."

I shake my head. "I came alone. I was hoping we could talk. About Reid—Reid Callahan? He's the best clarinet player I know, and he worked so hard, and you have to reconsider withdrawing his audition invitation. *Please.*"

Jenny's expression is compassionate, but more pitying than understanding. "Oh, Natalie. It's sweet that you came all this way for your friend. But I can't give anyone special treatment, not even on an old friend's daughter's behalf."

"Reid isn't my friend," I say.

Jenny closes her laptop, her eyebrows shooting up. "Oh?"

I take a seat and unzip my backpack. "Who evaluates the audition tapes? You?"

Jenny shakes her head. "A panel of masters students. I'm in the room for the in-person auditions. But no, I'm not involved in the initial screenings."

"Okay," I say. *That's* why she's so easily rejecting. She hasn't heard his creative piece, how Reid sent *a full orchestration.* If she listens, she'll get it. She'll have to give it back. "Well, I think you should listen. Before you decide for sure."

"I really . . ." She stands, picking up a stack of folders. "I can't. Not only is that *very* against the rules, I have an eleven o'clock. As I said in my email, Reid can still apply for Winter Institute." Jenny walks toward the door and shit, I am losing her. She holds the door open, like she expects me to get up and leave. "I'm sorry that coming all this way was a waste of time."

I don't move. I can't move.

Jenny walks away.

I follow her. She can't just *leave.* "Wait!"

"I know this is disappointing for Reid but you need to leave. Seriously, I don't know how you got in here in the first place. The only reason I'm not calling security, quite frankly, is because you're Aaron's daughter."

"It's my fault!" The words tumble out in one breath, the words I should've started with. "Reid's letter didn't get lost. My dad is his teacher. It was delivered to my house and I hid it. I'm the reason Reid didn't RSVP. He didn't know he had an audition."

Jenny holds her folders against her chest, her mouth parted, forgetting her annoyance for a second. "Why would you do that?"

"It's a long story," I say.

She looks at her watch. "I really do have an eleven o'clock. Wait in my office, okay?"

I exhale because it's not over yet. The chance is still alive. "Oh my God, thank you!"

Jenny shakes her head. "Don't thank me yet."

She's gone before I can thank her again.

I wait.

Text Fitz that it's going to be a while.

And wait.

Text Henry that he's going to have to start rehearsal this afternoon without me.

And wait.

Almost an hour later, Jenny returns with hot chocolate and croissants.

When she hands me a warm mug I . . . am confused.

"Only ten percent of applicants make it through the initial screening," Jenny says, picking up where we left off. "From the in-person auditions, one in eight applicants will be accepted. I'm telling you this to emphasize how competitive this program is. And that even if your not-friend Reid Callahan gets an audition, it is by no means a guarantee that he'll get in. But I think you know that."

I nod.

"So please, enlighten me."

I tell Jenny everything and it all sounds so ridiculous when I try to explain. I tell her how the clarinet always put Reid and me in opposition, and the circumstances that brought us together to make *Melted*. How working together changed everything. How I thought this audition was going to *ruin* everything. Because no matter how close we are, history can't be erased, and I jumped to the worst conclusion.

I tell Jenny it wasn't about Reid. It was about me.

"Wow. Okay," Jenny places her empty mug on her desk. That's how long I've been talking—a whole hot chocolate experience's worth of time. "That is a lot."

I exhale. "Yeah."

"You have his audition materials?"

My eyes widen. "Yes! . . ." I unzip my backpack and pluck my hard drive from it. "Here. It's all right here."

"I'm not making any promises," Jenny says. "But this seems to have been out of Reid's control, so I will listen."

"Thank you!"

"No promises," Jenny repeats, before pressing play.

Hearing Reid's *Melted* medley again? It evokes the same exact feeling I felt the first time I listened in Dad's studio. It's perfect. Reid *gets* it. Reid gets *me.* And I just . . . didn't get him. For so long, when I looked at Reid I could only see the boy who stole from me. Stole music, stole my dad, stole my best friend. No matter how many prank wars I initiated and won, I could never take back everything Reid stole. But that was never the truth.

If I can't fix this, well, *I'll* be the one who stole. A horrible, unforgiveable steal.

The music fades and Jenny's expression is perfectly neutral, considering.

I have no idea what this means.

I count and it is the most stressful twenty-two seconds of my life.

But then her expression shifts. "I think I understand the reason you drove all this way. They're remarkable pieces—both for someone his age and someone with no training at a private conservatory."

Remarkable! Reid is remarkable!

"Reid can audition in-person. Day two is booked solid before our deliberation, but we can squeeze him in at the end of day one. February sixth. It's the best I can do."

I jump from my chair and wrap my arms around Jenny. "*Thank you.* You don't know how much this means."

Jenny laughs. "I do. I can't wait to meet him."

I pay the audition fee and thank Jenny a million more times before we say goodbye and I am floating because *I did it.* Reid is going to audition. He is going to kill his audition and spend his summer here, living in Mozart during the day and sleeping in A Major, or whatever the dorms are called.

I don't know what this means for *Melted*'s opening night. I do know that I'm not giving up on this show, on my cast. We've come so far, we've faced every obstacle. We weren't supposed to exist. But we do. I—along with Henry and Fitz and the entire cast—will figure out *Melted.* I should have known we could from the start.

But first, I have a Moritz I am so excited to fire.

CHAPTER TWENTY-SEVEN

Fitz and I make it home in time for the second half of *Melted*'s first day of tech week.

Dad's expression is impossible to read when I enter the auditorium. So I turn to the stage instead and I am overwhelmed by the scene in front of me. Wow, it sucks that I have to rip everything apart now that it's all come together. The costumes are finished. The tech hasn't spontaneously combusted yet—no dead mics or blown-out lights. Makayla and Cherish's set looks incredible, a celestial canyon on steroids. Every cast member seems comfortable onstage, transformed into their characters. *Melted* has come to life, for real.

Reid is even here, onstage in his Moritz costume. Reid showed up for *Melted*.

Fitz and I sneak into the back row of the auditorium and it's kind of nice, to *be*. To watch *Melted* without my binder of notes, without putting my director hat on. Even if this feeling is only for a scene, until the lights go down and the props are reset.

Reid finishes Moritz's last scene, singing a reprise of "Hate Is a Closed Window." Reid is *nailing* the emotional performance. He might be—oh my God, he is crying! It's perfect. It's devastating.

Even more so now that I know it'll never happen.

I exit through the auditorium door and run backstage before the song ends. Reid exits stage right, so I want to be there to intercept him when he does. I make it there as Reid is singing the final notes. When he sees me waiting in the wings, he pauses for a half beat, almost like he's contemplating exiting stage left instead. But ever the professional, he doesn't.

"Reid."

He keeps walking.

I follow him out the double doors, to the hallway. *"Reid."*

He stops walking but doesn't turn around. "Not today, Natalie."

"We need to talk," I say.

"I don't want to—"

"Yes. You do. It's important."

I pull Reid by his wrist through the double doors and around the corner to Dad's empty classroom. He follows, reluctant, but, I mean, he has the strength to dig his feet into the ground and stop me if he really wanted to. So at least part of him wants to come. Inside Dad's classroom, I flip the light on and close the door behind us and drop my backpack onto the floor.

"Natalie, what do you—?"

"You're fired," I say.

Reid blinks. "What?"

"You're fired," I repeat.

"No," Reid says.

"Reid—"

"No." His eyebrows scrunch together. "I know I didn't show up for a while because I was pissed. I'm *still* pissed. But I'm here now. I'm *here* and I'm not like you. I'm not going to destroy this thing we built because I'm mad at you. It sucks, because you're getting exactly what you wanted, aren't you? It sucks that I want to be here, that I still care about this show, that I—"

"You're fired because you're going to Albany."

His eyes widen. "Wait. What?"

"Saturday. They can fit you in at the end of the day." I hold out my phone to Reid and show him the email that Jenny Nelson forwarded to me.

I forward the email to Reid. It contains a confirmation notice with his audition number and day-of instructions. "It's all set. I bet my dad will drive you there and everything."

Reid doesn't move for his phone. "What about *Melted*?"

"What about it?"

"Who's going to be Moritz?"

"That's not your problem."

Reid shakes his head. "It is."

"I'm firing you from acting and this being your problem."

"It's still *our* show," he says, his voice low. "You can't fire me."

"Reid, you have an *Albany Institute* audition. Take it. Be selfish."

Reid *ughs* into his hands. "This was never supposed to be an ultimatum."

"I know, and that's my fault. I'm so sorry. For ruining everything. Not just *Melted.* I should have given you the benefit of the doubt."

"Well, we've spent, what, a *decade* fighting each other? Skepticism isn't . . . surprising."

"Still. These last few months were different. I should have known that." I stand up and swing my backpack over my shoulder. I want to stay more than anything, try to get him to forgive everything and go back to where we were. But I know that's not fair. Not yet. Reid has his audition to focus on and I'll figure out a way to get *Melted* together and maybe, eventually . . .

"Nat—?"

I turn around, pressing my back against the door. "Yeah?"

He holds up the confirmation email on his screen. "How?"

"Groveling. Lots of groveling."

"You hate groveling."

Reid smirks, only for a millisecond, but I saw it, it *happened.*

I nod. "I do."

"I . . . have an audition?"

I nod again. "You do. Don't mess it up."

He takes a step toward me. "I won't."

"I know. For what it's worth, I'm not skeptical of you anymore. Not at all."

Reid is so close, I could reach for his hand and twine his fingers with mine. So close I could stand on my toes and press my lips to his and we'd be *Natalie and Reid* again. Not *Natalie vs. Reid.* But I can't read his expression.

The moment passes and Reid reaches past me, pushing the door open. "I never wanted to be skeptical of you," he says, exiting Dad's classroom.

Reid has an audition. He's taking it. That's what matters.

But I can't help but hear an edge in his voice that says, *I will always be skeptical of you.*

At the top of our next rehearsal, Dad shares good news and not-great news.

"Good news first," Dad declares. "Tickets are nearly sold out."

"Really?" I ask.

Everyone, cast and band alike, start cheering.

"Never underestimate the power of a strong word-of-mouth campaign," Dad says.

As it turns out, in an excellent and somewhat unexpected twist, the science teachers loved *Melted* on concept and latched onto the phrase *an environmental call to action.* The entire department purchased a section of the auditorium and encouraged their students to *support your classmates, support The Sunshine Project!*—with free tickets and an even more alluring offer: extra credit. Between that, the band's family and fans showing up en masse for their musicians, and the stellar digital marketing plan spearheaded by Makayla and Cherish—our audience came through!

My shoulders relax.

It's like the universe knows I can only handle one stressful thing at time.

"The less good news is that Reid can no longer perform as Moritz . . . because he has an audition for the Albany Institute!"

This means nothing to the cast, but the band kids are cheering.

After the excitement dies down though, reality sets in.

We need someone who can play Moritz.

"Why does Moritz have to be a dude?" Danica asks.

"I mean—" Henry says.

"Gender is a construct," Fitz says, looping her hair into a topknot.

"His songs are written for a tenor," Reid says. "It'd also leave only Kevin as the sole guy in the principal cast."

"Is that relevant?" Kevin asks.

"Imagine! A musical with less—" Danica *gasps* dramatically "—men!"

"What a tragedy," Fitz grins.

I chew on the eraser end of a Ticonderoga. "Okay. Fair point. But who even knows it well enough to be able to pull it off in time?"

Fitz smacks my forehead. Not *hard,* but she actually whacks my head like I'm supposed to be having a light bulb moment and I'm . . . not.

"Me!" Fitz says.

"What?"

Danica frowns. "Fitz, Moritz *sings.* Moritz *dances.*"

"But less than anyone else in the show. Just two songs! I will butcher them, no doubt. But I've been here from the start. I know the part. I can fill in. As for the dancing . . . it's not like Moritz is a *featured* dancer in any scene. It's fine. I'll hide in back."

"Our options are limited," I say.

"I can't sing, but I will act the shit out of his death scene," Fitz says.

"I'm into it," Emerson says, and I feel like a Proud Mom, watching her find her voice.

"It won't be a perfect show," Henry says. "But . . . they never were in the first place."

"It's not like the school committee won't see us giving it our all," Danica reasons.

I . . . totally agree.

"All in favor of Fitz playing Moritz?" I ask.

Everyone's hands fly into the air and I'm even madder at myself because it took *one* conversation to figure this out! A conversation that never would've happened if I didn't jump to conclusions. I inhale to steady my shaking breath. An impossible show made possible then impossible again is now possible once more—thanks to the team of people, *friends,* who love it as much as I do. I thought making *Melted* a musical would ruin it, but it became so much more than I could have dreamed. So it's not going to combust because Fitz will sing two songs off-key. *Two songs.*

I won't let it.

I guess it's only fair that the success of *Melted* will require a directorial miracle.

CHAPTER TWENTY-EIGHT

The rest of the week passes in the blur of Fitz's transformation into Moritz. I have to accept that Reid was not wrong removing Fitz from the musical. Because she shines with every monologue she delivers but cannot keep up with the choreography at all. So we have to reblock most of the dance numbers and dial back the difficulty of "Hate Is a Closed Window" so it's less dancing and more walking in rhythm. Still, it's fun seeing Danica and Fitz performing together. Even better that they're *not* playing siblings.

It's kind of a hot mess in those spots, but we're making the best of it.

I mean, that's how theater was always supposed to be. Silly. Fun. Us.

The night before *Melted* makes its debut, I am *terrified* in the best and worst possible way. I hope the school committee sees the heart in this show, despite our less than professional performance tweaks. But no matter what happens tomorrow, we made something out of nothing. HAVE A HE(ART) will have its moment. We'll raise money for an important cause. The show will go on.

Henry and I are currently sitting on my bed, our backs pressed against the wall and feet dangling over the end. Henry has his laptop open to calculus and—is senioritis not a thing? But Henry is always on a *mission*, and now that Mission: College Apps is complete, Henry's new focus is Mission: Conquer AP Tests so he can offload as many core requirements as possible.

I'm supposed to be writing up a titration lab report that is due Monday, to get ahead of it. But I can't focus, like, at all. I don't understand how Henry can have calculus brain right now, when *Melted* is less than twenty-four hours away.

"Time to turn our attention to Leo and Claire," Henry says, closing the calculus and scooting closer so we can share his laptop screen between us.

"Yes, please." I pass Henry a slice of pizza.

Henry always sleeps over before opening night. We eat an extra-large margherita pizza straight from the box, watch Baz Luhrmann's *Romeo + Juliet*, and make our *what if* list—detailing every possible consideration to ensure that nothing goes wrong tomorrow.

What if the mics all blow? We've got backup mics.

What if there's a costume catastrophe? We have extra safety pins for that.

What if Danica forgets her sunglasses again? We'll bring a spare.

There is no scenario we haven't already thought of, but we go through the list anyway.

When we finish, Henry swallows. "It's our last night before opening night."

I punch his shoulder. "I'm trying super hard not to think about that."

"Yeah, it's—" Henry bites into his slice "—weird. But we did it. It's happening. You made it happen. It's pretty awesome, Nat. Dare I say, *college essay–worthy*."

I shrug. "Maybe."

"Come on. You love this," Henry says, nudging my arm.

I exhale. "Yeah."

Henry presses play on our favorite Shakespeare film, except I can't focus on dashing baby Leo or the fact that Paul Rudd doesn't age. Instead, I'm thinking about how Henry is right, I *do* love this. The best part of this year will come to a crashing halt after this weekend. What is the point of going to school if it's not so I can attend rehearsals after? Every year there has at least been the spring play to look forward to, but not this time.

This year, *Melted* is all I have, and my chest constricts at the thought of letting it go. I hate that Henry is right, Reid is right, my parents are right—directing, playwriting, it's not a hobby. I don't think I ever *wanted* it to be a hobby.

I told myself it had to be.

In first grade, we traced outlines of our hands on a projector. Inside, we drew bigger, stronger, surer versions of ourselves. The standard *What do you want to be when you grow up?* question was written across the top in Miss Beckett's clear block print. *The future is in your hands.* In my hand was a Crayola drawing of my mom. She had just explained to me what she did for a living, that she gets to make up stories—and I remember thinking that was the closest thing to magic I'd ever heard.

It *was* magic. Until the words stopped.

That's the problem with art, with writing, with music. The thing I still can't shake. It's magic until it's not.

I press the space bar on Henry's laptop, pausing the movie right before the balcony scene.

"Bathroom," I say, springing to my feet and out of my room. But I pass the bathroom, running downstairs and hooking left to Mom's office. The door is closed but the light is on. I knock, two quick raps of my knuckles against the white hollow wood, before twisting the bronze doorknob and poking my head inside.

"One sec, Lee," Mom says, her fingers dancing on the keys.

I almost say *never mind* because I feel bad interrupting her flow. But I stay. My lips press together in a thin line, keeping the words inside until she's done. I stand with my back pressed against the doorframe, watching Mom write. It's still my favorite sight in the world, seeing Mom in the zone, absorbed in her work.

Finally, Mom flexes her fingers and takes a sip of tea from the mug beside her. "What's up?"

"Are you happy?" I ask.

Mom blinks. "Of course I'm happy, Lee. What kind of question is that?"

"You haven't published in five years."

"True."

"But . . . you're happy."

Mom arches an eyebrow. "I'm writing now, aren't I?"

"Yes, but . . . I don't know. Sometimes I think I want to try to make it in theater, for real. Because I don't want *Melted* to end or drama club to not exist. But then I remember what a creative slump looks like. What if I can't sustain it? Then what?"

Mom moves to the futon and pats for me to sit down next to her.

"It's not easy. I'm glad we didn't delude you into thinking it's going to be easy. Your father and I have certainly had our ups and downs on the path to our dreams. But the things that we love? They are always in our lives. Even when it's hard, we make them work in ways we didn't expect. Your father isn't in an orchestra, but he loves Lincoln Street Blues and he loves his students. And I've been in a creative slump because I churned out ten books in nine years and that is just . . . not sustainable." Mom laughs. "Burnout is real, and I'm working through it. I'm on my way back. It's not easy. But don't be a cynic, Lee. Don't be too scared to even *try*. The question is, do you love it?"

"I love it," I whisper.

Then Mom's arm wraps around my shoulders and she pulls me close. "I know."

CHAPTER TWENTY-NINE

Delia makes chocolate peanut butter pancakes for lunch the next day even though there is zero chance I can eat.

She flips pancakes on the griddle like a pro because she's the only one who has the patience to cook with Dad. He always made these on opening day. He would cook more than we could eat, and everyone would sit around the table, the four of us plus Henry, stuffing the butterflies away because these pancakes are that good.

Tonight, the curtain goes up at seven p.m., in six hours. The cast call—our *final* cast call—is in four. I'm restless, checking emails and double-checking my lists as though I can will nothing to go wrong or conjure something for us to do besides twiddle our thumbs and eat pancakes. There is nothing to do except count down the hours, the minutes, the *seconds*, until we are live. We're as ready as we'll ever be.

I hope Reid is too.

"Pretend these are the best pancakes you've ever tasted," Delia says, serving us at the table. "I'm not Dad, but I tried."

"Thanks, Dee," I say. I kind of love Delia a lot for trying.

Henry is already digging in, only pausing briefly to give Delia a thumbs-up, which makes her pump her fist in the air in victory. I cut a tiny bite so I don't hurt her feelings and drench it in maple syrup. But I'm not hungry.

Dad's absence is *so* glaring—but I can't be mad because this time it's my idea. At least he's active in the family group text, sending sporadic photos from Albany. One pointing at The Egg in the distance, Albany's performing arts center. A cheeky selfie in front of the Capitol, which looks more like a Newport mansion than a government building. The last one, Dad, smiling, hanging out with Reid.

All of them showing Dad, in Albany, not here for opening night. I wait for my stomach to do that twisty thing it always does seeing Reid and Dad together.

But it doesn't.

Is this what it feels like to not blame Reid for the chasm between Dad and me?

"Are you going to eat those?" Fitz asks, her face pressed against the sliding screen door. Danica stands behind Fitz, both hands on her hips. Delia unlatches the slider, assuring Fitz that there are plenty of pancakes for everyone. She forgot that Dad always halves the recipe. We are going to be eating pancakes for days.

"You can have mine," I say, pushing my plate to the empty seat to my right.

Fitz squeezes my shoulder as she walks past me. "Hey."

"Hey," I repeat.

"Eat your pancakes, Natalie," Delia instructs. "I'll make a plate for Fitz."

I place my phone on the table, facedown. "Okay, Mom."

Delia sticks her tongue out at me, everyone laughs, and for a moment the butterflies dissipate and everything is okay.

You've come a long way and no matter what happens tonight with the school committee, you should be proud. I am.
Sincerely, Mrs. Mulaney.

The email popped into my inbox one hour before call time. Seriously, Mrs. Mulaney. It's a nice note, but way to remind us there is pressure, like we don't already know.

"Y'all thought you could kick me off a stage!" Fitz says while doing her makeup. She has fifteen minutes to make her eyes match her vest. "Look at me now!"

I read her the email from Mrs. Mulaney.

"She *will not* rattle you," Fitz says, applying liquid eye shadow to her right eyelid. "It very well will *not* be our last show. When the curtain closes on our LHS drama career, I am damn well going to be the lead."

"It's what we deserve," I say.

"Truly," Fitz confirms.

"Fitz?"

"Hmm?"

"Thanks. For everything."

Fitz snaps a picture of us making goofy faces in the mirror. She smiles at her phone, her fingers flying over the keys as she proclaims that she's sending the picture to Reid.

"What? No. Why?" I ask, reaching for her phone.

She swats my hand away. "If you mess up your hair, I swear."

"Don't text Reid," I say.

"What? You look hot, Natalie. Very conductor chic. Besides, Reid asked for updates."

"He did?"

"Yeah. We've been texting all day. I'm, like, talk to your codirector. He said you're probably stressed enough as is, which is fair. Dude knows you—" Fitz's phone buzzes midsentence, lighting up with four new texts from Reid "—and *Neid* is not over!"

"It will be if you keep calling us that," I say, but my heart is doing a tap dance.

"I don't choose the ship name. The ship name chooses you."

"But, like, no."

Fitz winks at me. "You're welcome. For everything."

Twenty minutes later, the cast and crew of *Melted,* as well the art students facilitating the showcase and charity auction in the hallways, are all gathered onstage, in a circle, holding hands—because, is it high school theater without an energy circle? I don't think so.

It's my first time leading it though. I squeeze Henry's hand, sending the pulse of energy to my right. Henry squeezes Emerson's hand, who squeezes Makayla's. I track the movement with my eyes, watching it flow around the circle until it comes back to Danica. Fitz. Me.

Everyone is silent, the only noise the quiet hum of our hearts.

"Speech," Fitz coughs, not-so-subtly.

I swallow, wishing Reid were here for this moment.

"I . . ." My voice catches in my throat. *Do* not *cry, Natalie!* I tell myself. *Your makeup is perfect, Natalie! Tears are for emotional endings. Do not even* think *about getting emotional until intermission. Cry in the privacy of the sound booth. Okay, so Makayla will be, you know, doing her job in the sound booth, but she'll ignore your tears.*

"I'm so stupid proud," I say. "Everyone in this circle stood up to show the school committee that art matters. Everyone in this circle took a chance on our parody play turned parody musical to prove that it matters—that *all* our arts matter. Thank you for making it possible and bringing it to life with us."

Henry squeezes my hand and takes over. "When Natalie and I started writing together, I never imagined our show would be a musical. But I love this rogue musical that could. It's my last show at Lincoln and I could not think of a better way to go out. Give tonight everything you've got. I refuse to believe that LHS drama and all the arts end with *Melted*."

Fitz's hand breaks from mine and she claps, woots, screams, "Team HAVE A HE(ART)!"

Everyone echoes, "Team HAVE A HE(ART)!"

After we get the cheers and screams out of our system, I cue Makayla and Fitz to open the house. Henry and I peek through the curtains, watching the wave of an audience flood our theater.

I've never seen so many bodies in these auditorium chairs. Every seat is filled.

Enthusiastic science teachers and band parents are no joke. Wow.

Henry laughs when I tell him this. "Yeah. That's what 'sold out' means, Nat."

But hearing it is one thing. Seeing it is something else entirely.

I don't let go of Henry's hand until it's time to make my way to the orchestra pit.

Because with Dad gone too, I'm not just a codirector.

It's time for me to conduct a musical.

Time is weird.

Ninety minutes feels like *forever* when it's a run-through during tech week. Tonight, time flies. My heart is so full watching *Melted* unfold from the orchestra pit, I don't even have time to process my conducting nerves or allow them to fester. I'm swept away by Danica and Emerson's performance, by the way the set comes to life with proper lighting, by the small miracle that is zero audio problems. I'm so stupid proud, I nearly miss the cue to start the music for "Hate Is a Closed Window."

Everyone performs full out, with their whole heart. Every note, every line, every lighting cue—it's all perfectly imperfect. Fitz sashays in the wrong direction but plays it off like she meant to. Kevin botches his first line but recovers seamlessly. Arjun misses a lighting cue, leaving Emerson in the dark a minute too long. But the music is captivating. The "In Winter" tap routine is iconic. And Moritz's death scene is mesmerizing.

The audience roars to life when the music cuts and the lights fade to black.

Then it's time for the other clubs to have their moment to shine.

The Trebles perform a *Frozen* medley onstage during intermission.

In the hallways, an art auction is live.

The *Melted: A Meditation on Climate Change Anxiety* lit magazine is for sale.

Every piece has at least one bid in the auction and the magazine sells out before the curtain goes back up.

I can't even process how much money that is. For our clubs. For The Sunshine Project.

So I don't. I get back to my spot and conduct.

And before I know it, it's time for the curtain call. All night my back has been toward the audience, focused on the music. But now, as I walk onstage for my bow, the spotlight softens and I *see* it. The whole place is on their feet cheering. Two silhouettes even stand off to the side, their backs pressed against the white brick wall. Sold out, *plus* standing room? It's basically every director's dream come true. I think about how we used to barely fill half the theater—and how after tonight, I doubt we'll ever have that problem again. If we get the chance to do this again.

My eyes adjust to the blinding light and the crowd regains their features, including the two standing figures. I bite down on my lower lip, *hard,* to keep from audibly *gasping.*

Because the standing room silhouettes are Reid and my dad, who both have the widest smiles on their faces. I . . . Reid and Dad are supposed to still be in Albany.

Yet, they're here.

Reid and Dad are *here.*

I've felt the high of directing a great play. But nothing has ever come close to this. Being involved in so many different parts of the creative process—writing, directing, music—it's like a giant piece of my heart is embedded in *Melted* and out there for everyone to see. And it matters to them. This is purpose. This is magic.

I believe in you. I'll never forget the way Reid whispered those words to me, so softly, outside of Olive & Twist on that snowy December night.

I can't wipe the smile off my face.

I can't wait to tell Reid I believe in me too.

CHAPTER THIRTY

And just like that the curtain closes on *Melted: The Musical.*

The applause fades on the other side of the curtain, until the only sound left is the beat of hearts hammering against our chests. I wait for the overwhelming release of emotion that the final curtain always triggers once the adrenaline wears off. Except it's not wearing off.

Reid is here.

Dad is here.

"Natalie! Jacobson!" Fitz squeals. My eyes pop open as her arms wrap around me. "That was amazing."

Henry appears, stage left, his headset around his neck, insisting to get in on the group hug. And even though I still have to go find Reid and Dad, this is when the tears come, the overwhelming feeling I can't push down or swallow. Tears roll down my cheeks because, like, how lucky am I to have Henry and Fitz? The best people. *My* people.

"My *makeup,*" Fitz says, mad at the tears streaming down her face.

"The show's over," Henry says.

Fitz's shoulders slump with the disappointment of seeing her art slide down my face. "But it still would have looked great for Chao Down. Ugh. I assume we're going to Chao Down?"

I nod through the tears, because dumplings have never sounded so good.

"Reid's smile for you is the stupidest," Henry says.

"Did you know?" I ask.

Henry and Fitz shake their heads *no* in unison. The movement is too precise, too choreographed, and I would call bullshit, but I'm so happy I don't even care. I break the group hug first and Fitz is fake-annoyed until I remind her the quicker I change, the sooner we eat.

In my closet fitting room, I change out of *conductor chic* and into a thigh-length cobalt sweater and black leggings. Someone knocks on the door as I'm lacing up my combat boots. "One sec," I call because I'm already rushing, okay? We only have four fitting rooms, which are very much one-person-at-a-time size, as they are, you know, actual closets.

I toss my duffle bag over my shoulder and pull the door open.

It's not Fitz on the other side. Not Henry. Not even *Reid.*

It's Dad.

"Hi—" I start.

I don't get the rest of the words out because Dad pulls me into a giant bear hug and it's so unexpected, so . . . *not my dad.* But none of this is. He's here. Not in Albany with Reid.

Not schmoozing with Jenny at the meet-and-greet. Not with Reid at the concert prospective students were invited to. Dad was *so* excited to take Reid to Albany, to network with musicians who have performed in orchestras around the world.

But he's here.

I pull back from the hug first. "How?"

"Jenny fit Reid in after lunch instead. We made it back as fast as we could. Traffic was a *nightmare*."

"You're here," I say, still stunned.

Dad frowns. "Of course I'm here. Everything about *Melted* was phenomenal. Mrs. Mulaney even cracked a smile during the tap number. I'm pretty sure she loved it. You put so much work into this and it all came together. I'm so proud of you."

I wipe my cheek, catching a stray tear that escapes. "I didn't think you were coming home until the morning."

"We wanted to surprise you," Dad says.

"Consider me surprised," I say.

Dad scratches his beard. "I've never missed opening night."

"Well—" I swallow "—it's never conflicted with a Reid thing."

My cheeks flush, embarrassed that I'm still admitting how I feel, how much I *care*.

But . . . maybe continuing to call him out is the first step toward trying.

His expression softens. "Natalie, I'd *never* miss your

opening night, not for anyone or anything. I'm sorry if I ever made you feel that I would."

I study my dad. The creases in his forehead that exhibit worry. His mouth, pressed into a thin line. His eyes, glossy, like *he* could start crying at any moment—but also urgent. *I'd never miss your opening night.* He said that.

And he didn't. He means it.

This time, I'm the one reaching out for a hug, my tearstained cheek pressed against my dad's chest. I know we're not going to wake up tomorrow with a perfect relationship, but maybe we'll wake up understanding each other a little better.

My emotions level off until I hear the words "I love you, Nat" spoken just above a whisper and then the tears come once more.

A few minutes later, makeup fixed a second time, I head to my dad's car.

Once the cacophony of parent and teacher congratulations concluded, Dad tossed me the keys to his car and Mom said, "Be home by midnight." Henry and Fitz are already on their way to Chao Down with everyone. We'll push all the tables together "La Vie Boheme" style and order all the dumplings. It's an LHS drama takeover, now so much bigger because all the clubs are coming too.

On my way out, Mrs. Mulaney spots me and pulls me aside.

"Natalie! Wow. I am blown away. From what I could tell, so was the school committee."

"Thanks, Mrs. Mulaney."

"You've made your case. Every one of you. And . . . I'll be fighting for you too."

I nod and thank Mrs. Mulaney again, because as much as I've wanted to hear that for so long, right now all I want is for this conversation to end. All I want is to make my way to Reid. I cross everything he's still here. Pushing through the double doors, I fight the urge to overanalyze Mrs. Mulaney's words. She *sounds* optimistic. But it's not a promise. Nowhere close to a guarantee.

I need to accept the reality that there are no guarantees.

And stop using my fear of failure as an excuse to not even try.

My heart speeds up as I look for dad's car and—just like I hoped he'd be, Reid is there, his hands stuffed in his pockets. I walk toward him, my lips pressed together so I don't break out in a smile because he's *here.* He's still in conservatory audition clothes, black dress pants and a white button-down, the sleeves rolled up. He looks incredible.

Henry's right. Reid's smile *is* stupid. I hope it's also for me.

"You're not in Albany," I say as if that isn't obvious.

He shakes his head. "Nope."

"You're supposed to be schmoozing at the faculty meet-and-greet."

"It turns out I am not a schmoozer," Reid says.

"Okay. Okay, but you couldn't just *try* to schmooze for the most competitive audition of all time? How was the institute? How did it go? How did you even *make it back in time*? Did you—?"

Reid takes a step toward me. "Natalie. Pause. *Melted* was amazing. *You're* amazing."

He's so close to me, I could press my lips against his. So I do. Because against all logic, despite the mess I made, he is here. And it *was* amazing. What we made was amazing. *We* are amazing, especially together. And it's time I take a chance. In no time at all Reid's hands are on my waist and mine are around his neck and it feels right, this kiss, more than ever before.

He breaks the kiss. "Hi."

Now I'm the one with the stupid smile. "Hey."

"I killed my audition, for the record," Reid says.

"Of course," I say, lacing my fingers through his. "Tell me everything on the way to Chao Down."

"Wait," Reid says. "I had this whole thing prepared. A word speech."

I nod. "Word speech."

"Shut up. Okay." Reid runs his free hand through his hair. "So. Do you know why I started playing clarinet?"

I shrug. "I mean, it's my dad's instrument, right?"

Reid sees Dad teaching me the clarinet. Reid decides he needs to learn too.

That is the rivalry origin story I've always known.

Reid shakes his head. "It was *your* instrument. It was a reason to hang out with you."

I am, for once, speechless.

"I like you, Nat. I've *always* liked you. But for *ten years* you'd only give me the time of the day if we were competing for top spot, or pranking each other, or whatever."

"Or whatever," I repeat.

Reid swallows. "Now though, I more than like you. And I don't want to go back to the whatever, no matter what happens with the plays or conservatory or anything else. So I'd like to request an amendment. In *Natalie vs. Reid.*"

I cross my arms over my chest. "Okay. I'm listening."

Reid pulls a folded-up piece of paper out of his pocket. His copy of our rule book. "To the truce clause, specifically. 'Truces are agreed on with a double pinky swear. No pranking can occur during the seven-day truce period.'"

"We were weird kids," I say.

Reid nods. "My amendment is that we extend the truce."

"Oh?" I ask.

"Yeah. Like, a permanent truce."

"Permanent?"

Reid crosses out the very specific details of our old truce amendment in black Sharpie, rewriting it to say, "And no pranking can occur. Ever." He signs the updated amendment and holds it out to me.

"What do you think?" he asks.

"I don't hate it," I say, taking the pen out of his hand and signing our new amendment into law. Reid folds the paper back into quarters and stuffs it in his pocket, smiling. He steps toward me.

"So. Natalie. Truce?"

He crosses his wrists and holds both his pinkies out, double pinky swear. Serious as it gets.

I smile and latch my pinkies around his. And as I do Reid kisses me and I melt into this moment, high on an incredible opening night and the music we composed together and the possibility of so much more that we'll do together. The boy who I couldn't seem to get out of my life became the boy I never want to go away. So I answer him.

"Truce."

Acknowledgments

I wrote the earliest draft of *As If on Cue* in 2018 over the course of one summer, in a world where the sound of drafting was the white noise of a local coffee shop, where brainstorm sessions with friends were in-person, where research was getting spontaneous rush tickets to a Broadway show. Even during the hard parts, drafting this story about a struggling high school theater program and championing the arts was pure joy. I thought I had conquered Second Book Syndrome.

Then, Broadway went dark on March 12, 2020—and that was one of the first real wake-up calls, to me at least, that *oh . . . this is serious.* And while my characters live in an alternate universe that revolves around live theater—the process of revising this book very much existed in the reality that was 2020. To say it was *difficult* is a massive understatement. *As If on Cue* exists thanks to the support and encouragement from my team, family, and friends. It truly took a village—thank you, thank you, thank you.

Taylor Haggerty, you are the best cheerleader and advocate in the business. Thank you for your clear-eyed guidance and assurance that I will be okay in a year when *debut anxiety* took on a whole new meaning. Your wisdom and positivity is such a light. To the entire Root Literary team—I am forever grateful to be a part of this family.

Alexa Pastor, thank you for championing this story and loving Natalie and Reid as much as I do. Your enthusiasm and thoughtful guidance bring the best out in my writing. I am a better storyteller for working with you and I am so proud of what we created!

To the entire BFYR team—Justin Chanda, Anne Zafian, Kendra Levin, Karen Masnica, Lisa Moraleda, Katrina Groover, Chava Wolin, Michelle Leo, and Kristie Choi—thank you for all you've done and continue to do behind the scenes. Thank you to my publicists, Chantal Gersch and Milena Giunco, for everything you do to help my books find their perfect readers. And a massive thank-you to the art and design team—Krista Vossen for designing a romcom cover that dreams are made of and Carolina Melis for illustrating Natalie and Reid so perfectly.

To the people I wouldn't survive publishing without—Kelsey Rodkey, Rachel Lynn Solomon, Carlyn Greenwald, Auriane Desombre, Haley Neil, Sonia Hartl, Tara Tsai, Rosiee Thor, and Al Graziadei. Thank you for reading *As If on Cue* during various stages and always being a sounding board during the creative process. You're all such talented writers and amazing friends—this book is so much stronger for your feedback.

2020 debuts—what a debut year it turned out to be! I'm so thankful for the friendships made and solidarity found in our debut group. I can't wait to meet you all in person someday. Cameron Lund and Martha Waters, my 4/7 agent sisters—thank you for being down to organize joint events / commiserate / celebrate small wins. I swear, we're bonded for life.

To readers, bloggers, bookstagrammers, booksellers, and librarians—thank you for all the work you do to connect books with readers! Thank you for finding joy in my books and sharing that joy. In what has been an entirely virtual author experience, your tweets and tags are a reminder that all of this is real. I can't wait to meet you at events one day!

As If on Cue is a love letter to high school theater, so I'd be remiss to not shout out my theater program. Debra Wald, Zac Broken Rope, and Sarah Cullen—thank you for helming our small but mighty drama club. To the cast and crew of *Hotel Vladimir*, our ridiculous play that could was the inspiration for this story.

Sam, you are my person. I absolutely did not know what I was getting into when you approached me with a script—but collaborating with you was one of the best decisions I ever made. I love you.

And finally, to my family—thank you for your unwavering support and love. Vanessa, thank you for always being down to listen to my ideas in their earliest stages. I know I have a great first line when it meets your high standards. Mom and Dad, thank you for taking all my dreams seriously and always showing up—be it for dance recitals, school plays, or navigating Zoom and Instagram for author events. We don't choose our family. Every day I'm so thankful that you're mine.